# SUSAN GRANT

## THE WARLORD'S DAUGHTER

HQN™

Recycling programs
for this product may
not exist in your area.

ISBN-13: 978-0-373-77361-9
ISBN-10:    0-373-77361-7

THE WARLORD'S DAUGHTER

Copyright © 2009 by Susan Grant

www.HQNBooks.com

Printed in U.S.A.

Dear Reader,

Are you ready for another adventure to the lawless, dangerous Borderlands, the no-man's-land between two mighty civilizations that have just declared peace after a thousand years of war? This story follows *Moonstruck,* but it's not necessary to have read it first. If you have, then you'll recognize Hadley and Bolivarr. This time you'll also meet Wren. Imagine being the daughter of the Warlord, most hated man in the galaxy, wishing you're nothing like him while fearing that you are. On the run for her life, Wren falls into Aral's arms. The former battlelord, one of her father's minions, is already half in love with her. He expected to rescue her, but Wren wants her freedom. It was fun watching them learn to trust each other. Throw an ancient treasure into the mix, angry goddesses, a profiteering trader and the entire galaxy on their tails, and you have one hot adventure ahead of you. So fasten your seat belt and hold on. Let me take you away on another, unforgettable ride!

As always, I love to hear from my readers. Visit me on Myspace, Facebook, my blog, or at my Web site, www.susangrant.com.

Until next time—fly high!

Susan Grant

For Geo

**Also by**

# SUSAN GRANT

*Moonstruck*
*How To Lose an Extraterrestrial in 10 Days*
*My Favorite Earthling*
*Your Planet or Mine?*
*The Scarlet Empress*
*The Legend of Banzai Maguire*
*The Star Princess*
*Contact*
*The Star Prince*
*The Star King*
*Once a Pirate*

**And watch for Susan Grant's
next intergalactic romance,
coming in 2010 from HQN Books.**

# THE
# WARLORD'S
## DAUGHTER

# PROLOGUE

"THE WARLORD HAS SUMMONED his child." The bellow echoed in the reception hall of the battle-cruiser orbiting high above the planet Barokk, Wren's home. Bristling with weapons and curiosity, the imperial guard hunted for her with narrowed, speculative eyes. Down, down, down his gaze had to fall to find her.

Wren shrank back from the sight of the tattooed giant dressed in armor. Beads and twists of hammered metal in his braided hair gleamed like wet seashells. The red diamond piercing the side of his nose looked like a drop of blood.

Somewhere behind him was her father, at long last here to see her. Magnified by the thick lenses of her glasses, guards blocked her view like a forest of impossibly tall and thorny trees. The giant with the blood-drop jewel was the friendliest-looking in the bunch.

Wren's guardian, Sabra, returned his glare. Sabra feared no one, not even these ferocious-looking guards. "It's about time. Half a day has passed. It's one thing making his minions wait, but his daughter?"

"Hush, woman. Watch your words. You're speaking of the Supreme Warlord of the Drakken Horde."

"Absentee father is a more appropriate title. The last time he saw her she was three. It's been ten years."

The guard's glare was direct, angry, yet somehow appraising, as if he wanted to strike Sabra for her insolence but held back because he thought her pretty, which she was. If it were Wren, and if she were not the warlord's daughter, she would have felt the sting of his hand. Beauty was prized over brains in females. Sabra had both. Wren pushed on her glasses, turning her gaze to her new, too-tight shoes as the towering guard growled, "You are young to be her guardian, woman. And foolish because of your age. You'd be wise to keep your mouth shut and your opinions to yourself if you wish to see her to maturity."

"And you would be wise to—"

"Sabra." Ilkka, another guardian, touched her friend's arm to warn her into silence as the towering guard led their party into the grand reception hall.

Always there was a certain tension between the women that Wren didn't quite understand. They seemed almost competitive at times, but today she was grateful for Ilkka's interference. Sabra was fiercely protective of Wren. It was her warrior instincts coming out. She once worked as an elite operative in the Imperial Forces. She'd have been a wraith assassin if females had been allowed to serve in such a capacity. Instead, at a young age, at what should have been the beginning of an exciting career, she'd been handed what amounted to a position as a wealthy man's nanny, raising the warlord's daughter. A woman who wasn't cut out to be a mother and never wanted to be a mother had in fact been the best of mothers.

Still annoyed, Sabra muttered in Ilkka's ear. "In all these years he couldn't be bothered seeing how the child was doing with his own eyes? And after what happened to her mother. As if it was her fault she produced a daughter first."

"The warlord has done more for Wren than you like to admit, Sabra. There's a war going on."

"For over a thousand years this war's gone on. Please."

"And rather than keep the child on display at the palace he's kept her hidden away with a guardian, you, sworn to protect her to the last breath."

"I'll give him that. He's managed to completely isolate her."

The two guardians spoke as if she weren't there. They thought she couldn't hear their hushed voices. Wren's hearing was more acute than anyone realized to make up for her poor vision. Her ears caught each one of the whispered words, which revealed nothing she didn't already know.

The warlord didn't want her.

Wren's stomach hurt. Her fingers clawed at the folds of her gown. What would her father think, seeing her for the first time as a young woman? Would he be disappointed? If only she weren't so small. If only she weren't so shy. Sabra said her mother was a great beauty. Lady Seela had captivated all who saw her. Would the warlord expect Wren to turn heads in the same way? Worry crawled over her skin that she would not measure up to this god of a man who'd sired her.

"Be brave," Sabra urged. "Stand tall."

Wren did her best to be both. She was smaller than other girls her age. Scrawny and half-blind. "Some battlelord's runt," she'd heard others say when they thought she couldn't hear them. No one on Barokk knew who her father really was, and Wren was forbidden to say. "It's so you'll feel more like the other girls," Sabra would say.

Wren couldn't feel more different.

Step by step she moved forward. Her shoes pinched her feet. The dress made especially for today scratched her legs. Her scalp pulsed hotly, a headache from the braids in her hair. Running her fingers over the braids, she checked that they hadn't come undone.

Sabra took her hand and squeezed it. "Don't fuss with your hair. You are a beautiful girl, inside and out."

Flushing with pleasure, Wren shook her head.

"You are. Someday you will see."

"Take off her glasses," Ilkka suggested. "She'll look better without them."

"If her father wanted her to have proper medical care, he'd have taken care of it. Maybe he'll do so now, seeing how she struggles." Sabra gave Wren a gentle push forward and set her heart a-pounding. "You must walk in front of us now. Go to him. Pay your respects as we practiced, sweetling. You know the words."

Wren proceeded, step by cautious step. It was silent. She feared her heartbeats were echoing off the walls of the spaceship. A row of solemn-looking men stood to her left. Several had bodies where excess had taken its toll—paunchy bellies, jowls. Others were fit and strong. All were many years older.

Battlelords, Wren thought. They were the wealthiest and most powerful men in the empire after her father. Her husband would be chosen from amongst their ranks someday. If the warlord had invited them here, it was for that reason. Now she had to worry about impressing them as well as her father.

The guardians resumed their hushed conversation. Sabra was angry. "How long now before he hands her over as a trophy wife? Which one of those sadists will be the lucky bastard? Arkkane? Mawndarr, perhaps?"

*Sadists?* Wren almost whipped her attention to Sabra, then remembered she wasn't supposed to be hearing their gossip.

"Or the boy, Mawndarr's son," Ilkka mused. "Aral."

"Fates. Banish the thought."

"The boy is as good-looking as his sire."

Sabra made a disdainful noise in her throat. "I don't find brutality attractive."

One tall man, quite physically fit, observed Wren with a cold, appraising glare. The void of space outside the portholes looked warm and inviting in comparison to those eyes. White streaked the midnight-black hair that he wore in a ponytail not unlike like the others; yet somehow on him the style seemed more regal. Attractive he might be—for an older man—but the cruel set to his jaw and mouth made her shiver.

Battlelord Karbon Mawndarr. Based on the descriptions provided by Sabra and embellished by Ilkka, she knew it was him. The battlelord was so terrifyingly magnetic that she almost didn't see the sullen, quiet boy standing in his shadow. He was older than her by a few years, seventeen or eighteen at most. Aral…Aral Mawndarr. The battlelord's son.

*"He is as good-looking as his sire."*

*"If you find brutality attractive."*

Brutality? A merry dimple sat square in the center of

his chin, mocking Sabra's observation. Aral held his tall frame slightly hunched over as if injured. There wasn't a mark on his perfect skin, but his eyes were full of pain as they found hers. A searching look washed over his face and his cheeks turned pink, revealing a tender heart. A kindred spirit.

She gasped. In his face was everything she felt. She was just as vulnerable, just as out of place. Just as trapped.

*We'll find a way out,* he seemed to say.

She fought the almost overwhelming urge to grab his hand so they could both escape this place. Then she stumbled over her unfamiliar shoes. Only Sabra's quick hand kept her from falling. By the time she bashfully adjusted her glasses Aral had shuttered his expression. With his gaze frosted over, he was a miniature Karbon Mawndarr as he gazed down his arrogant nose at her. Even his dimple had flattened. The transformation was so swift she wondered if she imagined the look they'd shared. Stung and bewildered, she shoved on her glasses.

"Haven't you been taught any manners?" a voice boomed suddenly. "Look at me, girl!"

Wren blinked in the direction of the angry shout and caught a dizzying glimpse of a man dressed in black armor striding toward her. She saw boots, a flowing cape in fabric that seemed to dance with a light all of its own, and a pinched, disapproving expression on the huge man's face as he reached for her and yanked off her eyeglasses.

Everything around her clouded over, except for her father's hand as thick fingers closed around the glasses, crushing them. He threw the shattered pieces to the floor.

*You disappointed him.* Not only him, but all her

suitors. She felt their contemptuous stares raking over her, even Aral's whose soft, sad gaze had given her hope only to steal it in the next breath.

*"Well?"*

Enveloped in her blurry world, Wren made fists in the fabric of her skirts. Before she could receive the warlord's blessing, she had to pay respects. No matter how hard she tried, she couldn't recall the words she'd rehearsed with Sabra.

"Speak!" The booming voice again.

Wren quaked. Her mind was a blank.

The warlord's armor creaked. His voice was low and stern. "I expected more of you than this, Awrenkka."

Her hands fidgeted with her skirt.

A heavy sigh. "You can't see, girl. Are you mute, too?"

"N-no, Warlord."

*"Father!* Say it!" he roared.

"Father. Noble hero, dear leader, you are my light in the dark, my way and my reason. I obey you. I worship you." The words she'd rehearsed spilled out. "I will die for you."

She forced herself to meet his eyes. Somewhere in their blurred, dark depths she sensed a spark of approval.

The warlord's hand landed heavily on the top of her head. He could crush her as easily as he did the glasses, she thought. "You are my flesh and blood, Awrenkka. It means you are different from the rest. Better."

Different. She knew that. Didn't want that. But better? Her?

"Heed my words, daughter, and carry them with you all the days of your life. My blood is your blood. My DNA is your destiny. Do not forget it. Do not ever seek to escape it."

"Yes, Father. I mean, no, Father." She stopped, biting her lip, wanting to melt into the floor and disappear.

The warlord turned in a blur of black and strode away. She felt the eyes of the battlelords on her. Most of all, Aral's. Sabra was grabbing her hand in the next moment, whisking her from the hall.

On the shuttle ride back to Barokk, Wren struggled not to be sick. Everything was a blur. It magnified the other sensations—the peculiar odor of a spacecraft, the loud noise of the air flowing and the engine and, worst of all, the rolling and dropping and spinning. She hoped her stomach stayed down. She never wanted to set foot on another spaceship. She'd have to, of course, when she left to marry. Maybe the warlord would give up trying after today. Nursing the thought, she huddled in misery, haunted by the memory of Aral Mawndarr and the heady feeling their shared gaze had conjured, the whirlwind of joy and confusion. "Aral seemed different from the rest," she mused quietly.

Sabra stiffened. "Don't be fooled. He's a Mawndarr."

"But he seemed…kind."

Sabra squeezed Wren's chin between her fingers. Her tight grip made Wren wince. "He's a Mawndarr. They're vicious killers, all."

"But his son—"

"Don't be fooled. The boy will turn out like the father. A Mawndarr."

Shock rippled through Wren at the woman's vehemence. "I don't want to marry any of them. If Father makes me, I'll run away. I'll—"

"Hush. It won't happen today. Or even tomorrow. For now you will live safe with me on Barokk."

It was all Wren wanted. She never wanted her life with Sabra to change.

The guardian rested a cool hand on Wren's sweaty face. "Your father broke those glasses like they were so much trash. Even after he saw how you depend on them. You'll have to wait for the next supply ship to have another pair. Why didn't I have a spare made?"

Wren squinted up at Sabra, clinging to the woman she loved with all her heart, and the only person who loved her. After meeting her father she knew it for a fact.

Sabra sighed. "How will we manage until then? How will you see?"

"Through *your* eyes, Sabra," Wren answered without hesitation. "It's how I've always seen the world."

Suddenly Sabra was dabbing at tears. She'd never seen the woman show such emotion. Even her voice trembled. "You trust me, don't you, sweetling? You always have. You expect I will do the right thing by you."

Why wouldn't she trust Sabra? Bewildered, Wren tried without success to discern Sabra's meaning. Her guardian acted as if she wanted to say something more, something important, maybe even something she didn't intend. Then, as if she'd reconsidered, she drew Wren closer, holding her tight to her breast the way she did when Wren was small. "'Your DNA is your destiny,'" she muttered, repeating the warlord's words. "Poor child. That isn't a blessing. It's a freepin' curse."

# CHAPTER ONE

*Approximately ten years later*

THE WARLORD'S FLOTILLA drifted perilously close to the Borderlands, a no-man's land between two mighty civilizations that wanted nothing more than to stamp out the other's existence and take the spoils. Tonight one of them would. Battlelord Aral Mawndarr fully intended to be on the side of victory. Whether he remained alive long enough to savor the feat was another matter entirely.

His orders as a battlelord in the Imperial Fleet were clear: no ships must penetrate the perimeter around the warlord's flotilla. Today he'd disobey those orders and allow one particular ship to get through. An enemy ship. Today he'd commit the ultimate betrayal of his leader, setting in motion the downfall of the Drakken Empire. Today, yes, today, he'd bring peace to a galaxy that remembered nothing but war.

As a firstborn son of a battlelord, Aral had always been ambitious. It was ingrained in him. It wasn't until his father had beaten him nearly to death, almost beyond the reach of life-saving nanomeds, that he'd realized the direction his ambition would take him.

Every crack of agony of his father's knuckles across

his face brought Aral closer to this moment. Every bolt of pain from the shock-whip forged his vow to destroy what Karbon loved and respected most: his status, his power, his empire.

Once his loyalties had shifted from the madman who'd sired him to the Coalition, treason had been surprisingly simple. At first, the Coalition didn't realize that a single spy was behind the apparent lucky breaks that seemed to fall into their hands at the perfect moment. As a young Imperial officer, Aral allowed the Coalition victories that no one suspected he'd been behind. He made the Imperial Fleet bleed.

The warlord blamed blindly for the inexplicable, inconceivable defeats. Pretending empathy and offering tactical advice, Aral became a favorite. He ingratiated himself to the man, was a frequent guest in the palace, and eventually the warlord came to trust him as one of his closest advisors. Ultimately, he was offered the sweetest prize of all—the warlord's daughter.

He never stopped preparing for this day. By tomorrow, trillions would applaud his actions as heroic. Those loyal to the warlord would denounce him as a traitor. He was neither a betrayer nor a hero, but a man driven by reasons that were as selfish as they were private. Believers would say his deeds guaranteed him a place in the heavens regardless. Aral turned a deaf ear to such talk. His sorry soul hadn't the barest chance at salvation. He was a battlelord and all that came with it. He'd had to kill and order killings. He'd had to send men into danger for the greater good. Sometimes he'd even sent loved ones.

It had been five years since his brother had disappeared. Bolivarr had worked as a wraith, a member of the covert arm of the Imperial Army, passing him intelligence. And then, nothing. He simply vanished without a trace. Aral never knew what happened, or why, and there was no one to ask.

In his final communication, Bolivarr transmitted that he knew of ancient religious writings that told of a key to a secret "with the potential to destroy us all."

Except that it destroyed only Bolivarr.

Aral tightened his gut, recalling the data Bolivarr had sent. The self-destruct coding had delayed just long enough for Aral to memorize a drawing of five glowing marks, a pair on each side and one at the top. It was centered on a page with many lines of unfamiliar runes he'd glimpsed too quickly to puzzle out. He hadn't stopped trying; too much depended on figuring it out.

By the blasted fates, he would. His brother had died because of that knowledge; he was certain. The boy he'd protected from his father's cruel hand had grown up only to be struck down in violence by another's.

*I will win today in your name, brother.* In some small way, seeing his grand plan to its conclusion would justify Bolivarr's death, for Aral surely had not made peace with it.

"I have confirmation, Lord Mawndarr." Battlecommander Kazara Kaan, his second-in-command, took her customary spot next to him on the bridge. Kaz was one of only a few female officers in the fleet, and the only Drakken female in a leadership position. "The ship is through the perimeter," she said.

Aral's pulse jumped a notch at her words. He of course didn't let it show. No one would be able to say he'd gleaned the smallest bit of pleasure from what he was about to do. It was a grim task, but one long in the making.

He squared his shoulders. The leather and metal accoutrements on his uniform crackled and creaked with the motion. "Our business here is done, War-major. Give the order to egress."

Kaz called to the pilot. "On Lord Mawndarr's order—set course for departure. Max speed."

"Aye!"

Calmly, Aral placed his hands behind his back. There. It was done. He'd allowed the enemy to breach the perimeter. He hoped the warlord's affairs were in order. And his daughter's.

*Especially his daughter's.* Aral had waited ten long years to make her his. If wreaking vengeance on Karbon was the reason for his actions, then sweet Awrenkka was his reward.

VARTEKEIR VANTOS was lucky to be alive. Running supplies through the Drakken blockade in the Borderlands wasn't the safest of jobs—hells, even the military didn't want to risk their ships or their hides to do it, but coming nose-to-nose with an Imperial battle-cruiser, a gargantuan vessel a hundred times larger than his ship, wasn't something he'd planned on. Instead, here he was, docking his ship at the outpost as if it were just another day.

It wasn't the first time he'd run into unexpected company in the Borderlands. Usually, he could shoot or talk his way out of it, or simply disappear—aka run.

"Vantos, you're living on borrowed time." Keir heard the comment so often that he gave the name to his ship. He'd remind them it was his skill not luck that got him through, of course, but, hells, this time they were right. His abilities, his instincts, his hands had nothing to do with it. It was luck, damn good luck. Crossing paths with that battle-cruiser, he shouldn't have made it back at all, let alone in one piece.

Irritably, he scrubbed his knuckles across a rough chin. Blast it all. He needed sleep, and he needed a shave. But above all, he needed a drink. This particular outpost's watering hole would be open and ready for business, even at this hour, filled with Coalition fighter pilots and other blockade-runners, traders like him who specialized in getting critical supplies in an out of the Borderlands, the no-man's land between two mighty civilizations that wanted nothing more than to stamp the other's existence and take the spoils. The survival rate of the average "runner" was less than a year. Eight months, to be exact, from getting lured in by the prospect of sky-high profits to do a job the military wanted no part of to crossing paths with an Imperial ship where every captain was either a sadistic killer or a trigger-happy psycho, and usually both. Eight months from that first border run to the last. Keir had been at it for four and a half years.

He focused his bleary eyes on the docking bay looming in his forward window. A double beep-beep in his ear piece told him that outpost security interrogated his craft one last time. All military bases double– and triple-checked craft coming in on final approach. The Drakken had blown facilities into micro-chunks using bait-and-switch tactics before.

Today security deemed him one of the "good guys," a stretch in anyone's imagination (in Keir's opinion), opening the clamshell doors to allow him through. With a shudder and a solid click of the locking mechanism, *Borrowed Time* slid into place.

How badly did those blasted Drakken ding up his ship?

Keir shut down the drive core and shoved out of his seat, pulling a nanopick from his pocket and slipping it between his lips. A fresh burst of mint woke up his mouth as he pushed up and out the hatch and jumped down to the platform. Luranium had a distinctive odor when burned to a crisp. The air around the hull stank of it. He stalked to the aft engine pod and appraised the damage. "Blast my ass."

"They did." The crew chief on duty whistled as she took in the condition of his ship. "Talk's all over the station that you ran into an Imperial battle-cruiser." The chief's eyes shone with misplaced awe as she waited for Keir to confirm. "And instead of blasting you into so many atoms, it fired a warning shot and let you go. How'd you manage to do that, Vantos?"

"I didn't do anything. They barely stopped to say hello. By the time I realized what happened, they were running away as fast as their little plasma core could carry them."

"You'd better tell the commander."

"*Your* commander." Keir was civilian, not military, and he made damn sure the people he worked for kept that straight. The star-major and his officers were always trying to shake down Keir and the other runners for intelligence information. Keir revealed what he thought he should—for the good of the Coalition and all that—but he was always careful to hold on to his, ah, trade secrets, as he liked to call them, the little things that kept him alive. People assumed he didn't care if he lived or died. He had news for them—he did. Taking on risk kept him from thinking too hard on his past, or even the future. But one thing was pretty clear in his mind—he intended to be around awhile to enjoy life. "Yeah, I made the required encounter report. There wasn't much to tell."

"Still, Vantos, a runner facing down an Imperial battle-cruiser and *they* blinked first? The news is already spreading. You're gonna be a hero around here."

"Look, they ran, and I ran. Hero stuff is for you boys and girls to do, not me." He wanted no part of it. Something about seeing both parents show up in body bags sucked the glamour out of "duty, honor, galaxy." He'd stick with "No commitments, no promises," and maybe "Stay under the radar," too.

Pleasure and freedom made life go around, anyway. At sixteen, he'd dedicated his life to the pursuit of both. At twenty-eight, he saw no reason to change.

The chief inspected the ship as she spoke. "What happened with you and that battle-cruiser seems to confirm all those rumors coming in. They're saying there's been a revolt. Drakken believers have overthrown the warlord."

Keir cracked up. "If you believe that, sweetheart, then I'm a virgin. Better yet, you are." Unlike in the Coalition, which was ruled by queens believed to be descended in an unbroken line from real gods and goddesses, in the Empire, religion was a dirty word, and had been ever since the goddesses fled the Drakken worlds eons ago to escape religious persecution. It split the settled galaxy in two, provoking a war that had raged ever since. Billions of believers still worshipped in secret. If they were caught, they were murdered on the spot. Now, after all this time, they'd finally decided to fight back? "Look, chief, I'm not religious, but I sure hope those believers enjoy their few minutes of fame. The warlord's going to crush them and love every blasted minute."

"I dunno, Vantos. There might be something to it based on what happened to you out there. Battle-cruisers don't run away. The Drakken are desperate, scared. Maybe you should stay out of the Borderlands for a while. Take some time off."

"Aw, chief. It almost sounds as if you're worried about me."

She rolled her eyes, telling him he was right, as she bent over to peer at the underside of the damaged engine. Probably calculating how much she was going to charge him for the repairs. True to form, she pulled a data-pad from the pocket of her flightsuit and started punching in data. "Nearly severed the pod. Do you have any idea how close you came to not making it back?"

"Some," he said dryly.

"You'd never know it, seeing how you're standing here giving me dirty looks about how much you're going to have to pay to repair the ass you almost got blown off. Every week you get closer to buying the farm. Go over to my kit and grab a paint stick. Go on. I'll help you repaint your ship's name from *Borrowed Time* to *Out of Time*."

"Bite me."

She transferred data from her pad to the outpost's main computer. "I would, but you never let me."

"I never said no. You just didn't want it on my terms."

"You mean a quickie and goodbye? You're right. I like my men to stick around for a while."

"I'm not the sticking kind."

She stopped to look him over. "If the war ends, it's going to change everything. Most of us will go back to being civilian. There'll be no more blockades to run. Don't you ever want to settle down?"

"Give me one good reason why."

"A family. A place to call home."

He stroked a hand over *Borrowed Time*'s fuselage. "This pretty little ship is all the home and family I need."

"That's no life, Keir."

Women. They were always trying to domesticate him. He let the chief get away with it because she was one of the best damn mechanics around. "I'll be in the bar. Just send the bill to my datapad. And stop listening to those crazy rumors. There isn't an atom of truth to them."

The war over, my ass, Keir thought, scouring fingers through his hair as he sauntered into the bar. The place was filled to capacity with military pilots and a few runners. He caught the bartender's eye. The man nodded, pouring him a double shot of house whiskey as a cheer went up. Then someone started singing the Coalition anthem and the whole group joined in.

Keir cringed at the show of patriotism. He wanted a drink, not a reminder he was on a military base. It was a simple arrangement: he used them, and they used him. That's as far as it went.

Keir sniffed his whiskey in anticipation of the first of a good many drinks when it hit him that the singing was due to the scene playing on the entertainment screen on the opposite wall. Every blasted gun-junkie in the bar had their eyes on the screen.

"Did you hear?" the bartender said from behind him. "They've confirmed it. The war's over. The Drakken issued a full and unconditional surrender."

"Don't believe it. We've heard fairy tales like this before—new battleships guaranteed to pave the way to victory. Did they? And what about outposts fool-proofed against terror attacks? Tell the families of the people who promised they'd be home for dinner that day and ended up skulled instead."

Like his parents. Keir clenched his abs as if a boot were headed for his gut in a bar fight. The son of two soldiers, he had grown up eager to defend the Coalition from the Drakken Horde, the embodiment of all evil. Orphaned, he changed plans. Sacrifice was noble, but where did it get you? Nowhere. After a few months kicking around the galaxy, dogged by grief, he ran into some civilian traders. He used the last of his credits to get one of them to teach him to fly. As a pilot-trader, he could do some good for the Coalition without the need for anything remotely heroic.

Instead of killing Drakken, he profited from them, first as a gun runner then eventually running the gauntlet of their blockades. Every time he got through their nets, every time one of the creeps took a shot at him, he cele-brated not pinning on Coalition rank at sixteen and picking up the fight where his parents left off.

Now they were saying the war was over?

Fighting a sense of disorientation he couldn't blame on whiskey, Keir stared up at the entertainment screen. Sure enough, various politicians and officers briefed journalists on a foiled abduction of the Goddess-queen Keira. Prime-Admiral Zaafran, commander-in-chief, spoke from a dais.

As far as Keir could tell, the warlord kidnapped the queen, helped by traitors inside the palace. His grand plan was to marry her to his son, combining her divine blood with barbaric Hordish blood to create the most powerful dynasty the galaxy had ever known. It seemed the warlord's massive ego hadn't accounted for how many billions worshipped the goddesses in secret, his own guards included. When they realized the queen was in danger, it was all over.

"It in effect broke the dam holding the faithful back," Zaafran finished. "The warlord's blood hadn't even cooled when Drakken believers began pouring out of the shadows. Thus, in an almost bloodless coup, the Drakken Empire crashed, bringing peace to a galaxy that remembers nothing but war."

At the sign of eternally stoic Prime-Admiral Zaafran showing real emotion himself, there wasn't a dry eye in the house. Or a sober one. The celebration became deafening, the rah-rah fight songs worst of all, drowning out the rest of the news stream.

Keir slugged back his whiskey in a single swallow. All he'd wanted to do was have a drink in peace. Blasted hells. He'd had no idea it would be literally.

## CHAPTER TWO

"Peace. Bah! It will never last. The only trustworthy Drakken is a dead Drakken."
—Admiral Brit Bandar, Coalition war hero (remarks issued off the record at the commencement of Galactic Reunification Hearings)

THE DOOR TO WREN'S BEDROOM crashed open, rattling the eyeglasses sitting on her bedside table next to a stack of old, dog-eared storybooks and a barely operable datareader. She fumbled for her glasses, sliding them up her nose in time to see her guardian slamming the windows shut and drawing the shutters closed. "Up, up—*now,* Awrenkka. We have little time and much yet to do."

"Ah, Sabra, but it's barely light." She groaned into her pillow, not yet ready to leave its soft warmth. She'd stayed up too late with her nose buried in a book.

Sabra yanked off the covers. "You are in danger."

"Here on sleepy, little Barokk?" She opened one, skeptical eye. Little of excitement ever happened on this all-female, sanctuary of a planet. Unless one considered making sand paintings and knotting shell jewelry, reciting poetry and learning Drakken history exciting.

The boom of a ship entering the atmosphere tore

through the chill, foggy streets outside the chalet. Wren shot up in bed. "A ship, Sabra. Hooray." Wren swung her feet off the bed as Sabra rooted through drawers, pulling out items of clothing—the ugliest garments she could find by the looks of the worn, faded cloak and battered boots adding to a growing pile. "It's been ages since we've received supplies. Months and months." She yanked her arms through a filmy robe, hugging it close to her breasts for modesty in her haste to reach the window. A cargo freighter meant fresh supplies and a glimpse of men—wild, virile, unsuitable men. "Let me close enough to see this time. Please, Sabra. Just looking isn't *dangerous*—"

"Wren, no." Sabra snatched her arm and spun her back before she reached the window. Wren grabbed her glasses to keep them from slipping off. A glimpse of Sabra's face revealed something she'd never seen there before: fear.

"Ah, dear Goddess…" Sabra made a circle with her fist over her heart then kissing the knuckle of her index finger. "Watch over this girl, for she knows not what stalks her. Help me to keep her safe. I can't tell if I am being selfish or wise, but I am veering off my path to help her find hers. Blessed Goddess, I remain your servant. In your name I so say."

Dumbstruck, Wren stared, both aghast and fascinated at the sight of Sabra praying. Sabra was a believer. Wren had suspected as much but never worked up the nerve to ask. In the empire, the warlord was worshipped. In the Coalition, they worshipped the goddesses, who were believed to be divine beings in human form, descended from those who fled the Hordish worlds eons ago to escape religious persecution.

A sense of betrayal competed with a burning curiosity about the most significant woman in her life. "You withheld information from me."

"To keep you safe. I could not allow you to develop practices that would endanger you in a battlelord's household. Wives have been beaten to death for far less."

"You never even gave me the choice to take that risk or not!" Even Sabra wanted her kept dumb and docile.

"And to keep me safe, sweetling, to be able to protect you. Believers are murdered on the spot."

"Not on Barokk," Wren argued uneasily as the world and the life she thought she knew tipped more and more off kilter.

"No?" Sabra shoved a bra band in her hands. "There are believers here in abundance. Have you ever seen anyone pray? Those who would murder them live amongst us, too."

Dozens of faces flitted through Wren's mind— teachers, guardians, servants and the girls, who prayed in secret, who would kill them? Religion was seen as a threat to the very survival of the Drakken Empire. As the warlord's daughter, was she not tasked with defending the empire against believers? Wren squeezed her hands into fists, watching the play of sinew and muscle. She'd been taught how to fight, from hand-to-hand combat to handling blades and guns. No matter how many times Sabra assured her that the skills were for self-defense, Wren's aversion to violence manifested itself in clumsy attempts to learn the moves.

"The warlord insists," Sabra would tell her, and the training would resume. Was this eventuality why, her kin gunned down in cold blood, necessitating her escape? Or were the lessons to prepare her to fight in the warlord's name? The possible answer left her shuddering.

Sabra shoved a many-times-mended blouse at her. "Put this on."

"That's a rag," Wren protested.

"Wait until you see the pants." Sabra pulled it over her head.

"I won't dress until you tell me what's happened."

Sabra took hold of Wren's arms, tightly, to the point of pain. "The ship you heard is neither a freighter nor Drakken. It's Coalition."

Wren gasped, her gaze automatically jerking outside. Their age-old enemy here? A sickening sense of vulnerability competed with blunt, primitive shock.

"I was summoned with the other guardians to the governor's office during the night. The captain briefed us from orbit. They aren't here to attack but to evacuate. There's been a revolt. The Empire is no more. We gave the Coalition our unconditional surrender—five months ago."

Horror sucked the air from Wren's lungs. "We're first learning of this now?"

"The entire quadrant has been isolated by a blockade. No one could get in or out, or any outside news."

That explained the absence of supply ships. Everyone had assumed the usual delays. There was plenty of stored food on isolated Barokk. No one had yet begun to worry about shortages. "It's a lie. The warlord would have tried to warn us. He would have come for me, made sure I was safe first." But he hadn't. His utter disregard stung.

"Sweetling." Sabra lifted her hand to Wren's cheek, a touch to comfort as well as steady her. "The warlord is dead."

Wren recoiled as if the words themselves were a physical attack. "And Rorkk?"

"Your half-brother, too. Assassinated, both of them. My sorrows, sweetling. The warlord was, after all, your sire."

Tears didn't fall. Terror didn't squeeze her chest. Only quiet outrage boiled at the atrocity committed against her family. To whom did she owe such composure—her murdered father or Lady Seela, the legendary beauty he'd impregnated and cast off for producing a daughter before a son?

"Get dressed. We're to meet Ilkka in the shed. We've hidden emergency supplies there."

Wren sorted through her wardrobe, her mind reeling. Her mind was fuzzy at the edges. It was hard to think. Sabra snatched a pair of shoes from her hands. "No, Awrenkka, not those shoes. The sturdy ones—the ones you wore to the mountains last autumn. And these pants, the ones I chose for you, not those."

Irritated, Sabra tossed the cloud-soft pants across the room. "Aren't you listening to me? The Imperial Palace is under Coalition control. It means the warlord's private records are under their control, too. As soon as they figure out he has a daughter, they'll come for you."

Thunder rattled the windows. A landing ship.

Panic flared in Sabra's eyes. "We must leave—now."

*They'll come for you.* The warning cleaved through the fog in her brain. They wanted her—*her.* They would do to her what they did to her family and quite likely injure or kill protective Sabra in the process.

"Hurry!" Wren snatched the thick, heavy boots from Sabra's hands, shoving her legs into an equally rugged pair of pants. Sabra cinched the laces on her boots so tight that Wren winced. Grabbing two travel cloaks, the woman took her hand and pulled her out the rear door. The early dawn light was frosty and still. No birds sang. They were frightened into silence by the foreign roar of the ship. It emanated from the main square.

They tumbled into the dark shed and slammed the door closed. The musty air held fast to the tang of stored vegetables and the dust of many decades. Her guardian leaned against the door and let out a shuddering breath. "Now we can prepare and finish disguising you."

"Answer my questions, Sabra. What happened to my father? How did he die?"

"He brought it upon himself. His greed, his arrogance—" Sabra stopped short of saying worse, relaying instead a convoluted tale of kidnapping and treachery beyond comprehension. Queen Keira, stolen to be her half-brother's wife, her divine blood mixed with that of the house of Rakkuu to create the most powerful dynasty the galaxy had ever known. The queen was worshipped as goddess, as was her mother and, before that, her grandmother and so on. The sheer logistics of pulling off such a brazen feat would have required traitors within the Goddess Keep itself.

No wonder her father had long ignored her. It seemed he was a very busy man. And now he was dead. Betrayed by his own minions, his closest advisors and the people he tried to exterminate in a sweeping campaign of genocide.

Wren struggled with Sabra's incomprehensible statements. What was true and what was propaganda generated by the Coalition captain who'd briefed them remained a mystery. "More secrets." Wren heard the accusing edge in her voice. "How many more will you keep from me?"

"There are more secrets than you can ever imagine, dear one." Sabra's eyes seemed unfathomably old as she searched her face. She looked haggard. She wasn't young anymore, but she hadn't looked her age until now. "Once I thought your having too much knowledge was dangerous. No longer. I see now that your naïveté is dangerous. Forgive me, child. Forgive me. The galaxy will turn to you next, Wren. Your blood is the last link to the warlord. The Coalition will put you on trial and execute you. Alive, you pose a threat to any treaty, no matter how it is exacted."

"Bah. A threat in the Coalition's mind only. Our people will never follow a female warlord."

"Perhaps not, but mated to a man of the right credentials and ambition, you could start a new dynasty. Loyalists will do all they can to resurrect the empire. All they can to win. They will do all they can to find *you*."

"If I were to join them, Sabra, and I won't. Father's dead. I'm in charge of my destiny now. I say who I will marry or who I will not."

"If Drakken believers find you first it won't matter what the Coalition or the loyalists desire. The believers will make you suffer in the most gruesome way in retaliation for what was done to them. Then there is the risk of attack by rogues and pirates. Times are desperate, child, and will become more so before they become better. The Coalition captain told us that displaced Drakken soldiers by the thousands are filling their free time—and their pockets—marauding. If word gets out that you're alive, I fear they may try to hand you over to a pirate lord who'll auction you off to the highest bidder."

Pirates, believers, loyalists and the Coalition. "Is there anyone *not* hunting me down?"

Sabra clasped Wren's chin between her fingers. The intensity of her amber eyes reminded Wren of a long-ago day when she'd warned her about the Mawndarr family. "Finally you see the danger, stubborn girl."

"Not so stubborn," Wren admitted in a whisper. "Scared."

"For good reason." Sabra's voice roughened with emotion. "Awrenkka e'Rakuu, you are the most wanted woman in the galaxy."

BATTLELORD KARBON MAWNDARR *threw the woman face-down onto the dining-room table. With one hand buried in her luxuriant blond hair, he unfastened his trousers.*

*Rigid with horror, Aral stood paralyzed in the entryway. Father was hurting Nanjin! Her cries had lured him from the far side of the mansion. Nanjin was his favorite teacher, and Bolivarr's, too. In the short time she'd been with them she'd become one of the few good things in their lives. Living in this household was hells— his father, a source of terror, and his mother? A sneered name, usually accompanied by a curse spat from his father's lips. She'd died in childbirth delivering Bolivarr. Fates had mercy on her soul, it seemed. With the absence of any kind of permanent female in the home, the boys delighted in Nanjin's attention and affection.*

*Nanjin screamed.*

*Aral sprinted across the room. "Don't!" He took his father's shirt in his fists and tried to pull him away from the sobbing teacher. The man was solid, a large man. "Let her go. Father, please."*

*Karbon snarled at Aral as he glared over his shoulder, his face plum red and murderous. His acrid breath and his pink eyes told Aral he'd been drinking sweef. The liquor was distilled from the berries of a type of conifer and mixed with an additive used to lubricate machinery. Homemade stills abounded on military ships. It was cheap, easy to make. Abuse rotted the teeth not to mention various internal organs, unless one was as wealthy as Lord Mawndarr and could afford nano-meds to reverse the damage. Sweef was poison, the drink of space-hands and pirates, not the upper class. But sweef didn't play favorites. It was equally addictive no matter what one's station in life.*

*The teacher tried to wriggle free. Karbon slammed her down with the fist Aral knew so well. Then he fastened his pants and turned around. "You better have a good reason for interrupting me, boy, and thinking you can tell me what to do."*

*"You're hurting her." Aral swallowed hard. He was losing nerve with each breath but trying not to show it.*

*"Is that what you call it?" The man smiled. "Perhaps it is time for your first lesson in pleasuring a female." His hand shot out so fast it was a blur. Those thick strong fingers gripped Aral's neck and cut off his air supply. He was lifted by that hand as if he weighed nothing. Sputtering, he clawed at the fingers around his throat, trying to pry them open.*

*Cra-ack. An open hand slapped across his face. And again. He tasted the familiar tang of blood. His vision quickly dimmed, going from red to gray to black.*

*He floated in and out of broken dreams.*

*Then awareness seeped back. The pressure around*

*his neck had eased. His vision returned as his pants were yanked down around his knees.*

*Shocked, he pushed away, but his father slapped the back of his skull, making his ears sing with agony. "Go on. Do her. You're a Mawndarr. Prove it. Make me proud."*

*Aral's throat hurt too much to allow him a gulp of shame. He was fifteen. He'd not yet been with a woman.*

*Another blow. "Move, boy! Do you need me to show you how?"*

*Horror and self-loathing sickened Aral. He refused to show his fear. Showing fear always made it worse.*

*"All right, then. If you can't make her cry out, I will." His father brought a knife to the woman's long, slender neck and pressed the edge to her jugular....*

"AH, FATES. *No!*" Aral lurched upright off the chaise upon which he'd fallen asleep, expecting to see his open, shaking hands glistening with blood. There had been so much of it.

Aral's pulse hammered in his skull as he blinked to awareness. He was in his luxuriously appointed, shipboard quarters. Alone. He'd merely sought a few hours' rest. *You should know better.* Just when he thought he was safe, his past would bring him to his knees. He'd tried every kind of tranq and sleeping elixir over the years, and any targeted nanomeds he could beg or steal from the Coalition. None worked. None made his nights a time of rest.

He'd learned to compensate for the lack of sleep by strengthening his body. For Aral there was an added benefit to working out—a few dreamless hours of rest. But it took sheer exhaustion to get him there. He savored the pain, took it in. This pain he controlled. This pain *he owned*.

Self-inflicted torture, his second-in-command Kaz argued. Perhaps. The stronger his body, the more finely honed his muscles, the more he could hold off the effects of his tortured thoughts. His impending madness, he often feared. Perhaps he was deluding himself, but if anything, physical exertion placed his focus where it did some good—his crusade.

He stalked to the shower and stood under the gush of water, seeking elusive peace as the blood still roared in his head. A weapon lay within arm's reach. He'd far outlived the lifespan of a traitor and a spy. Well aware was he of that fact, every blasted minute of every day. Guards watched over him around the clock, but one must never become complacent or trust fully. He'd not dreamt of the rape in some time. Of all the incidents in his life orchestrated by his father, that one had been the most disturbing. It was a turning point. It was the day that had started him down the road that led to here and now.

The nightmare reiterated his greatest fear: losing Awrenkka to Karbon. She was more like him than anyone alive, a product of evil who had somehow held on to her humanity. She needed his protection as much as he was compelled to offer it to her. He'd find her, and in doing so he'd save them both.

He hoped he wasn't too late.

The memory of the day he met her remained crystal clear. His beating earlier that morning had been particularly harsh. Ever mindful of other's opinions, his father had pumped him with enough nanomeds to erase the visible bruises. Why, they were about to have an audience with the Supreme Warlord of the Drakken Horde, after all. Impressions were everything. One couldn't have their sons limping or bleeding, could one? Especially a son on the short list of possible marriage candidates for the warlord's daughter.

Aral had been forced to stand there with the battle-lords as the warlord paraded the girl in to tantalize the men. The older men had recoiled in unison at the shy, undersized girl and her huge thick glasses. "She looks like an insect," Karbon had remarked later when they were in private.

The girl had walked past their group, noticeably unsure of herself as she sneaked peeks at the men. Then her focus landed on Aral and stopped. She may have been wearing cumbersome eyeglasses, but he scarcely noticed them at all. Her eyes were the clearest, purest violet-blue, and utterly unguarded. That gaze grabbed at his heart, stealing his breath.

She was the most beautiful girl he'd ever seen.

But it was more than that. He saw a girl much like himself, both of them completely cowed by their fathers, in their thrall and utterly terrorized. Like him, she must have thought there was no escape. He quite remembered thinking: what if *he* were her escape? He, Aral Mawndarr, would rescue the warlord's daughter.

Then he panicked. Ridding his face of any traces of besotted fascination, he aimed his coldest expression possible at her. She appeared stung, then disenchanted. He knew then his tactic had worked. After all, he'd had the best example in the galaxy from which to learn such a glare.

He'd wanted to find her and pull her aside outside the ears of her chaperones. He'd explain everything. But of course, that was impossible. If he showed any interest at all in her, his father would have noticed and campaigned to marry the girl himself, if only so Aral couldn't.

Marrying Karbon would have been the death of her—if not physically, then of the spirit. He'd saved her. She just didn't know it yet.

Exiting the shower, he scoured a towel over his skin as he glared outside a nearby viewport. Outside was a dark, frigid void, much like him. His reflection glowered fiercely back at him. He looked too much like Karbon. Those looks had served him well when he'd needed them to. Being feared made him more efficient.

*She'll fear you, too.*

Most likely, yes. But her alternatives were worse.

By now Coalition intelligence had swarmed into the palace and ransacked the warlord's records. After all, he'd all but handed them the keys to the palace on a platter. Evidence of another child would shock them. Paranoid to the extreme and ashamed he'd produced a daughter before a son, the warlord had never officially recorded the existence of his eldest. The public knew only of Rorkk, a younger brother. Learning of Awrenkka was one thing. Finding her would be another matter, however. The warlord had been quite smug telling Aral of the false leads he'd left for anyone who tried to find his daughter.

It wouldn't stop the Coalition from casting a galaxy-wide net to catch her. Aral was banking on his arms being the very last place they looked.

## CHAPTER THREE

THE STARSHIP in Barokk's main square rumbled ominously. Men's shouts told of soldiers patrolling the streets—Coalition soldiers—all because of the warlord's kidnapping of Queen Keira for Rorkk's wife. Did he not consider the effect such a brazen crime would have on the balance of power in the galaxy and the faith of trillions of people? Did the man's ambition have no bounds?

Wren swung between being in awe of her father, despairing she could never live up to his expectations, and the insinuations Sabra had made of his true nature. If the warlord was truly this evil, this despicable, then what did that make Wren? Whose blood dominated—his or her mother's? She knew nothing of Lady Seela other than that she was a great beauty. It was obvious Wren didn't take after her at all. She was her father's daughter, then. "Perhaps those wanting to see me dead are justified. Who's to say the warlord's evil doesn't flow in my veins and simply hasn't manifested itself yet?"

Certainty stole over Sabra's features. "Impossible."

"I fear what may lurk inside me."

"You have a pure and open heart, dear one."

"You can't be certain."

Sabra lifted a hand to Wren's cheek. "Do you remember, long ago, returning from your father's battle-cruiser after he broke your glasses?"

"Yes. I was sick to my stomach." Wren adjusted her glasses. More than space sickness had nauseated her that day. Meeting all those potential husbands; seeing grave, young Aral Mawndarr's gaze change from openly curious to cold; knowing she'd humiliated herself in front of him and the others, as well as disappointed her father, she'd tried to bury the memory without success. Yet, Sabra had remained constant then and all these years since, her anchor, as she was now.

"I didn't know how you would manage without the glasses. Then you told me that you saw the world though my eyes, and that you always had. Ah, sweetling. You trusted me utterly. I saw it in your face. I felt it in my soul. It brought me clarity for the first time. I saw my true mission—to protect you, to keep you innocent of evil. It changed everything." She was rummaging through boxes Wren had never known they owned, choosing some items, discarding others. "Your father never thought past his reign. He never planned for an overthrow. So when you were small, Ilkka and I decided that we'd make sure you got to safety in the event anything happened to him."

"You mean making sure I went with loyalists. A battlelord."

Awkwardness tempered Sabra's grave nod as she opened a small box filled with a small cache of jewels. "That was then. My view of what I considered safe changed. It changed when I changed. I love you like a daughter. Gods save my soul. I'm taking you on that Coalition ship."

"Does Ilkka know?"

"She will. We'll all go. We'll disappear amongst thousands of others just like us. It's the only way. I'll not sentence you to a life of misery." She drew a dagger out of a leather case and brought the blade to Wren's hair. "It must be shortened—to your chin or higher."

Wren might be the most wanted woman in the galaxy, but it seemed if her guardian had anything to say in the matter she'd soon be the most unrecognizable.

"Wait." She grabbed her guardian's wrist, stopping her. Dark, gleaming brown with more than a hint of flame-red, her hair swung loose just above her bottom. It was one of the few physical attributes about herself in which she took pride. Cutting it off seemed so…drastic. "It's all happening so fast."

*Will you take charge of your life, or will I always have to care for you?* The question—the dare—burned in the woman's eyes.

A flash of weak sunlight preceded Ilkka ducking into the shed with them. She closed the door behind her. The tall rangy guardian was left silhouetted against the light seeping though the wall slats. More than Sabra's friend, she was a backup caregiver in case anything happened to Sabra, as well as the only other person on Barokk who knew Wren's true identity. "I've readied the hopper. It's hidden behind the grain tower. We'll fly out from under their noses. We'll wait on the southern continent for loyalists to come."

Loyalists. The word alone was chilling enough, let alone contemplating a future with no free will.

"Plans have changed," Sabra informed Ilkka. "We'll evacuate with the rest. She'll be safer in that camp than in the clutches of someone we don't know, or trust."

"Clutches." Ilkka rolled her eyes. "Such drama, Sabra. Please. She cannot be allowed to fall into enemy control. You of all people know that. The loyalists are our future. Her future."

"My destiny is not yours to decide—not anymore." Wren's protest drew surprised glances from both women. The quiet mouse had spoken. She quite liked the feeling, yet a small voice warned her to keep control, to not complain, to *be good*. "There will be no husband. I'm free now."

"Free?" Ilkka laughed. "The warlord's daughter, free." Her expression turned frighteningly serious then. "Your bloodline is too precious to lose. Don't you understand? There *will* be a marriage, and you will do it for your people. Your empire."

Wren had long since accepted the fact that she'd be married off to a stranger, one who viewed her as a possession and a marker of his status, not as his love, his wife. Once, she thought there was hope for her dreams when she met Aral Mawndarr, but he turned out to be like all the rest. She'd accepted her fate without much complaint, never admitting the true extent of her terror. Now everything had changed. Her future was even more uncertain and dangerous than before, yes, but it was *hers*. For the first time the prospect of freedom danced before her, and by the fates, she wasn't going to let Ilkka, the greedy old crone, take it away from her.

"Give me the dagger." Wren extended her hand. Sabra offered her the blade. This time, no convincing was required. Wren grabbed a handful of thick, glossy hair and sliced through it.

The first cut was raspy and loud. The rest she refused to hear. A few hacks later her beautiful hair lay in a pile at her boots. What was left tickled her neck, falling just shy of the bottom of her chin. Wren removed her glasses to blow off bits of hair from the lenses with a puff of air.

Sabra gathered the rest of their things while Ilkka paced angrily by the door. "Drakken currency is worthless now," Sabra explained. "There is some jewelry." She tied one pouch to Wren's belt and the other to hers.

"Thank the fates you thought of bringing valuables." Mortified, she realized she would have run with only the clothing on her back. Everything on Barokk had always been taken care of—arranged, repaired and pushed along. She'd never had to do anything, to plan. "Without you, I'd be lost, Sabra," she whispered.

Sabra crushed Wren close, wrapping her in strong arms. "Whatever happens, child, I am here for you. I will die for you."

Wren shook her head violently. "If anyone dies because of my kin, it will be me."

"Come on, come on, or we'll all die here," Ilkka urged.

Sabra pushed a travel cloak into Wren's shaking hands. "Keep your eyes down and let me do the talking for you."

Through the slats, she saw how quickly the fog had thickened, magnifying the rumble of a starship. It was a day to stay inside, sip warm soup and read, not fly away into the unknown. Her stomach rolled. The memory of her space sickness on the journey to see her father hadn't faded. She grew queasy with the mere thought of leaving the ground and all the accompanying forces on the body the feat required. What choice did she have? The ship was her only escape.

They headed for the door. Ilkka took Sabra by the elbow urging her to the side. "I'm no traitor. Allowing her to board the Coalition ship...it isn't right."

"It is *my right*. I'm her guardian. I'm entrusted with her survival."

In the background, the Coalition ship idled noisily. The other villagers were loading. They should be amongst them. It was Wren's chance to escape before her enemies caught up to her. "Sabra," she said. "We have to go."

"We will."

Sabra's assurance drew a disbelieving glare from Ilkka. "Think about what you're doing. She has the key to the treasure."

"*I* have the key. It's in my safekeeping."

"I'm not stupid, though you clearly think me to be. Only she can unlock it. The value is unimaginable. You cannot release it into Coalition possession. It's the last thing of worth the Empire has—besides her."

"The treasure doesn't belong to us. It belongs to Wren."

"And she belongs to the Empire."

Wren's gaze jumped from woman to woman as they played tug-of-war with her. The argument about treasure sounded too far-fetched to be real. It was like the old days when she'd tell Wren bedtime stories. Wren was wiser now. "You never told me about a treasure, Sabra."

"Because she wanted it in her control, not yours," Ilkka said.

"A lie!" Sabra's face was flushed with anger. The two former warriors faced off. Tension crackled. "It was too dangerous for her to know. I will tell her when it's safe to do so."

Ilkka shook her head. She turned to Wren, almost

with pity. "She kept it all to herself, didn't she? You don't know any of it—what Sabra is. What you are."

Wren shook her head.

"For one, your mother, Lady Seela, was—"

"Don't say it!" Sabra shoved Ilkka away. She extended her hand to Wren. "Come—come now. Hurry."

Ilkka regained her footing and grabbed Wren by her shirt, throwing her backward before her fingers met Sabra's. Wren fell over a crate of harvest tubers, spilling the pile of shorn hair and landing thankfully clear of the dagger. Her glasses were lost somewhere underneath her sprawled legs. Blurred figures and grunts of effort warned her of the worst—the two guardians were fighting over her.

Panicked, she hunted for her glasses on her hands and knees. She needed to see. She needed to—

A low, guttural cry of utter agony and despair filled the shed and chilled Wren to the core. *Sabra...* Wren's fingers closed around her glasses. She shoved them on. The scene came into focus: Sabra was down, writhing. Ilkka loomed over her, her arm raised high. Something metallic glinted in her hand.

Outrage built in Wren's chest, a breath-stealing swell of red-hot fury. Doubt evaporated in the fire of anger. It filled her with the desire to protect. To punish. Her pulse drummed it. She'd never felt an emotion so pure. The dagger was in her hands before she even formed the thought of what she intended to do with it.

Ilkka glanced over her shoulder. Not a smidgen of remorse appeared in her cold blue eyes. That coldness changed to disbelief as the dagger sailed across the shed and sank deep into her back. She made no sound. Her eyes remained accusingly on Wren for a few seconds more. The spark of life dimmed, lingered for a fraction of a second, then winked out as she crumpled to the ground.

Ilkka had died where she stood, holding the gaze of her killer. It was the most dreadful sight Wren had ever seen—life leaving a human body. Life that *she had taken.*

A moan had her wild gaze swerving back to Sabra. She was alive! Her heart clenched with raw despair as the echo of Sabra's cry repeated again and again in her mind. She dropped the dagger and ran to her guardian's body, crouching next to her. Sabra was panting as if in terrible pain.

"Where is the wound?" She slid frantic hands under her cloak. Her fingers collided with the blunt end of a dart embedded in the woman's stomach.

She yanked it out. It was a thin, bright blue cylinder.

"Poison," Sabra explained in staccato gasps. "Deadly."

"Fates. What do I do? Is there an antidote?"

Sabra was quivering from head to toe, sweating profusely. "My pouch. The p-pendant." She paused to cry out softly.

Frantic, Wren removed Sabra's pouch and dug inside. Her fingers closed around a chain. The metal was unusually cool to the touch. She pulled it out. A flat, black oval pendant hung from the chain. On its flawless surface, five tiny points of light glittered like stars on a summer night. Like a tiny constellation, they formed an obvious pattern—two lights on each side and one at the very tip. A little arrow. Despite her racing heart, despite her fear, the piece was eerily mesmerizing. "Here—"

"*Yours.* The key."

"To that treasure."

"And all that is lost…"

"But I don't want riches," Wren insisted, and choked up. "I want you."

Sabra's lips trembled. She, too, fought emotion. "Find Ara Ana. Make the galaxy whole." The words made little sense, but the ferocity in the dying woman's eyes told her that every word was important, terribly so. "Promise me." She grasped at Wren's blouse weakly, willing her cooperation with that intense gaze.

"All right. I'll find Ara Ana. I will."

Sabra nodded, the tension going out of her pain-racked body. Her eyes closed.

"Who is she? Sabra—where do I find her? Tell me." The woman shuddered and went still.

"Sabra!" Wren gave her a hard shake. She pushed on Sabra's chest then blew into her mouth, filling the woman's lungs with air. Panicked, she pumped her chest some more. It was no use. Sabra was gone, wasting her last bit of strength on talk of treasure, of keys, *of nonsense.* "Blast your secrets! Blast you!" Grief lanced Wren's heart. "I don't know where to go."

Soldiers yelled to one another in the streets. Their Coalition accents sounded crisp, foreign. It jolted Wren from her grief. She lifted her glasses to wipe away tears then looked around the aftermath in the shed. Ilkka lay facedown, the dagger in her back.

Several soldiers walked by the shed close enough for her to hear the sound of gravel grinding under their heavy boots as they went door to door, yard to yard, looking for stragglers. She couldn't be found here amongst the bodies. It would generate questions. Questions were dangerous.

She was dangerous. She saw the life fading from

those blue eyes all over again. She barely remembered the act itself, she'd been so driven to kill in that moment. *The beast was rattling the cage.* Shame heated her face and pressed on her soul. She was her father's daughter.

*"My blood is your blood. My DNA is your destiny."*

Unlocking a treasure was also her destiny, according to Sabra's dying words. She looped the pendant around her neck and hid it under her blouse, securing it under her bra band. It must be worth a fortune. It certainly looked as if it was. The last thing she wanted was such a valuable object in her possession, let alone the treasure it opened. People would fight to have that treasure in their possession as they would fight over her. Yet, she'd said she'd find it—and someone named Ara Ana. Worse, she'd promised to make the galaxy whole again, when she was the person most likely to tear it apart.

Blast her promise to a dying woman.

She fastened the travel cloak over her shoulders. Then she took Sabra's pouch and tied it to hers. Shoving open the door of the shed, she fled the stifling air and the stench of death. She fled evidence of what she was.

Lurching into the streets, she merged into the procession of refugees and didn't look back. An immense starship loomed ahead, and with it, a new and unnerving future.

# CHAPTER FOUR

ARAL PACED in the elegant confines of his study. Kaz was stretched out like a feline in one of the sinfully plush seats, observing him with the patrician features of their class, much like his but without the invisible scars, physical and mental, left by his father's harsh hand. The furniture and every inch of this starship was a far more obvious reminder of his father. After being forced to leave his battle-cruiser at war's end when the order came for all remaining Drakken vessels to be taken out of service for dismantling or study, he moved with his massively pared-down crew to a smaller, civilian ship owned by the Mawndarrs. He changed the name from *Blood Run* to *Nevermore,* but its origins weren't so easily erased. The craft both repulsed him in the memories it held, and also cheered him, for Aral's mere presence here meant that his father wasn't. They'd never been able to share the same space. Or even space itself, based on how many attempts to kill each other they'd each launched. The older man wouldn't be launching much at the moment, Aral knew. Karbon was running for his life from Coalition pursuers. Aral, on the other hand, enjoyed diplomatic immunity for having helped the Coalition in the war, though to this day they hadn't shared his crucial role with the public. A Drakken hero? It was a quite a new concept for most of them.

He tugged on the hem of his uniform jacket. The plush carpet muffled the sound of his polished boots. Old boots. New uniform. The disparity brought home just how much he'd changed the galaxy. He served in the Triad Alliance Forces now. On his chest was an emblem depicting a silver triangle, each side edged with a different color—blue, black and red. The Triad, an alliance of three civilizations. Blue represented Planet Earth, the birthplace of Prince Jared, Queen Keira's consort and the passenger on the ship he'd allowed through the perimeter. Earth was a newcomer to this once two-sided game. When it came to tech, Earthlings made the Drakken look downright advanced, but it had been kept safe from attack in the months before the end of the war, protected under its status as a Holy Shrine, thanks to it being the birthplace of Queen Keira's consort. It was quite an achievement for such a far-flung, water-covered little rock. Few Drakken had heard of Earth until their prince killed the warlord. The black side of the triangle represented the former Coalition, and the red the former Drakken Empire. Red, for blood, he thought. The warlord's legacy would not soon be forgotten, even in this new Triad.

For now, the Coalition provided most of the resources and infrastructure in these early stages of reorganization. Earth was too small and backward, of course, and the former Drakken Empire was in disarray. Simply put, the Coalition was still in charge. They had, after all, won the war.

Aral, on the other hand, had not yet won his. His battle was, and would always be, intensely personal.

"Please have a drink."

Aral halted at the artificial voice. A glass of untouched Menarian whiskey sat on the smart-table next to Kaz. It registered his proximity and predicted his intent. "Please have a drink," the table intoned a second time. It was a ludicrously expensive piece of furniture his father had stolen from a Coalition vessel. The Empire lagged woefully behind their enemy in non-battlefield technology. The Hordish fleet had made up for it in sheer, primitive firepower.

"Please have a drink—"

"Blast it. If I wanted a drink, I'd have taken it." He pressed two fingers to his forehead. "Fates, I'm arguing with tables now." Maybe he was as mad as his father. He drove a hand through his hair.

Kaz was far more serene as she sipped from a crystal glass of hideously expensive Menarian whiskey. "Perhaps the table has a point, Lord Vantos." Her voice held the faintest hint of concern. "Join me here while I finish my whiskey, at least." She patted the snowy cushions.

Aral fought the desire to sink down, close his eyes and fall asleep, if only so he could awaken and find out that Awrenkka was already here and he wasn't having to slay monsters across the reaches of space to claim her. "I will rest when I have her."

Kaz studied him over her glass. "Have you considered the possibility that she won't see your crusade to protect her the same way you do?"

"No."

Her eyes, black like his but with a brown tint compared to his gray, glinted with amusement. "And if she is as stubborn as you?"

"Kaz," he warned.

She reacted with a very female sigh and proceeded to brief him as she did each and every day. "'You are a selfish, violent race of religious zealots responsible for eons of war,'" she said, quoting data from the latest news stream beamed in from the central galaxy. "'The Coalition may succeed in silencing me, but the bad blood between my people and yours will live on.'" She glanced up, appearing rather smug. "Apparently, Battlelord Arkkane was unrepentant until the very end."

Once, many years ago, there had been talk of marrying her to Arkkane. That ended as soon as she began serving in the military. For a female to do so was considered a disgusting aberration. Males didn't take orders from females.

The daughter of a senior officer who lived on the Mawndarr estate, Kaz had been a friend of his and Bolivarr's since childhood. Later, she and his brother became lovers. Aral was still captaining a battle-frigate and training Bolivarr when Kaz started coming along on a few raids off the record to be with him. She proved to be a master tactician. When Aral rose to the rank of battlelord, he chose her as his second. Every Drakken commander knew a strong arm was necessary to keep a Hordish crew in line. The punishment for defying a battlelord was death, and not in a particularly merciful fashion, either. He made it clear that to disobey Kaz was to disobey him. It took only one insubordinate spacehand to get his point across. After that, Kaz was accepted in her position and, eventually, respected in it.

As for Arkkane, he deserved what he got. So did they all. Yet, Karbon continued to elude capture even after Aral had given the data necessary to track him down.

Aral was fast losing patience with them. Karbon should have been cornered by now. At least he'd been able to keep Awrenkka protected behind a blockade the Triad had erected at his suggestion to prevent pirates, loyalists and looters from harassing the people in that sector. They never guessed the real reason for their efforts was to keep his bride safe.

"Allow yourself a bit of pleasure, at least, for this latest execution, Lord Mawndarr. Arkkane was one of the worst. He was responsible for the massacre of millions."

He did feel a trace of satisfaction, but without Karbon in custody, it was hollow.

*Eeep…eeep…eeep.*

Aral's personal communicator device rang. He and Kaz exchanged a hopeful glance as he inserted the PCD into his right ear. The hardware had been given to him by the Coalition for his use in this postwar joint effort in espionage. The Empire hadn't anything as small and convenient—or secure—for communications. "M here."

Several tones indicated that his voice required authentication before the call could commence. The procedure was typical for high-priority, classified calls. Due to his distance from the Ring, it took some time for the signal to go through. Finally, an artificial voice announced, "Authentication verified."

A real voice came on next. A familiar one. "Greetings, M."

"Z," Aral acknowledged. During the war, he hadn't yet met the individual he'd come to know as Z, but his bets had been on Prime-Admiral Zaafran himself. It pleased him when after the war ended he'd learned he was right. For old times' sake—and perhaps out of respect for the enormity of what they'd accomplished in secret—they kept up the act, but it was no longer necessary.

"We've got Mawndarr."

Aral closed his eyes for the briefest of moments. He noted that the admiral didn't say "your father." That would have personalized things. No one really wanted to think too hard on a son selling out his sire.

"We'll delay the execution until you arrive. You've worked hard for this, M. We all have. I look forward to meeting you in person."

Karbon was in Coalition hands and about to be executed as a common war criminal. He'd waited a lifetime for this moment. It would seem the perfect climax to all his efforts to be able to stand in front of Karbon and take credit for his downfall, to savor the singular, exquisite pleasure of seeing the man realize that his own son had betrayed him. Betrayed them all. Yet Aral didn't want to watch the spectacle, even to gloat. All his life his father had twisted his thoughts and actions to use against him. The man would no doubt do the same if Aral were to have any personal role in his execution. Let him die alone and without the satisfaction of last words directed at his son. Yes, let him die as so many had suffered and died at his hands.

"That's all right, Z. I'll pass."

"No last words for the battlelord?"

"No. My presence isn't necessary."

Zaafran's pause revealed his shock that Aral would skip the execution. "Certainly your identity can be kept secret, if you so desire it."

Aral had already taken steps to ensure exactly that. Of course he wouldn't embark on a mission to rescue the warlord's daughter in the persona of Battlelord—*former* Battlelord—Aral Mawndarr. He'd assume the identity of a Borderlands Patrol agent posing undercover as independent trader with Kaz as his loyal mate. The ruse gave him the authority to move freely in the camp, as well as make arrests if need be. *Nevermore* had been retrofitted with a Triad transponder code to mimic a typical cargo ship and allow passage through checkpoints. He'd obtained fake identification in the form of data squares. It helped to be a spy; he'd made connections over the years. Helpful connections, Zaafran tops amongst them. In fact, it was Zaafran's help in this matter that allowed him to obtain everything he needed for this one last mission. The prime-admiral was all too happy to assist Aral in tracking battlelords. Through the top officer, Aral had assembled everything he needed for his raid on Zorabeta.

"Go forward with the execution without me. I have a bit of a schedule conflict, you see. It turns out I must take care of some unfinished business. It's a personal matter." *Deeply so.*

He could tell Zaafran was anxious to know more, but gave him the respect of not asking questions about his "personal matter." They would not, of course, have been answered.

"I have one last request, then, M."

Aral stifled an impatient sigh. This is what he feared. His service to the Triad would be never-ending. Little did they know he'd disappear soon enough, never to be heard from again. He'd live out his days with his wife far from prying eyes and assassins' reach—on both sides of the freepin' war. "Tell me what you require, Z."

"Find the warlord's daughter. Deliver her to me, dead or alive. I've got my people looking in every conceivable nook and cranny, but so far there's been no sign of her—or what happened to her."

Aral stopped in his tracks, his blood going cold. He knew her existence was no secret to the Coalition. Hearing Zaafran voice his desire to see her imprisoned and executed for her father's crimes was another matter.

Aral kept his voice smooth. "I'll find her, Z. You have my word." It was, after all, the truth.

# CHAPTER FIVE

"The existence of a surviving child of the warlord,
if in fact true, looms as a grave threat to continued galactic peace. Our first responsibility must
be to eliminate such a menace."
—Prime-Admiral Kemp Zaafran, Commander-
in-Chief of the Triad Alliance

"WHAT A HELLS HOLE." Keir Vantos didn't find himself
staring very often. He'd seen too much in his twenty-
eight cycles for much of anything to surprise, horrify,
or intrigue him. But *this,* he had to say, was stare-worthy.

Horde, Drakken Horde, everywhere. For a thousand
years his people, the Coalition, had warred with the
Drakken Horde. Now here were hundreds of them, displaced, confused and even frightened, milling about in
a hastily set-up refugee camp. There were similar camps
all over the Borderlands, the disputed space between the
worlds of the Horde and the Coalition.

Not disputed any longer, he thought, twirling a nanopick between his lips as he lounged in the shade of
*Borrowed Time*'s wing. He could escape the sun, but not
the odors of too many bodies, strange perfumes and
other scents that defied description, not that he cared to

try. How the hells were they going to blend into Coalition society, or civilized life period, the grand plan of the overly optimistic reunification politicos? Tattoos covered the men as well as the women. They wore jewelry in places any sane human wouldn't dream of piercing. And their hair—name it, he saw it. Blending Drakken into mainstream society would be like mixing oil and water.

That was the reunification panel's problem. One man's headache was another man's profit, Keir always said. The past few months he'd carved out quite a nice little niche supplying the ships that supplied the camps. But why be the middle man when he could bring in cargo directly? Now he was a direct supplier. He might have to work a little harder, but it was worth it for entertainment value alone, being able to sightsee in the camps.

The odors of unwashed bodies and fear drifted in the weak breeze. He wrinkled his nose. It smelled as if the Triad would need more cleansing supplies, and soon. He took out his datapad and typed in the information.

*Keir Vantos, provider of shower soap and scum swipers,* he thought. Gods. The very idea sucked the last vestiges of his good mood away—not that hauling toilets across the light years had done much for his spirits or his pride lately anyway. He needed a shower and a nap. Hells, he needed a lot of things he wasn't going to be able to do much about right now, like a real bed and maybe even a woman who wouldn't mind joining him there for a few hours' playtime. His lips curved. Maybe if this gig of supply running to the camps worked out, he'd be able to swing a little R and R next month. Tropics, playful ladies, tall drinks. He couldn't remember the last time he took a vacation. The reason used to be that the money he was making was too good to pass up. Now it was because the money he was making wasn't enough.

He went back to supervising the unloading of his ship. He'd been at it all morning, and the workers weren't done unloading yet, ensuring a paycheck at the end of the day. No, it wasn't the kind of money he used to make running the blockade. Then again, no one was shooting at him, either. Least of all Drakken. They were crammed into these camps now, awaiting transition into mainstream Coalition life, whatever the hell that was. Good luck to them. Keir hadn't yet found anything close to mainstream that suited him—and he doubted he ever would. Mainstream, domestic contentment, mom, pop and kids—it was tied too closely with every bad memory he had.

Dust tickled his nose and made him sneeze. When were they going to get the roads around here paved? Maybe he ought to suggest hauling in asphalt. Every refugee's boot hitting the dirt churned up fine dust. It burned his nose and eyes. The blistering heat only doubled the pleasure, he thought with sarcasm, swiping a hand across his face. Add a cold drink to his list that began with a nap and ended with getting laid. Except it looked like an icy beverage was as elusive as everything else he'd like. If there was a bar in this hell hole, it sure ain't anywhere where he could see.

"Well, well, look at this. The former blockade runner is now a chem-toilet runner."

Keir swung a dark stare in the direction of laughter. Two ensigns stood, chuckling at the chem-toilets being carried off his ship. Mardem and Zarren had been fighter pilots assigned to the last outpost he'd served before the war ended. They'd toasted cheating death many times in the bar there. It had been months since he'd last seen them. Seemed like an eternity.

He jumped down from the gangway. "Hell, yeah, I'm running chem-toilets. Guns or butt-catchers—what difference does it make? It's all good money." That last part was a partial lie, but no need to come clean about it, not with those grins on their faces. There was money in supplying the camps, but it wasn't good. Peace had changed everything. He now had to worry about making a living when before he'd turn down offers. He peered at the docks and the long rows of cargo craft. In and out they'd roared all day. "I don't see any fighters. Just cargo-freighters docked from here to tomorrow. Don't tell me you're trash-hauling, too?"

The pilots swore, looking sheepish. "Not much action these days," Mardem admitted. "People are being RIFed left and right. It's the biggest reduction in force in history. We're lucky we're still in the service let alone bitching about what we get to fly."

"I told you rocket-jockeys about the benefits of being civilian. You wouldn't listen."

Mardem shrugged. "I wouldn't know how to be civilian. I never expected I ever would be civilian. I wanted to be a fighter pilot all my life. I don't want to do anything else. Who dreamed this damn war would end—" he snapped his fingers "—like that, overnight, with no warning? Blast it all, Vantos. I'm not done killing Drakken."

Keir's parents weren't either when the Drakken killed

them. No one was ever done killing. That's why the war went on for over a thousand years. That's why he'd pulled out of it. He'd quit. Not because he was a coward. Because if anyone ever put a weapon in his hands and dropped him in front of a Drakken, he couldn't guarantee he wouldn't pull the trigger. He didn't like being spring-loaded to kill. Innocents got killed that way.

Keir pulled a fresh nanopick out of his pocket. "Look, when the time comes, and it will, and you get booted out of the service on your ass, come talk to me. I'll give you rocket-jocks civvie lessons. Set you up in the business."

"And we can be chem-toilet haulers like you."

Smirking, Keir swore. "What's taking up space in *your* cargo hold, rock-jock? Troops? Plasma bombs?"

Mardem cleared his throat. "Dehydrated vegetables."

Keir cracked up. The ensigns joined him after a moment or two of feeling sorry for themselves.

They glanced back at the Drakken flowing by, an unending influx arriving from worlds beyond. Zarren shook his head. "At least a third of them are suffering from diseases we eradicated generations ago. The average citizen hasn't a single nanomed in their blood."

"Hells, even pets have nanomeds," Keir said.

"You can't help but think of them as animals. They treated each other worse than they treated us. The warlord made sure he and his imperial officers were protected by nanos. Screw the rest of the population."

Keir pulled the pic from between his lips. "Seems they already did. Is this a surprise to anyone?"

"Broken limbs, colds…" Zarren took an accounting of the refugees as they trudged past. "Tumors…scars…"

Those things humanized them. Turned the enemy into people.

*Vantos, is this you talking?* These refugees' compatriots had tried to shorten his lifespan so many times over the past dozen years that he wondered if he'd ever be able to live and work with Drakken like they were regular people. Now he was thinking they were. Underdogs, even. The Drakken race was tied to every bad thing that had ever happened in his life. It wasn't something a man shook off overnight.

"Listen up, Vantos," Mardem said. "We had a secret briefing today—need to know only. You need to know."

"No, I don't." Military secrets came with too many obligations.

"Yes, you do, buddy. Vantos, for years you've given us pilots inside information from your runs. You helped us, and we never gave you nothing in return."

"Didn't need to. It evened out in the bar."

"No way in hells. And you know it. We relied on you more than our intel people on where the Drakken were hiding. You single-handedly cut the rate of ambush in half. So here's something in return." Again he cast his gaze around as if nervous someone was listening. "We had a briefing today. Top secret. But you're one of us." The ensign glanced at his friend and lowered his voice. "The boss says to keep an eye out for the warlord's kid."

"The son was killed."

"He has another. A daughter."

Keir choked. "Gods, are you serious?"

"Headquarters wants her. Bad."

"I'll bet." Who wouldn't want the ultimate war prize: a piece of the old man? The queen and her consort killed him in self-defense. That pretty much stole the ultimate satisfaction from the Coalition high command. "It was his daughter. Look at who the guy employed. I'd have kept her hidden, too. I'm surprised we haven't found out where by now."

"The palace records are a flargin' mess, in code and disorganized. But they're working on it."

"By the time they crack the code, she'll be long gone," Keir said.

"She is. That's why they're going to offer a bounty to anyone who can bring her in. If anyone can, it's you."

"A bounty, you say." Keir tried not to look too eager. Anything that combined an adrenaline rush with profit got his full attention. "How much?"

"Fifty million queen's credits."

*"Fifty?"* Keir wheezed. "Fifty million? Hoo, baby."

"They're announcing it soon—tomorrow or the next day—but I'm telling you now. Off the record, Vantos. You'd better not say anything to anyone."

"Say something? Are you blasted kidding? Competition's something I don't need."

"That's why we want to give you a head start," Mardem said. "For old times' sake."

He had a blasted run to make, a roundtrip to the depot and back. He needed the money and couldn't get out of it. But he'd be back. "Give me something more, Mardem. How about a physical description?"

"No one's got any pictures, but they showed us a composite based on the parents. Over ninety percent probability it's what she looks like. Gorgeous, tall, blond. Hazel eyes, or green. A real bombshell."

"In that case, I'll definitely keep an eye out for

her. She's going to make me a rich man. I'm half in love already."

Mardem snorted. Then he took a call on his PCD. "They want us back in the hangar. See you around, you crazy runner." Mardem bid him farewell with a salute and walked away with Zarren.

Keir called after them. "You rocket jockeys take care of those vegetables!"

Zarren flipped him off. Chuckling, Keir walked back toward his ship. Fifty-million queens! With that kind of money in his pocket, he'd be able to quit this damn gig and head out to points unknown, maybe start his own transport company—high-risk stuff, that sort of thing.

*If* the warlord's daughter was still alive. If the Triad didn't get to her first, the believers would. They had scores to settle.

And Keir had a living to make.

If they'd resorted to a reward for the warlord's daughter's capture it meant the high command had exhausted all leads. Why? He racked his brain, trying to look at the puzzle from all angles. Maybe the warlord's daughter wasn't statuesque or even blond. Maybe she'd lived a low-key life under an assumed identity. Maybe, just maybe, she was nothing like what anyone thought and that was why no one had found her yet.

The thrill of discovery shot through him. *You're on to something, Vantos.* Screw toilet patrol. The minute he got back to Zorabeta, he was going hunting. It may not be as exciting as running the blockade, but fifty-flargin-million queens were his if he was right about this, and he was getting the feeling he was. The entire galaxy was headed down the wrong path. But not him. No, not Keir Vantos, runner extraordinaire. If anyone could see alternative ways in—and out—it was he. Let everyone else look for a bombshell. *He'd* search for the girl no one suspected.

## CHAPTER SIX

THE JOURNEY TO ZORABETA was interminable. Wren
found that this new loneliness was almost harder to
bear than her grief for Sabra. Feeling like an outsider
was nothing new: on Barokk, she hadn't been old
enough to be accepted by the guardians and was too old
to be peers with their charges. When Sabra was alive
the sensation of not fitting in hadn't been so acute. Onboard the ship, crammed into the underdecks with
hundreds of other refugees, she'd never felt so alone.

The voyage was made longer with delays and re-
routes due to blockades and unrest in the Borderlands.
Traveling by spaceship was no better than it was the
first time on the trip to meet her father. Space-sickness
soon consumed her. Finally, someone noticed and
called for help.

A medic and a guard rousted her from her narrow
bunk. She'd lost track of how long she'd lain there,
curled on her side. Startled, she felt for the hidden
pendant. It was still there.

"I'm going to administer a dose of nanomeds," the
medic said, making her sit up. Others gathered around
to watch. Some she knew from Barokk, others were
strangers. The ship was beginning to fill up. At some

point she guessed they'd reach capacity and head for Zorabeta. "They're microscopic computers targeted for health issues. You were going to get them in the camp anyway." He rooted through a bag of supplies and pulled out a small stick that reminded Wren uncomfortably of the poison dart. "Everyone in the Coalition is inoculated at birth. Your medicine was so backward that none of you were. Well, some of you Drakken have nanos—high-ranking Imperial officers, battlelords and the like. That's how we find the ones trying to escape. The hardware in their blood gives them away."

Her father and his men had had nanomeds, but he never saw to her care. If he had, the Triad would have detected the nanomeds. For once she was glad to have been neglected.

She fought dizziness and upset stomach as he pushed a stick against the inside of her elbow. It hissed and left behind a spot of blood. "You should feel some improvement now," he said.

The magical creatures were inside her now. Nanomeds. She stared at her arm, opening and closing her hand to see if she could detect any differences. She couldn't, but she felt better almost right away. "Thank you," she breathed in awe.

The medic turned away to remove his gloves and reapply a cream to his hands. He wiped it off carefully with a cloth, cleaning every part of him that had come in contact with her. He did so in a way that reinforced the perception that the Coalition considered Drakken animals. It was reinforced by an air of superiority—a thousand years' worth of righteousness. The Coalition served under goddesses, divine beings, whereas the Drakken followed the orders of mere mortals.

The medic packed up and left. He wasn't rude, but he wasn't friendly, either. Probably the last thing the medic wanted was to treat a Hordish barbarian kindly, but did so because it was his orders. Someone above him, someone even above the captain of this ship, wanted peace to take root, despite the hatred between the two peoples. It was cause for celebration. And also concern, for it meant they wouldn't give up trying to find her—the warlord's last surviving child. When it came to peace, her mere existence put it in jeopardy.

AT THE NEXT STOP, new arrivals had everyone atwitter. Wren stood with the others as refugee after refugee came aboard. These newcomers were pale and silent. They didn't interact with anyone, not even the guards. Their eyes were blank. Dead. It was as if they'd retreated inside themselves.

"They survived a massacre," some whispered.

"Everyone was skulled."

"What does that mean?" Wren asked.

"Naive girl," a woman scolded.

"Consider yourself freepin' blessed for not knowing," another said. "I saw people who were skulled once. At the base of each one's skull was a little circle of soot— a hole if you looked closer, about the size of your fingernail. Nice and neat. But if you saw the other side, the face, there was nothing left."

Wren fought a fresh wave of queasiness, the kind that came from squeamishness and horror, and that meds couldn't fix. What she felt when her fingers found the dart embedded in Sabra's stomach. What she felt when she watched the life leave Ilkka's eyes. The consequences of hate.

Most of the Barokk citizens listened on along with Wren in appalled silence. Like her, they'd been insulated from the horrors of war. Wren said, "But they're Drakken."

"You *are* naive. They're Drakken, but they're believers."

Wren blushed hard and clamped her chatty lips closed. She was hungry for answers about her new world, the world she knew nothing about, but not to the point she wanted to risk revealing her identity.

An eavesdropping guard said, "'Skulling' is Hordish slang for blowing people's brains out." His cheek began to twitch. Surrounded by his former enemy, he gripped his rifle uncomfortably tight. "It was a favorite game of your battlelords. They did it to demoralize us, but all it did was infuriate us. Unlike us, your own believers wouldn't retaliate, and the warlord knew it. They were defenseless. Still, he set out to kill every last one of them. What you see here was probably the last of it, thank gods. The last victims of the holocaust." The big guard made the sign of the goddess. "May the likes of that monster never arise again." He kissed the tips of his fingers and sent his prayer to the heavens as Sabra had done.

Murmurs went around. It took a moment before Wren realized that the others were mumbling prayers and thanks that her father was dead. A few began to weep.

She'd held out a small, selfish hope that the Coalition's and the Drakken believers' loathing of the empire drove them to lie, to exaggerate, but seeing the skulling survivors told a different story. Little wonder she was the most wanted woman in the galaxy. She felt sick in the pit of her soul. Sweat broke out on her forehead. She pushed on her glasses. Then she tore them off, not wanting to see the blank expressions of the survivors—survivors of her father's atrocities.

Not wanting anyone to realize who she was.

No one else she'd met so far wore glasses. Only her. How long before someone on the warlord's ship that day remembered she'd worn corrective lenses? She must not be found—by anyone. Found and used. Found and fought over. And risk waking the beast inside her.

She no longer had dear Sabra's eyes to see. She needed her own.

*EEEP...EEEP...EEEP.*

Aral was lying on his stomach in bed. *Eeep...eeep... eeep.* What was that blasted sound? He opened an eye and scanned the environmental panel by his bedside. Indications were normal. *Eeep...eeep...eeep.* He rolled onto his back, actually desiring to return to slumber for once. After a nightmare earlier in his sleep cycle, he'd actually fallen back asleep. It had taken well over a hundred push-ups to exhaust himself to do it. A shot of whiskey and a longing glance at a vial of sleep meds and he was back to sleep. A memory of his father's sweef-glazed eyes and the stink of it on his breath was enough to convince Aral not to drink more. Nor would he take the risk of medicating himself with the arrival at Zorabeta imminent. He needed all his wits about him to see to Awrenkka's safe rescue today. Today!

*Eeep...eeep...eeep.*

"What is that freepin' sound?" It was coming from his closet.

The PCD, he realized. After his last conversation with Zaafran, he'd stowed the thing. The man had been trying to reach him continuously. For what—to see if he'd captured the warlord's daughter yet?

*Eeep...eeep...eeep.*

He stalked to the closet and growled, "Open." His closet presented a fresh uniform on a spindly robotic arm. "No."

The uniform disappeared back into the darkness and a soft, black civilian suit glided forward. It dangled from its hanger. "Next," he commanded to the sound of the muffled beeping. In which pocket did he leave the PCD, and what the hells did Zaafran want now? If it concerned whether he'd sighted the warlord's daughter, very soon he'd be able to answer in the affirmative.

It was nothing he cared to share with the prime-admiral, however.

Several clothing combinations rotated by. At the thought of Awrenkka, his grogginess began to clear, and his foul humor at being woken from the rare if brief stretch of sleep. If his innards felt sliced by razors at times, she was the salve—the mere thought of her—as she had been that day when he was little more than a boy.

His spare uniform swept stopped in front of him. *Eeep...eeep...eeep.* The beeping sound was loud and sharp.

He fished the PCD out of the pocket where it had been forgotten, grasping it in his fist. For a fraction of a second he considered answering the call. Karbon was gone. There was no reason to be connected by an umbilical cord with the Coalition anymore. With a flick of his thumbnail, he deactivated the power crystal. "The recipient of this call is unavailable—permanently," he murmured, mimicking the computerized female voice that came on to authenticate all communication. His work with the Triad and for the Triad was done. It was his turn at life now. Yes, and Awrenkka's.

AT ZORABETA, guards boarded the ship. They barked questions and entered information into what Wren learned was called a datapad. She fought to remain calm despite the trembles in her belly.

"Name?"

"Wren Senderin." It had been Sabra's last name. It was both a way to remain anonymous and honor the memory of her guardian.

"Birthplace?"

She supposed answering "the Imperial Palace" was not a good idea. "Barokk."

"Occupation or special skills?"

Sand painting, reciting poetry, serving tea to battle-lords, carrying on the Rakkuu bloodline? Purveyor of Rakkuu DNA? Or, perhaps, guide to a priceless treasure. "No."

He punched in something on his pad, then handed her a data square. "This is the address of your tent when you arrive in the camp. Single, childless women only. No men allowed."

She slipped the data square in her pocket. The guard gave her another. "Take this to the medical tent. They'll fix your eyes."

How she'd ached to be freed of her handicap. She closed her eyes and whispered silent thanks for her sudden good fortune—not to the goddesses but to anyone, divine or otherwise, who would listen.

"There's no cause for worry. It comes with no obligation. The medical care is being donated by relief organizations. Top-notch surgeons volunteered to help you Drakken."

Fates, he thought her worried. "Good sir, I am so happy I am speechless."

His gaze warmed as if he thought she was sweet. Perhaps there was a time she might have agreed; now she knew better. "I don't know if you'll like what you see here once you can," he said. "This dump isn't the most scenic place we've got. But you're Triad now. Things like eyeglasses gotta go."

She took the data square and tucked it away in a pocket. Then she was standing at the top of the gangway, staring down at the spectacle that was Zorabeta refugee camp.

There was a sense of wildness in the camp, of too many people under not quite enough control. Strapping armed Coalition soldiers sauntered amongst the hundreds of bedraggled Drakken, inserting a layer of fear and respect that seemed a very thin barrier between calm and chaos. The odors of too many bodies in need of washing, strange perfumes and other scents that defied description tickled her nose.

A ship screeched overhead. The docks themselves were a noisy place. Trader-pilots relaxed in the shade of their ships, chatting with friends, waiting for freight or simply waiting, looking bored and hot. Others watched the streams of refugees go by. In wonder, she stared at the ships taking off and landing all around her, and the men and women who piloted them to all corners of the

galaxy—and maybe even beyond, she thought with a
twinge of envy. She'd never been anywhere outside the
books she devoured. And when she finally did have the
chance, it was under the worst of circumstances.

"Come on, miss," one of the guards below called up
to her. "You can't stand there all day."

A cluster of guards watched her, their expressions
amused. Someone gave her a push when she hesitated.
She stumbled. Her glasses almost slid off. A panicky
push with one finger put them back in place. It took
every ounce of guts she had to step forward. The short
walk down the ramp seemed miles long and took an
eternity. Then she set foot on the ground.

Despite all her fears, despite all that was as yet
unknown, she was free. Not a daughter. Not a wife. Free.

Then, with a deeply indrawn breath and a determined
push on her glasses, she hurried forward to lose herself
in the anonymity of the camp.

## CHAPTER SEVEN

"We 'Earthlings' are new to the vast galactic arena. What we lack in experience, we make up for in courage and hope. Today we celebrate a promising future, joining our new allies in their wish for enduring peace."

—Laurel Ramos, President of the United States (address at Unity Day festivities at the United Nations, New York)

"Hell, yeah, I traded my slot in the Thunderbirds to serve on the *Unity*. Wouldn't you, sir? Star ships, hot alien chicks…we're talking a new frontier. I always wanted to be a space cowboy."

—Major Ruben "Tango" Barrientes, USAF pilot (courtesy *Air Force Times*)

AN EXPLOSION ROCKED the ship. "Enemy targets in all quadrants, Captain."

Triad Captain Hadley Keyren noted the first hint of panic in her lead pilot's voice. There was no time to ponder his terror, or even hers. The time for second-guessing was after a battle. That was, if you had an after.

Her battleship was surrounded. Enemy ships were

everywhere: a rogue battlelord and his loyalist buddies. How had they so thoroughly caught her off guard? Were they that good, or was she that green?

Her vote landed somewhere in between. Her promotion was only weeks old, and everyone knew how Drakken battlelords fought.

*With black, godless souls and no mercy.*

Sweat tingled on Hadley's temples. She fought the same tendrils of panic she'd heard in the pilot's voice. Half the bridge crew was glancing at her where she stood. They waited for the order that would save them, waited for the order that would turn this losing battle around.

*Goddess, guide me through this.*

But the gods who she'd prayed to all her life were curiously silent now. She was on her freepin' own, as her Drakken friend Rakkelle would say.

If only Rakkelle were here. She'd know what to do.

A flash of light. "Incoming!" the weapons officer shouted. Hadley caught the edge of the command console and braced herself. That one almost jarred her molars loose.

"Impact—aft left control pod!" the engineer called out.

"Seal off the pod!" Hadley ordered.

"Done."

Hadley smelled something burning. Her ship or her pride? Both were equally at risk at going up in smoke.

"Lost two more fighters, Captain."

Blast it. They were decimating her defenses, killing her crew. The war might be over, but this one was just beginning.

She stalked to the front of the bridge. There was no

way they were going to fight their way out of this one. They were either going to be a casualty, or…

"Ram it." She made fists. "Pilot, spin her around, on my mark—"

"Ram it?" Stunned would describe the man's expression and tone. Well, it beat panic.

"Turn this baby around, Lieutenant. We're going to hit that monster's ship with our damaged pod to keep our good side functional. Do it."

"Yes, ma'am."

The bridge crew was silent as the pilot obeyed her order. Alarms wailed distantly through the damaged ship.

"Aim for just forward of their star drive." She was crazy. She knew what the crew was thinking. *We're going to die anyway—might as well die trying.* Hadley had grown up on a farm on Talo, an outlying provincial world where the sun and the seasons formed the framework of life, not machines. She used to drive fruit to market in a centuries-old truck. Once, road pirates tried to steal the load. Her brother rammed them. Hadley never forgot. He had showed her how. It was just never applied to a starship.

Before this moment.

They were moving full speed when they hit. The impact threw her sideways. She pulled up to her knees. Metal screeched on metal. The vibration rattled her bones. Sparks lit up the starboard view ports. "Jump speed—now," she ordered. They needed to accelerate away or they were dead. "Jump, jump!"

Grimly in the midst of chaos, she took stock of statistics. Her fighters were still out there. They'd jump without their mother ship. They'd make it to the other side even if the command ship didn't. Maybe this wasn't a victory, but it was a draw; her crew and ship were a total loss, the battle-cruiser was heavily damaged if not an outright hull loss, and her fighters would have survived.

The ship shuddered as it struggled to accelerate. She thought it was going to come apart. The speed crawled higher, but it wasn't yet at the necessary velocity to jump to hyperspace and safety. The battle-cruiser's fighters pursued them like a swarm of angry bees.

"Go," she whispered to her ship, her hand in a fist, her stomach twisting, wasted, her uniform jacket damp with sweat.

Then…then finally…the stars stretched out into streamers, and they were gone. Breaths later, they dropped out of hyperspace in a non-hostile region.

It was utterly silent.

The lights came up on the bridge, and her instructor walked toward her. She couldn't read his expression. "I'll pack my things," she told him. Now that she'd failed, she'd be assigned somewhere else.

"Captain Keyren."

"Yes, sir." She stood tall. Might as well look good while receiving the news that takes away your dreams, she reasoned.

"Congratulations," he said, taking her hand. "You passed. That was a hell of a risk, but I saw no other way out."

"I passed…"

"Yes."

"I passed captain school…"

"Now all you have to do is wait for your ship to come out of dry dock."

*Cloud Shadow.* Her own ship. Her first command. She was going to be a captain. *Oh, my goddess.* "Thank you, sir. Thank you." She turned to the shaken crew and saluted them. "And thank you."

They were still too shocked to say anything as she walked out of the simulator. Beaming, she pushed into the busy corridors of the Ring, the headquarters of the former Coalition military and now the Triad Alliance. The frosty planet Sakka, home to the palace of the goddess-queen, glowed large and luminous outside the view ports.

"Well, sweet thang, you look like you've been through hells."

She braced herself at the sound of Tango's voice. Sleeves rolled up, the Earthling's uniform was just shy of being too tight, but snug enough to show every muscle on his body, and then some. He caught up to her, laying his arm over her shoulders.

She lifted his arm and dropped it. He reacted with his "aw, baby" look that she'd long since learned to ignore. The Earthling Major Ruben Barrientes, aka Tango, was tall, blond and insufferably cocky. "I have been through hells, as a matter of fact," she told him. "Hells and back."

"I'll bet. I heard you pulled the quad profile. Don't feel bad. No one gets out of that one."

"I did."

"It's what separates the men from the boys," he continued, oblivious to her comment. Then his steps faltered. "Holy shit, Hadley. You did? You *passed?*"

She grinned.

*"How?"*

"Rammed it."

"You rammed the ship…"

"Yes."

"A freepin' Drakken battle-cruiser? Are you crazy?"

"Guess I am." If this is what crazy meant, she had to say she quite liked it.

"You owe me a drink in the bar later—and I don't mean one of those fruity girly drinks, either. You've got no excuse. Your boyfriend's still in the hospital." He winked at her, then continued on down the corridor.

Once upon a time when they were both newly assigned to the *Unity,* Tango had both horrified and fascinated her. His flirtation had her emotions roiling. Handsome and so very foreign—Texan, to be precise— he almost managed to get her into bed. But there was a complication. A tall, dark and dangerous complication: Former Imperial Wraith Bolivarr, who she didn't realize at first was the love of her life.

Why would she? Bolivarr was Drakken. She was Coalition. He wore tattoos of a wraith, a highly trained covert operative. Wraiths were masters of deception and of survival. Their own military feared them along with everyone else. She on the other hand was a country girl from the rural planet Talo. Her past was an open book, whereas his was a mystery. Bolivarr knew nothing of his life prior to being found beaten unconscious, naked, and left for dead in a back alley on a down-and-out mining world with nothing but wraith tattoos and a virulent hatred of the warlord's regime giving hints to his past. He was rescued by Drakken pirates who ended up being assigned to the *Unity,* where he and Hadley had met in the final days of her assignment.

Bolivarr suffered from thought-suppression. It blocked secrets he wasn't supposed to remember. The people who had done it to him were probably dead. It made her sick to think of beautiful Bolivarr used as a tool for the warlord, much like the coalition's now-banned REEF assassins. The difference was that REEFs had hardware installed; they were bioengineered. The Drakken didn't have technology that advanced. Meds and sometimes surgery were used to alter the brain. The technique was cruder, the results often unpredictable. And, as in Bolivarr's case, the reality was always cruel.

Bolivarr willingly suffered for the chance to recover his memories. The treatments were rigorous frustrating, and often painful. There was always the risk they'd cause more damage than what had already been done. He'd do it for the chance at a normal life, to be able to, once and for all, know who he was. He didn't know how long healing would take. "If the meds don't work, I might need surgery. And then perhaps therapy, depending."

"I'll wait for you," she'd whispered. "I will."

They continued to see each other between his hospital stays and her shipboard duties. Sometimes they had days on end to be in each other's company, sharing her quarters or his, acting as if they were already married, which she hoped one day might happen. Other times, like now, they were apart for weeks, with Bolivarr stuck in the hospital after suffering seizures, and her attending captain's school. While she worked at earning her captain's stripes, Bolivarr endured experimental treatments of every kind in hopes of uncovering his past. So far, they'd uncovered nothing but nightmares.

Hadley hurried through the corridors to the medical wing. Her heart gave a happy little leap at the sight of Bolivarr, in bed, quietly intense as he sketched on a datapad. His eternal calm was probably part of his training to be a wraith. She tried not to dwell on what else he was trained to do. A lock of black hair hung over his forehead. She itched to brush it away, and to feel his warm embrace.

For once, he didn't sense her presence. He was too focused on his drawing. The stylus scratched over the surface, then he paused to ponder his work. He appeared confused, even troubled. Her heart went out to him. To not know who you were, or what secrets your mind kept hidden, was awful.

He needed a hug. Hells, she needed one after the morning she'd had. She bounced inside and landed on the edge of the bed. No medical assistants in sight. They'd have shooed her off. He glanced up, and she caught him midlaugh, kissing him full on the mouth.

Goddess, the man could kiss. Luckily, no one stormed the room to investigate. His pulse must be off the charts, she thought, because hers sure was.

"You just kissed the Triad's newest ship captain," she murmured against his lips.

He moved her back to look at her. He was so handsome when he was happy that it stole her breath away. "Congratulations, Captain Keyren."

"That's Hadley to you."

"Hadley my *love*, you mean. Let's go out tonight to celebrate your achievement. Dinner, even drinks." They weren't big drinkers and as a rule stayed out of the bar. It was more than she could say about the rest of the Drakken he'd come aboard with. System-wide there was a ban on sweef in effect, the homemade rotgut liquor inexplicably loved by so many Drakken military.

It was distilled from a type of evergreen tree—and tasted like it. The smell alone made Hadley's eyes water. Worse, sweef was highly addictive and rotted teeth. She'd seen Tango consume a shot on a dare once. Fighter pilot bravado. Bolivarr had never touched the stuff. Um, that he remembered. Then Bolivarr's face fell. "If I can convince them to let me out of here for a few hours."

"I'd rather you get well. We'll celebrate when you're out of this hospital."

"We'll celebrate more than that." His eyes turned dark as he lifted her hand to his lips and pressed a kiss to the underside of her wrist. "I want to kiss you everywhere," he said. "And I mean everywhere."

A med tech entered the room. They jumped apart. Hadley felt warm from her blushing face to her curling toes. They remained silent until the tech finished replacing some supplies and left. Then she melted into laughter.

She pointed to the datapad Bolivarr had turned upside down. "What are you working on?"

"An unfinished drawing of an unfinished thought. A half-remembered dream." He turned the datapad so she could see it. Five circles formed an elongated pentagon. "This keeps showing up in my thoughts. I don't know why." He showed her some other sketches. "Runes. I think. I don't know." He groaned and dropped the pad. "I want to know, Hadley. I'm tired of waiting. Maybe this is the key. Maybe this will unlock everything."

She ached with the frustration he must feel not being able to remember. "Every tiny piece remembered is one closer to finishing the puzzle."

"I know." Sadness flickered around his features despite his smile. Bolivarr was such a gentle spirit, shy and sweet with those tragic eyes. It was exactly that aura of innocence that had won over her heart. She wanted to erase the melancholy that was always a part of him. Even when he was laughing it was there in the background, as if he missed something terribly. Or someone.

He'd been a wraith, a loner by profession, but maybe there were loved ones in Bolivarr's life. Or a lover. Even a wife. She tried to dismiss her worries as silly, futile jealousy, but what if there was someone who meant so much to him that even with total memory loss, he grieved their loss? What if? It scared her. After all, she may very well have lost her heart to someone whose heart already belonged to someone else.

Together they studied the drawings, most of them of the same five small circles, and some with borders filled in creating pentagons of various sizes. "It looks like an obelisk," he said, his focus back on his drawings.

"Without the border, those five marks remind me of one of the patterns my grandmother and her friends used to weave into their quilts and paint on pottery. Something that ancient warriors wore on their armor, I think. The guards of the birthplace of the goddesses, or some such thing." Her home planet Talo was a rural world with a tradition of folklore and fairy tales as rich as its farmland. "Life was a bit slow, you know. At night there was nothing else to do but make quilts and make up stories."

"I for one am glad you had no night life. You might have found a man long ago and I never would have had the chance to be with you."

"That's too sad to think about."

"I know."

"So let's not."

In the next instant he was using the stylus furiously, filling in the sketch he'd made, drawing a border around them then scratching it out. Then he stopped, throwing down the stylus to rub his temples. "It's something from my life before. I'm sure of it."

"Something bad?"

He shook his head. "Something I'm supposed to know."

"A wife and three children." Her finger tapped each point of light in turn. "One, two, three…and mama and papa. See? And those are their names."

"In runes?"

"Who knows? Maybe you had a family."

He chuckled. "I don't think so."

"You don't know that."

"We've been through this, Hadley. I was a wraith. Wraiths are married to their work." He tucked her hair behind her ear, tenderly. "I told you not to worry about that stuff."

Yet a familiar unease tugged at her, and that jealousy she couldn't help. After the first seizure when he'd thought his memories were returning, he told her he wasn't married. Despite what he insisted, there was no guarantee Bolivarr was single. True, there was no marriage tattoo, a Drakken custom, but his body art told only part of a story that his mind had no way of validating. "All I'm saying is that you can't be sure."

"I'm sure about you, love." His hand slipped deeper into her hair, loosening it from her regulation, battle-bridge chignon as his soft mouth brushed over hers. "Sure that I can't wait to make love with you again."

She sighed, melting, awash in tingles. Smiling against

her lips, he pulled her into a full-on kiss despite the threat of a medic walking in on them at any moment.

The kiss was so delicious that her ears rang. It took a few seconds to realize only one ear was ringing, and only because her PCD was chiming in it.

"Keyren," she answered crisply as Bolivarr's thumb traced distracting circles on the inside of her wrist.

"I hear congratulations are in order, Captain."

The deep and familiar voice set her heart to kicking even harder. *Zaafran,* she mouthed to Bolivarr, who dropped her hand at the mention of the famous name. She shot straight up. "Prime-Admiral Zaafran. Thank you, sir."

Zaafran was the highest-ranking naval officer in the Coalition—and now the Triad Alliance. He was a peer of Admiral Brit Bandar's, the Coalition's most beloved war hero and Hadley's personal hero. She remembered the emergency drills, growing up on Talo. Then one day the drill was real. They were under attack. The entire squadron of Hordish ships was destroyed by a single warship under the command of Admiral Bandar when she was still only Star-Commander Bandar. The admiral saved Hadley's planet. From then on, Hadley was determined to model her life after the admiral's. She became the first female from folksy, clannish Planet Talo to win an appointment to the Royal Galactic Military Academy, and the youngest graduate to be selected as Admiral Bandar's executive officer. The miracle of Hadley's existence was having had the honor of serving in a capacity to make her hero's life easier. Although it had always been her dream to someday rise up through the ranks and captain a ship of her own, she'd learned so much from watching in her day-to-day routine as Admiral Bandar's assistant. That Zaafran, a contemporary of Bandar, would take the time to congratulate her, a mere newbie captain, left her in shock. She couldn't imagine that her passing the check ride would be such news. Unless he, too, was surprised. *Talo girl makes good.*

Hadley beamed and almost missed the prime-admiral's request. "I have some work for you, Captain," he said. He sounded weary, stressed.

"Of course, sir." She deflated slightly. Likely all he needed from her was to escort another group on a bridge tour of the *Unity*. No matter that she was awaiting re-assignment; she was still in demand in her former role. That meant getting stuck escorting VIPs and the press, both virtual and real, around the huge ship, the first of its kind combining all three sides of the Triad.

"Report to my office for your briefing."

"Yes, sir. Um, any word on when the *Cloud Shadow* will be released from the shipyard, sir?" She could feel him smile at her impatience, but, hells, she couldn't wait to take command of her first ship.

"That is in fact one of the reasons I would like to see you."

"It is? I mean, it is, *sir?*"

"*One* of the reasons, Captain Keyren."

She blushed. *Shut up, Hadley.* "Yes, sir. Understand, sir. On my way, sir." She ended the call and spun back to Bolivarr. "The prime-admiral wants to see me in his office. Little ol' me."

"Little ol' *Captain* you," he reminded her.

She grinned. "This is the Ring, Bolivarr. The central command headquarters of the largest military in the galaxy. As much as I'd love to get a big head over making rank, around here captains are as common as a queen's penny-credit."

She combed his hair off his forehead, but the glossy black locks flopped forward as they always did. He'd go back to his drawing the moment she left, she knew. Why had he dreamed of the circles? Or, rather, remembered them? Maybe it was the first crack before the wall inside his head crashed down. She loved him. She wanted him to be healed. Why then did a feeling of dread accompany his discovery?

She transformed her worry with a bright smile and pressed another quick kiss to his lips. "I'll see you later."

She scurried down the corridor, fixing her hair as she went. Two lift rides, several long, curving corridors, and a retina scan later, she was being escorted into Zaafran's suite of offices. His lair was abuzz with military personnel of all ranks. It was the heart of the Ring. He waited for her in a quieter, more private section with a dizzying view of the outer ring and the ice planet below.

In the seconds before his aide called out her presence, she glimpsed a mature, fit man concentrating on a datapad. The glow illuminated deeply etched worry lines between his brows. His usually immaculate uniform was ever so slightly wrinkled, as if he'd been in it for days. She imagined the days and long nights that he did indeed sleep in his uniform, if he did sleep at all, when it seemed the Hordish tide would sweep over their worlds.

"Prime-Admiral, Captain Keyren has arrived," the aide announced, saluting and backing away.

Captain, she thought. *It sounds wonderful.*

The prime-admiral's expression eased instantly.

Worry lines became smile lines that bracketed his mouth. He strode toward her, his blue eyes shining. She snapped to attention and saluted.

His PCD began to beep at the same time several datapads on his desk demanded attention with a variety of chimes. He slapped his PCD with impatient fingers. "Joss, hold all calls." Frustration roughened his voice. "Unless, Star-Major, it's to tell me we've got him. I don't care which one—either Mawndarr will do."

She studied him as unobtrusively as she could, trying to figure out, without actually appearing baffled, the source of the normally unruffled officer's distraction. Apparently it wasn't her or something she had done— this time—thank the goddess. She'd stuck her neck out before. She was doubly determined to toe the line and stay within the lines. No one trusted rogue officers. It was a career-ending reputation, for sure. Hadley wanted her career more than anything.

He exhaled and turned back to her. "A convicted battlelord is on the run. You'll hear who soon enough— Karbon Mawndarr."

"I'm aware of the name, sir. Admiral Bandar mentioned him now and again." Usually in between swearwords and vows to "see the monster strung up and castrated."

"During transport to his war crimes trial, he escaped. Obviously he had help—from the inside. It's a humiliating blow for us, and a boost in credibility for the loyalists." He folded his arms over his chest to sit on the edge of his desk. "Now I've lost contact with the man who helped us capture him." A pained look shadowed his eyes. "His son."

"You think he betrayed you and helped the battlelord get free, sir?"

"He has the brains and the knowledge. Blast it all, I never thought he would betray me. I trusted him."

"And if he didn't, sir?"

"Then he's a target. I've issued a galaxy-wide warrant for his arrest. I had to think long and hard about it and decided it was for the best. If the son wasn't involved, arresting him will keep him alive. Mawndarr will know who sold him out. He's too clever not to. Blast it, I don't want him walking free. If anyone has the power and cunning to start up a resistance movement, it's him."

"Resistance to what, sir—peace? The Drakken aren't being treated as a defeated nation. They're sharing in the Triad."

"The loyalists would see to the rebirth of the Drakken Empire. With the warlord's daughter out there some-where, and now this monster, possibly aided by his son, they very well could."

And ignite a thousand more years of bloodshed and oppression? "There are billions of believers who won't let that happen, sir."

"Nor will I allow that to happen." He made a fist, rotating it with restrained anger in his palm. Then he seemed to transform, his expression brightening once more. "But that is not why you're here, Captain. The reason is one of new beginnings. Hope. Congratulations, Captain. Not only have you passed captain's school with an outstanding ride, you're about to head out on your new ship the very same week."

"Yes, sir! I am honored, sir. And blasted excited," she

blurted out next, clamping her teeth together to keep from spewing any more inappropriate expressions of emotion.

The edges of her superior's mouth twitched, his eyes twinkling. He hadn't disapproved and seemed to somehow find her excitement amusing. "Now, I'd like you to keep that trademark enthusiasm of yours channeled into this mission, even if it's not what you expected."

That meant she wouldn't like it. She'd been in the military since she was a teenage cadet. She knew all about making flarg smell sweet. "Yes, sir."

"An ancient artifact has come into our possession. An urn. We found it behind enemy lines, lost to us for millennia. It dates back from before the Great Schism, perhaps touched by the hands of the goddesses themselves."

His description raised bumps on her flesh. So little predating the war had survived. The few items left were preserved in temples or the palace, cared for by priestesses, and loaned to various museums for public viewings during special times of the year. Since the war ended, news had come of the Drakken rich and powerful hoarding many more such artifacts, plundered and otherwise, on display in personal residences and ships, and others used dismissively as decorative objects or stepping stones in gardens.

"I'm sending you off to explore its origin. We've run an exhaustive analysis of the relic. Priestesses translated the runes. They reveal coordinates to a planet previously uncharted, deep inside Hordish space. We anticipate that the site will be of enormous religious significance. At the very least, it promises to provide a wealth of information from the days preceding the Great Schism, the very birth of our society. A high-priestess will serve as your advisor and an archeologist as your first officer."

She did her best not to blurt out her dismay. An archae-ologist first officer? She'd have hoped her second in command would be a qualified bridge officer, not a scientist. This was an expedition, not a mission. Zaafran didn't expect her ship to be anywhere near any kind of action, even with an infamous battlelord and the warlord's daughter on the lam and threatening peace.

"It will be an ideal first interstellar experience for space cadets from the academy," he went on, "as well as a first mission for a new captain."

Her thrill at taking command fizzled a little more. Since when did captain duties include chaperoning a bunch of teenagers? This wasn't even an expedition—it was a school field trip. She bit her tongue so as not to voice the thought. The really exciting, most thrilling missions were a thing of the past. She might as well get used to a peacetime military like Brit Bandar and the others had gotten used to.

Actually, Admiral Bandar had more or less retired into a position as commandant of the RGMA. For now at least, married, and pregnant and sitting at a desk was her escape from this fate, Hadley realized. She, on the other hand, was about to launch her career. Doing what? Patrolling for common space thugs and babysitting cadets? Not that she didn't want the end of war—she'd fought for it and had seen friends die for it—but did peace have to be so blasted *boring?* How would she ever make admiral—an admiral worthy of respect—at this rate? It was her life's dream and she wouldn't let it go—not yet.

The prime-admiral's silvery hair and piercing blue eyes glowed in the muted light as he laid a large datapad on the table. He activated the holovis feature. "Display map." Five lights appeared in front of them, three-dimensional and glowing as they floated in midair. They formed the general shape of two sides coming to a point.

Goddess! She grabbed the edge of the table to steady herself. It was very nearly the same pattern Bolivarr had sketched: five dots arranged in a pointed shape. "And runes," she murmured. Some that Bolivarr had scribbled, as well.

"It's Sakkaran."

"The ancient tongue of the goddesses. I've heard of it but haven't ever seen it."

"We have so little examples left. Only a few of our highest ranking priestesses know how to read and write it. There's no more use for it, really, but they keep it alive for the sake of history. The Agran Sakkara was originally written entirely in runes, all four volumes. Many believe that the original volume, the fifth, wherein the origin of the goddesses is revealed, still exists, somewhere on one of the ancient worlds, behind what was once enemy lines."

"Do you mean the lost scripture, sir?"

"Yes. The revelation of *everything*."

Hadley lifted a brow at the longing and awe that crept into the admiral's voice and eyes. "I didn't expect you to be such a lover of fables, sir. Isn't treasure part of the legend, too?"

He nodded. "I was an ancient history major at the academy. Not many know it. A fable the lost scripture may be, and the treasure that surrounds it, but to entertain the promise of such a discovery, to dream of it…it is what our weary, war-ravaged people need. To know the goddesses existed…that they *were real*. That true goodness exists, Hadley." A faraway look softened his gaze. Then he blinked back to the briefing room. "Or that goodness once existed, at any rate. Gods know we could use some now. Now, Captain Keyren, no more sidetracking me with fables and legends of yore."

Her? She grinned. "No, sir."

He activated the holo. "Display image for Mission Origins." A misty sphere glowed on the holo, mostly water and with several good-sized, life-sustaining continents. "Ara Ana," he said. "Your destination."

"Ara Ana? That's the birthplace of the goddesses. It's a myth. It doesn't exist."

"That's what you've been told. We all have. But what if it's real?"

Hadley clasped her shaking hands behind her back. On the heels of her surprise and wonder came the uneasy knowledge that Bolivarr knew of this, too—an ancient artifact from possibly pre-Schism days. Bolivarr was Drakken. A wraith. How would he come into possession of such knowledge—and why? Had he discovered the information accidentally, or on purpose? How many other people knew that the birthplace of the goddesses and possibly the lost scripture might actually exist—to be plundered or revered, depending on the discoverer?

"You are correct, however, Captain. We don't know the name of the planet or even what's there. But why not launch an expedition with great fanfare—keeping your actual destination secret, of course—and give the people a bit of hope? It will serve as a diversion from all the reports coming in from the Borderlands lately."

Yes, the evidence of massacres and skullings, whole

cities wiped out, starvation and sickness, poor little Drakken children who looked old at eight—they were old, after what they'd endured—and now of two, honest-to-goddess monsters on the loose who'd see to the continuation of those atrocities.

Mawndarr, she thought, and the warlord's daughter.

"Yes, sir, we could use such news, sir." Suddenly her mundane archaeological field trip took on meaning.

"Our presumptive Ara Ana lies at the fringes of the Uncharted Territories," he continued.

Hadley stood straighter with interest. The Uncharted Territories—the UT—lay beyond the Borderlands. It was a region of space at the rim of the galaxy that was so remote that it remained virtually unexplored, mostly due to war and the inability to use enemy-controlled wormholes. It had been a lost region of space for thousands of years, a region now on the verge of discovery. It would take weeks of traversing through wormholes in space to get there.

And she'd be tasked with keeping teens out of trouble for the duration. Goddess help her. So much for "meaning." She'd be lucky if she kept her captain stripes after this.

Zaafran read her expression. "Perhaps it's not the mission you envisioned, Captain. I know you young captains, champing at the bit for action, pirates and the like—but I don't have a single other ship to spare. But, by the gods, I'm damn curious about the site. I envy you. I'd go myself if I didn't have the Triad to run."

"You're just saying that to make me feel better, sir."

"Maybe I am." He smiled. "Enjoy. When you return, we'll see about something a little more challenging."

"Yes, sir." When she proved herself, he meant. Her focus returned to the five dots. Bolivarr's dots.

*"It's something from my life before."*

*"Something bad?"*

*"Something I'm supposed to know."*

Hadley squared her shoulders. "A request, sir. I'd like to add Battle-Lieutenant Bolivarr to my crew."

His brow rose.

That brow lift said it all. Bolivarr was a model officer. Yet ever since Hadley had been promoted to captain, she had sensed that her relationship with Bolivarr was frowned upon. Subtly. Like Zaafran's eyebrow lift. No one ever came out and told her not to see him, but she feared that any day now she'd be forced to end the relationship, especially if Bolivarr's memory returned and revealed he'd committed war crimes. It was close-minded and unfair, but she'd have little choice if she were ordered to give up Bolivarr in order to keep her command.

"The amnesiac wraith?"

"The former wraith, sir," she corrected as tactfully as she could. "He's been seeing the same pattern in his dreams and thoughts. There's a good chance if he comes along on this mission, it will open up his past. He'd be of great help, sir. He's a history buff like yourself, sir. In fact, the Drakken people as a whole are known for being enthusiastic collectors of antiquities."

"Particularly of antiquities that belonged to us," Zaafran commented dryly, shifting his attention to a bank of tall, curved windows that looked out at the massive sweep of the Ring. Hadley remembered quite acutely how disorienting that view was the first time she ever glimpsed it. "So you think his memories may provide more information essential to this mission," he said.

"Perhaps even the lost scripture."

"In Drakken hands. Burn the thought." He paced a few steps and stopped. "The world the goddesses left behind is behind the border—what once was the border. Bolivarr could very well know what we don't." He paced a few more steps, halting again. "It might make sense to add him to the crew roster."

Hadley squeezed her hands hidden behind her back. *Please.*

"You will be far from civilization, Captain, as you know, and he suffers seizures. He may be a liability more than he is an aid to this mission."

"Medication's controlling the seizures, sir. It's been weeks since he had any. We'll have a physician onboard. I'll ensure he's thoroughly briefed by Bolivarr's medical staff. I know the position of chief of security has not been filled as yet. Bolivarr is eminently qualified for the position." Probably overqualified. "He ran security on his last ship before the *Unity.*"

"That was a pirate ship."

"Then who better to assist in avoiding pirates during our transit than a former pirate himself, sir? Bolivarr will be an asset to the operation. Certainly, with cadets onboard, I'll want the safest ship possible—and so will their parents. And if we come upon treasure, having worked with pirates, Bolivarr understands the security measures needed for its safe collection."

"It is obvious you've given this much thought."

"Yes, sir." Actually, it was all off the top of her head. Good thing she could think on her feet. Or in her boots, as Admiral Bandar used to say. "I think there's more to be gained by having Bolivarr assigned to my crew than leaving him behind. I know my request is highly irregular, but I didn't get this far by thinking inside the box."

The prime-admiral's eyes sparkled. "No, Captain, you did not." He rubbed the length of his index finger across the bottom of his chin as he considered her proposal. Then he dropped his hand. Sighed. "If his doctors say he can go, I'll add him to the crew."

*Goddess, yes.* "Thank you, sir. Thank you." Hadley remembered her decorum and came to attention. "I hope you find the person who needs that information on Mawndarr's escape."

He nodded in weary thanks. "So do I, Captain."

Even as she saluted again, he'd activated his PCD. She whirled on a heel and marched out of the office. Her darling Bo had long hoped for a way to unlock his past. Mission: Origins, aptly named, could very well be it.

# CHAPTER EIGHT

IN THE MORNING, Wren had to leave the cool, shaded safety of the sleeping tent. No one was allowed to stay inside during daytime. The crowded tents were sanitized then. Soon after being roused from her cot, she was forced back outside into the heat and noise with the other stragglers. "Be back at dusk for curfew."

Another day out in the open loomed. She had to get rid of her glasses. She was too obvious in her current appearance. A bad haircut, yes, and old clothes, but the glasses were a dead giveaway for anyone knowing what to look for. Now was the perfect time to get her eyes repaired. The medical tent would provide shelter and safety until curfew.

"No more appointments are available," the tech there said, running Wren's data square. "Come back later."

"May I stay here and wait?"

He shook his head. "Against the rules."

She turned back into the streets. The air was stifling, the dust choking. There were thousands of people around her but she'd never felt more isolated. Her energy began to flag. And her spirits. She gave her glasses a push with the tip of her finger and forced her feet to keep moving.

The breeze and Wren's boots churned up fine dust.

It burned her nose and eyes. A scan of the crowd revealed only disinterested faces. Yet, the sense that she was being watched or followed nagged at her. She was trapped in this camp. Everyone who glanced at her became suspect. They became her hunters.

Every moment she was stuck out in the open increased her risk. She'd never realized how draining fear was.

Never mind her. This was what it had been like for her father's subjects, namely the believers, every day of their lives.

At the docks, pilots and others made sport of mocking the refugees. Their defeated enemy was being paraded before them as they gloated. Shame thickened her throat. It embarrassed her to see her fellow Drakken this way. Their appearance and condition contrasted so sharply with the obviously much better off Coalition. *Look at us.* This was what happened when making weapons of mass destruction took precedence over society.

She'd seen nothing like these people on Barokk, of course. She realized that her father's aim had been for her never to see the way real Drakken lived—and especially not the damning evidence of his reign of terror. If her life had turned out the way it was supposed to, she never would have known of it. She would have gone straight from Barokk to a battlelord's household, never realizing anything else existed. Sabra had further assured her ignorance by keeping so many secrets over the years, keeping her horribly innocent of…everything. The woman had done it to protect her. Out of love, but it was wrong. Wren had a new life now. She vowed never to be kept in the dark again. And never, ever in anyone else's control.

The pendant pressed to her skin, a constant reminder

of that last, terrible day on Barokk. The things she'd learned and not understood whirled in her mind all day and all night. Ilkka had been about to reveal a secret about Lady Seela, her mother, a secret so harmful that Sabra wouldn't let her do it. Was her mother as vicious as her father, and Sabra meant to protect her from the knowledge? She'd always spoken of her mother in loving, reverent tones. More lies, lies and secrets. No matter the reason why they were perpetuated, Wren resented it.

She'd have the final word. She'd find that treasure her family had apparently accumulated and donate it anonymously to the people who cared for war victims. Every last coin, every priceless jewel. She wanted none of it. She couldn't rid herself of her family's genes, but she could unload their wealth and, in that small way, try to atone for what they'd done.

To do that, she had to get out of the camp. She held fast to that goal, her first outside the basic need to survive. Her first made as an independent woman.

As she made her way through the streets, a genuine sense of excitement rippled through the camp. "Have you heard?" people were saying to each other. "The warlord has another child. A girl child."

Fates. Wren kept her shoulders hunched and her face down.

"They're offering a bounty for her arrest."

A bounty. As if the motivation to find her wasn't enough. Double fates.

"How much?" someone asked, craning their neck to see.

"Fifty million queen's credits."

A roar went up. "Fifty *million?*"

"A fortune."

"A man would never have to work again in his life with that kind of money in his pocket."

"Or a woman." The females in the crowd laughed and cheered.

*Bounty* and *millions* rang in Wren's ears no matter where she turned. People were plotting and planning how they'd spend their share of the reward, never imagining the very woman they sought was in their midst. Refugees and guards alike searched each other's faces, wondering if this girl was the one, or that one.

The crowd clustered around the data-generated likeness displayed on the screen reserved for camp news, warnings of infractions and the like. Normally gatherings of any size were forbidden. The Triad was willing to bend the rules to make sure she was found. No wonder she'd been able to slip past without detection. They were using a sketch based on her parents: "Highly attractive," read the notes, "tall, blond, hazel eyes. Or possibly green…"

All her life she'd bemoaned the fact she hadn't inherited her parents' looks. Now she couldn't be more relieved. How long before someone figured it out? The bounty had turned everyone into a potential captor, from the refugees to the guards.

THE TRIAD WAS OVERWHELMED by the influx of refugees all through the Borderlands. Refugee ships were being rerouted so often it was difficult if not impossible to know when one would dock. The galaxy it seemed was in disarray even now, months after the surrender. To

Aral all that mattered was data showing the vessel that picked up the citizens of Barokk had already arrived, beating him here. He had the location of her sleeping quarters after narrowing down by age and description what false identity she was using: Wren Senderin. As a presumptive law enforcement agent he was privy to the data. Due to the camp's rules of emptying the sleeping tents during daylight, Awrenkka was now one of thousands milling in the streets of the camp. He'd wait for her. While he waited, he'd search.

No one raised an eyebrow at his activities and inquiries. It was, so far, nothing unusual. Criminals poured into Zorabeta and the other camps with regular Drakken. The Triad wanted them winnowed out as best as their strained resources permitted. Little did they know that a former battlelord was about to do them all a favor by taking the warlord's daughter off their hands.

He and Kaz walked along the docks. A group of traders loitered nearby with those he was certain were off-duty soldiers. Sharing drinks, they made a sport of Drakken-watching, snickering about the backwardness of the refugees.

"Each new load gets worse and worse," one observed to more half-drunken laughter.

"Their women wear tattoos, too."

"And they pierce body parts you don't want to know about."

Never was the gulf between the two civilizations more apparent than in this camp. The differences didn't stop at skin and jewelry. Hair was another visible reminder of the gulf between their peoples. Drakken hair was most often worn beaded, braided, or knotted, or some combination of all three. Most high-ranking military officers favored a more conservative style, however. Kaz wore her hair the same way she always had: short. He'd insisted on her removing most of her jewelry, however. Dutifully she'd complied, leaving only the two small ruby-red diamonds, one in each earlobe, that had been a gift from Bolivarr.

Aral dragged a hand over his own hair. Cut short, it was freepin' hard to get used to. Every day of his adult life he'd combed his hair into a neat ponytail tied at the base of his neck out of habit and sensibility more than style. Practically living in an Imperial Navy uniform, he'd had no need to give a thought to fashion. He'd had far more important things on his mind. By keeping to a life aboard ship, he'd bypassed, or, rather, avoided, time on his planetside estate and the frivolous social whirl that came with it. Only when visiting the warlord did he have to play that game. The palace parties, the drugs, the rich food and drink, the women, the tournaments, it was all what he'd like to forget.

Yet, with meeting Awrenkka imminent, he couldn't help wondering what she'd think *of him*. Would she find him pleasant to the eye, or frightening?

Did he care?

It blasted well felt like it.

"You had better not meet her wearing that face," Kaz cautioned in a private tone. "You'll frighten the girl."

"She's not a girl. She's a mere two years younger than you. Four younger than I am. We are not girls and boys by any means."

Kaz shrugged blithely, but he sensed she did so to hide her hurt at his sharp words. They rarely quarreled.

Not since the dark months after Bolivarr's death when neither much slept due to their efforts to find him. It was almost a relief declaring him dead a few years later, though no less painful.

He shook his head, feeling fatigue dragging him down, and causing him to act intolerably to his friend and valued officer. "Kaz, sorry. I need sleep."

"Nightmares?"

"And what little sleep I did get was interrupted by that blasted PCD."

"What did Z want?"

"I didn't answer."

"Was that wise?" she queried carefully as a good second ought.

His quick, soft laugh sounded weary, even to his own ears. "Probably not." He sighed. "Kaz, he wants me to help capture Awrenkka. What else could it be? Everyone else of importance is dead." The name Karbon was left unspoken. "Whatever new information he cares to share can wait. I'll contact him before we leave for good. He'll thank me for my service and that will be that." He peered into the glare of the harsh sunlight that was as bright as two suns. It felt like acid poured on his raw nerves. "I can't be like this around her," he confided. "She won't understand. I'll try to sleep with some of those new meds later."

"Later? *She'll* be with you later. It's your wedding night. Sleep with her, not your meds."

"It won't be that way with us so quickly."

One inky, perfectly formed brow lifted. "Where there's attraction, there's desire. Where there's smoke, there's fire—"

"Kaz, it's bad enough I don't know the first thing about

the care and feeding of a wife. I won't compound things by forcing myself on her like a common barbarian."

"Don't let too much time pass—waiting, being cautious, thinking you'll know when the time is right. You won't. Each day together is a gift that you may never have again. There's no warning when it happens, Aral. You know that."

He thought of her and his brother. "When one doesn't move on with life, isn't that waiting, as well? Being cautious?"

Her mouth tightened as she flicked a speck of dust off her simple, dark flight outfit that she'd somehow managed to keep immaculate despite the wretched conditions. "Point taken." Then she squared her shoulders. "I should not have brought up such a personal subject while on duty."

"You seemed fine until it got too personal *for you*."

"My apologies for not being more professional."

"Professional? Bah. We were friends long before we were shipmates, Kaz. In fact, the very first time you boarded a ship of mine it was through illegal means. You stowed away to be with Bolivarr."

He was glad to hear her husky laugh. "You knew about it. You sanctioned it. So technically, it was not stowing away."

"Technically—*selfishly*—I needed the extra hand onboard. I looked the other way."

"Hardly. Late-night sech matches over bottles of whiskey don't exactly equal looking the other way." She laughed softly, her eyes sparkling. "Such good days those were. All three of us were partners-in-crime, not only your brother and I. Don't rewrite history." Though he knew if she had the power, Kaz would write Bolivarr back into their lives. They all would.

Her smile faded to a pensive gaze and she turned her focus back to the streets. "Perhaps it's time we did close the book on the past, Aral. We'll write new books. Today you'll begin your first chapter."

"Look at them—look!" Untiring of the parade of bedraggled Drakken, the group gathered nearby grew louder and rowdier. Now they were ridiculing some of the Drakken wounded in countless attacks, injuries old and new. The Coalition hadn't been spared such wounds, but unlike common Drakken they'd had access to the medical care to mitigate damages and repair them.

"That one's missing an arm," one of them observed. "Did he leave it at home?"

"Ignorant oafs," Kaz snarled. "Put them in the Empire under the warlord's rule and see how long they'd last."

They were lucky they'd never had to know what such a life was like. Aral wouldn't wish that on anyone. Life under the warlord's thumb was something no human should have to suffer. Yet, they had for thousands of years, the last warlord arguably the worst of the lot. That his people were adapting to new circumstances with tentative hope said more for the Horde than the Coalition that defeated them.

"Shut the flarg up, Oreksen," one of the traders admonished the group who was making fun of the war wounded. He stood in the shade of his ship, *Borrowed Time,* when the men switched from poking fun at tattoos and dress to injuries. The ship's name was somehow familiar, but then Aral's mind held on to many more details than he should, details he often wished he could forget. "That's just plain disrespectful," the trader said.

"Touchy today, Vantos?"

"Yeah, I'm touchy."

Aral asked a nearby trader, "Who is that man?"

"Vartekeir Vantos. The guy's a legend, the longest lived runner we ever had."

Ah. So that's why he was familiar. Aral spent a lot of time shoring up the blockade. He was supposed to keep runners from getting through to supply forces on the other side. "Supposed to" being the key words. As "M" he'd done little he was supposed to for the empire. He'd been too busy ensuring its defeat. Over the years, many of the Coalition vessels had become familiar to him. *Borrowed Time* was one of a few that kept showing up in his sights. Lucky for Vantos, it appeared. He'd survived the war.

"Ex-runner. War over means game over." Vantos threw a hatch closed after checking the contents within then turned back to the man he'd rebuked. "I'll run my fist through your face if I hear you saying anything else about those people's injuries. They're civilians, for blasted sake."

He walked over to Aral and Kaz, wiping his hands on a greasy rag. "What a hells hole, eh?" He turned to Kaz and winked. "But I have to say the view around here's improved dramatically in the past few seconds."

Kaz's mouth thinned in annoyance. She was a battlelord's second. No man would dare speak with her in such a brazen manner—if he wished to live to the end of the day. "Pity I can't say the same."

Vantos quickly covered his surprise with a laugh. "Most women appreciate a fine view."

Kaz turned her disdainful gaze back to the crowd she was supposed to be searching. Her dismissal broadcast that, one, she wasn't "most women" and two, his flirtation was beneath her regard.

"That hurts. I'm going to be sore tomorrow." The trader's manner might be deceptively casual as he gnawed on that infernal nanopick, but his probing eyes gave him away. He was curious about Aral, wanting to know more. "Interesting crowd," he hinted, moving his chin in the direction of the incoming refugees.

"Extremely," Aral said.

"Looking for someone?"

"I enjoy people watching."

"Ah."

More laughter erupted from the group of traders who clearly hadn't tired of watching the refugees. To the sound of guffaws, one of the crowd-watchers called out to his cohorts, "And look—that one's wearing eyeglasses!"

Glasses? Aral knew of only one being who wore them. His blood surging, he jerked his gaze around to a petite woman making her way through the crowded streets. She wore her hair loose and shorter than the other women. The wind kept picking up strands and blowing them around her face, teasing him with a peek at a pale slender neck and the curve of her jaw.

She was too small to radiate the kind of magnetism she did. She should be lost in the crowd; instead she was the eye of the storm as chaos spun around her. Maybe it was how she seemed to avoid interaction with everyone else, or the way her brown hair reflected the sunlight that bounced too harshly off everything else, strands that glowed red where the light hit it.

Just as he remembered.

A bolt of recognition, of anticipation, electrified him from head to toe. Awrenkka. At last.

# CHAPTER NINE

WREN STOLE sideways glances at the other refugees and the traders at the docks. Who were enemies? Who were friends? A trio of traders stuck out for not laughing at the refugees. One of them, a handsome, boyish trader-pilot, bantered with a more subdued, tall and striking couple. The male of the pair caught her attention. He was tall, muscled, with slits for eyes and a hard mouth. In profile, he looked carved of stone. A human weapon, there was nothing soft about him. He belonged in uniform. On him trader garb—boots, leather flight jacket, trousers worn slung low around his hips and cinched by a thick leather belt—was a joke.

Wren pushed her windblown hair off her face, unable to pull her eyes away. *Don't do this. It's too dangerous.* She couldn't risk drawing their attention. The other, boyish trader noticed, pulling some sort of thin stick out of his mouth to look at her. Then all three turned to look at her in unison. The tall, dark-haired trader stepped forward, as if to get a better view. As the crowd jostled her, she stared back. She knew that face, those eyes. *Blacker than midwinter's eve and as haunted.*

A punch of recognition, of déjà vu, hit hard. He looked like Aral. Fates, yes. Aral Mawndarr but with short hair and all grown up. The lost boy who'd touched her heart, only to crush it.

Impossible. The real Aral was a battlelord and most likely dead. Word was that the Triad had killed or sentenced to death all the warlord's top leadership—really, a type of genocide, of mass murder, too. Or did the definition depend on what side of the border the orders originated? If Aral *had* evaded getting caught, which she doubted, the very last thing he'd do was show up in a refugee camp to loiter in wretched conditions and with those he'd consider far beneath his exalted self, like these dockside traders. She'd never forgotten the callous way he'd dismissed her, as if she were miles beneath his regard. Seeing this look-alike reminded her of a very real danger: real loyalists on the lookout for her.

Ducking away, she let the crowd swallow her up. She wanted to run, but it would draw too much notice. She used her small size to wind past the other refugees and get as far away from the docks as possible. She had to get out of this trap of a camp, and she needed to do it quickly. Time was not on her side.

AWRENKKA. HE'D FOUND HER! A few thumps of his thundering heart later, she was gone, her violet eyes burning in his mind like an after-image of a too-bright light.

Why was she alone? Why had her chaperones abandoned her? Something inside him twisted at the sight of her small frame swallowed up by old, oversized clothes. She didn't belong here in this camp. He knew the kind of sheltered life she'd led, yet she didn't cower or skulk. It made him proud. She deserved a future, happiness.

Was he capable of giving it to her?

He hadn't an example on which to base anything approaching a normal husband-wife relationship. He certainly wasn't going to revisit the horrifying circumstances of his childhood. It hit him that he'd never extrapolated his rescue of her beyond the vague details of fleeing with her somewhere quiet and remote to live out their lives in peace, blessed peace. Now that the reality was upon him, he wasn't sure how he was actually going to accomplish it. The devil was in the details.

He crushed the compulsion to go after her. The overly curious ex-runner was watching him. The man's lingering perusal was sharper and more inquisitive than before. Aral tried to act as if he wasn't affected by the sight of Awrenkka. His success in doing so was questionable.

"Well, I'll leave you to your business here," the runner said. "I've got some of my own." He nodded in farewell to Aral and gave Kaz another wink. "See you around, sweetheart."

"Boor," she muttered, then she turned to Aral.

"It's her," Aral said. "Awrenkka."

"The small woman with the glasses, yes. She fits your description, aside from the short hair."

"It's her. I'm sure of it. Ten years has changed her, but not enough." Ten years had changed him, too, in fates knew how many ways.

"Did she recognize you?"

"It's hard to say." She'd given him a double take, however. Well, he'd know soon enough. He turned his gaze back to teeming throngs of refugees where Awrenkka had vanished. He'd lost her, but it was for the very last time.

KEIR'S MIND RACED as he strode away from the docks. The man and woman he'd encountered were covert operatives, both of them. He knew the look; the camps were filled with undercover law enforcement types, covert agents, spies, assorted fugitives, opportunists, and trusted former Drakken. His guess was that they were former high-class Drakken. They didn't act anything like the bottom-feeders filling the refugee camps. Yeah, blue-bloods. The first clue was their precise queen's tongue, carefully covering up their accents—a little too carefully. And the woman with the flawless skin like white marble and the red luscious lips, she was a cold one, all right. Exactly the kind of woman he avoided. Of course he did. She was Drakken.

He replayed the scene where they'd all stopped to look at the woman wearing the antique eyeglasses. It was clear that little refugee was a person of interest to the pair, and thus a person of interest to him. Fifty million queens rode on his guess why those two agents were in lovely Zorabeta. They were searching for the warlord's daughter, too.

WREN FLED THE DOCKS, intent on eluding her hunters, both visible and not, as memories of Aral Mawndarr haunted her. Seeing the trader who resembled him so closely was disconcerting. The day on her father's ship came back, and the few heartbeats of a glance she'd shared with Aral. That encounter had launched years of daydreams. There had been a real person before he disappeared behind that frosty sneer. She'd glimpsed him. Yes, a person a lot like her.

*We'll find a way out.* In her fantasies, he'd snatch her

hand and they'd be off. Together they'd leave their nightmares behind. Her belly gave a small, tight twist at the poignancy of that childish wish. It was Sabra's fault, filling her impressionable young head with fairytales that made her so susceptible to the fleeting gaze she and Aral had shared as teenagers.

*Enough silliness, Wren. Enough acting like a teenager with an unrequited crush. Aral is dead. The battlelords were hunted down and killed, every last one.*

The pleasant scent of incense came as a surprise and a contrast to the bleakness around her, pulling her out of her thoughts. A priestess walked past, incense drifting in her wake like her robes. Smoke gray and pearlescent, they billowed around her body from head to feet. There was strength beneath that silk. Her skin showed the lines of a long life. Her serene, ageless eyes were paler than the heat-bleached sky. "May the goddess be with you," she told Wren as she passed, bestowing blessings on all within reach.

"And also with you," others called back to her.

As if connected by a string, Wren followed at a distance. The peace she'd felt in the sister's presence was too wonderful to surrender so easily. It touched her, luring her.

Eventually the priestess disappeared behind the flap of a large tent. Inside, Wren glimpsed women resting, talking, and, to her delight, reading books. It was a makeshift temple. Ah, to be safe inside in the cool of the tent, immersed in learning the religion of the goddesses. The desire to join them almost made her step inside. To be able to be a priestess and spend the rest of her life in solitary, quiet prayer and study was a powerful draw.

Her presence in the sanctuary would have been an insult to these women, reading the *Agran Sakkara,* the bible of the religion that her father and the rest of her ancestors had worked so hard to eradicate.

She backed away from the entrance, trying to forget the sense of peace inside, the sense of belonging there and not here. Not in this life she'd been dealt. This camp.

She lingered, wandering outside the tent like a stray dog. The usual signs of day-to-day life were scattered around the perimeter: large containers of drinking water, assorted boxes, and freshly washed robes fluttering in the breeze on the drying racks.

Disguises for the taking.

Even as she recoiled from the idea, she embraced it. Wearing one of those robes would afford her freedom of movement and instant respect from even the guards. Believers were given credit for the hated warlord's fall, after all. If Wren were a priestess, she'd have the same advantages.

She turned her eyes to the heavens and whispered in her best attempt at a prayer. "I have to make sure the treasure doesn't fall into the hands of the wrong people. And—" she swallowed "—that I don't fall into the hands of the wrong people."

*Sorry, Sabra.* She plucked one of the outfits off the drying line and dropped it over her head. The robe swallowed up her small frame. It took a fistful of fabric for her to raise the hem high enough to keep it from tangling in her boots. She'd barely gotten the garment over her head when footsteps thumped behind her. There was no time to pull on the hood.

"Hello, miss."

It was another refugee, not a guard. She tried to slow

her bouncing heartbeat. He was thin, almost emaciated like so many people here, with heavy tattooing on one side of his face and a Drakken eagle on his forearm, revealed by his rolled up sleeve. Former Imperial Army, she knew the look. He was one of the lucky ones, or one of the smart ones, to have made it into the camp. His counterparts were either running for their lives, trying to eke out an existence as a pirate, or awaiting execution for war crimes.

"I said hello."

"Hello," she mumbled back, and scooted past him. The smell of food alerted her to a mess tent in front of which snaked a long line of refugees waiting for a meal. Keeping her eyes down as piously as possible, she took a spot at the end of the line.

Instantly she was urged to go to the front. "You first, sister."

"But—"

"Please, sister, go on ahead."

Dressed as a priestess, she received assistance at every turn. She was given a tray and as she proceeded down the line items were plopped onto a plate until it was full. She took the meal and searched for some shade, one hand grasping the hem of the robe to keep it high.

Boots crunched behind her. The ex-soldier was back. She'd thought she'd lost him.

"We were on the same ship," he said. "They kept you women away from us space hands—smart move on the captain's part." He glanced in one direction then the other and leaned closer. "You came from that all-female school planet, didn't you? You weren't wearin' priestess robes."

She scurried away. The robe tangled with her boots.

She hoisted the hem higher with one hand and almost dropped the tray.

He kept pace with her. "I took you for a virgin. Even then. See, I'm never wrong about that."

Her cheeks blazed. She hurried away from him, winding through the crowd with her tray of congealing food. She couldn't afford to attract attention, and that seemed all she was able to do.

A hand grabbed her shoulder, spinning her around. "I'm not done talking to you, sister." The soldier's eyes were angry, his mouth hard and unhappy. It wasn't so much rape she feared, but an incident leading to her being discovered. "Not all of us spent our days killing believers. Some of us were good and loyal soldiers. We kept the Coalition from invading your all-girl world. Invading *you*. How about a little respect?" He twisted his fist in the fabric of her robes and jerked her toward him. "C'mon, little sister, give me some because I know you ain't really no priestess—"

Wren shoved the tray into his face. Sputtering, he wiped cooked vegetables from his eyes. "You freepin' bitch. I'm gonna take you behind the tents and—"

She drove her knee upward. His strangled cry barely registered before she rammed his chin with the heel of her palm. He hit the ground hard, sitting there stunned.

Dust choked her and coated her glasses. The crowd moved back, forming a human arena for the fight. They were cheering, the noise thunderous. He was going to ruin everything. He was going to get her caught and killed.

He got back up and charged her. She raised the tray above her head, consumed by a primitive, bloodthirsty urge to finish him off. She hit him across the head. The impact traveled up her arms and made her teeth clap together. He went down again, got up, and then passed out.

Booing shook her back to reality. What had she done? Shame squeezed her lungs in an invisible vise. Once again she'd loosed the beast inside her. She'd lost control of her temper, and it was ugly indeed. At least she stopped before she killed this time, but it was little consolation. The incident drove home how dangerous she was. She couldn't even get a bite to eat without causing horrifying behavior in someone else. Maybe she ought to turn herself in to the authorities right now and save the galaxy from herself.

She blinked at the crowd churning around her. Male, female, everyone was an enemy in that moment. Army veterans stalked past, glaring and giving her dirty looks, believers tugging on her sleeves, pleading for blessings and reacting with expressions of disbelief when she didn't know how to respond. A sea of people. Of strangers. *Of hunters.*

"Move on! Show's over!" Guards had arrived to disperse the crowd.

The necessity to remain free overwhelmed every other thought except a gut-deep compulsion to find safety. She dove headlong into the crowd. The trailing fabric of her robe tangled around her ankles. She tripped. It sent her glasses clattering to the ground. Instantly they were crushed by the boots of someone in the throngs of people.

Blindly she ran a few more steps—and slammed into a solid body. "Whoa, whoa," the man said. Gasping, she tried to twist free. "Don't be scared. I'm only trying to help, sister. I'm a trader, not a cop. I saw you earlier near the docks. You weren't in the order then. Now look at you. A priestess." He chuckled. "I usually have the opposite effect on women."

It was obvious he didn't believe for a minute she was a priestess. With her hood off and a fight she'd just fled, just how believable was her disguise now? Not very. Not only that, she couldn't see.

The shouts of the guards came closer. The trader called to them, "It's about time security got here."

She tried to bolt. He wouldn't let her. "Hey, hey. They're not going to hurt you."

"No," she gasped. "No authorities."

"Why? You in trouble with the law, sister?" He seemed amused by the prospect. "Don't worry. I got you covered. I'll take care of this and then we'll go have a drink—I mean, for you a glass of water, right?" He acted as if they were in on the same joke. "Stay here."

A guard's boots crunched closer on the gritty street. The crowd had cleared a wide circle. Everyone knew the look of police activity and wanted no part of it. "So, what happened here, Vantos?"

Vantos. That was his name. He knew the guard, a female.

"The creep wanted a piece of something she wasn't willing to give."

"That right, sister?" the guard asked Wren.

Wren nodded.

"Disgusting." Wren relaxed a fraction as the guard's fingers tapped on her datapad. "Even a priestess isn't off-limits around here. We've had incidents like this all day. Must be the full moons. He looks nice wearing your lunch, though. Good job, sister. I hope what happened here makes the rest of them think twice about thinking they can take advantage of the females in this camp." Then she held out her hand to Wren. "Your data square, please."

Wren hesitated. The guard would see she wasn't identified as a priestess, or even a believer. Her excuse was going to be that she was a new apprentice. "I got you covered," Vantos assured her softly.

"Thanks for intervening," the guard told him. "That's not like you."

"Blasted right. Subduing the local populace isn't my job. It's yours."

"I know, I know. You've told us enough times. You do your thing, and we do ours, even though you slept on our outposts—"

"After running *your* supplies cross the blockade—"

"—and drank in our bars—"

"Listening to your pilots drink toasts in *my name* for saving their asses from another ambush your own intel didn't have a clue about," Vantos argued, motioning Wren to hand over her data square.

The guard took the data square as Vantos continued to engage her in conversation clearly designed to distract. The guard sighed as she inserted the data square into her reader. "You should be dead, you know."

"Yeah, well, that's on a lot of people's wish lists it seems."

"Vartekeir Vantos is a legend as a runner," the guard explained to Wren.

She sensed the dark look cast in her direction. "I used to run the blockade you Drakken set up in the Borderlands to cut us off from the front. That was then. Now

I'm freelance trading with the camps because there's not enough Coalition around to do the job—or do it right. I'm the one who brings in the supplies to the camps that you Drakken go through faster than we can keep up."

"Like chem-toilets," the guard teased.

"Chem-toilets are easy money. I like easy."

He was a freelancer. A man with no love lost between himself and the military establishment. He wore his lack of loyalties like a badge of honor, and bragged of his love of easy money. Profit was the way to this trader's heart—and quite possibly her way off-planet, she thought with sudden hope.

She knew as little about profit as she did men. What would be fair to offer? No refugees were supposed to leave. Putting him at risk would cost her. If the jewels weren't enough, she had treasure at her disposal. The fact that she didn't know exactly where it was didn't matter. Someone like Vantos would figure it out.

"You got an appointment, sister," the guard commented. "Med tent. Vision repair. That right?"

"It is. Yes." Just as she contemplated using it as an excuse to leave the scene of the fight, Vantos took her arm.

"I'll escort you," he said gallantly. She began to feel thankful that she'd bumped into this trader of all the others, though a strong sense of self-preservation kept her from trusting him or anyone here fully. "Like you said, the sister needs to be seen by the doc."

"Her appointment's not for two hours."

"I've got it covered, Ellie." As he urged Wren along, she tripped over something that sounded hollow and metal. He kept her from falling. "You really can't see, can you?"

"No," she mumbled, ashamed.

He steered her up to the med tent. "The sister's got an appointment."

"Data square," the med tech said tiredly.

Wren felt hope drain out of her. "It's with the guard."

"I can't help you without a data square."

They turned back.

"Hold on, Vantos." The guard was calling. She caught up to them, breathless. "There's a problem with her data square."

A problem. Wren gulped. Her blood roared in her ears.

"I'll handle it, sweetheart," Vantos murmured. "Don't tell me—they double-booked her for med exams."

"No…" The guard scanned her data reader. "Her ID's been flagged by Borderlands Patrol."

Flagged? "What does that mean?" she asked weakly.

"Hard to say, sister. It could be an administrative issue, or maybe they want to ask a few questions."

Vantos argued. "I saw the whole thing. She was forced to defend herself. Since when is that a crime?"

Her crime was being the firstborn of the most hated man in history. A death sentence. She had to escape Zorabeta—now. Everything hinged on it. Peace itself. "Help me," she whispered to Vantos.

A strange cough came out of the trader's throat. "Help" may have been the wrong thing to say. What did one say to a man she fully intended to use? It was for a greater purpose, for the good of all humanity, keeping her from starting another war, but it was using all the same. Another trait she'd inherited? The more she found out she was like the warlord, the more she wanted to prove herself the opposite. But she needed Vantos.

Needed to use him. Maybe when she was done with the man she'd make it up to him. Somehow.

There was no time to waste. She'd go right to the bribe without any preliminaries. "I want to buy passage on your ship." She fumbled for one of the bags of gems. "I will pay half now, and the other half upon arrival." She sounded so matter-of-fact as preternatural calm flooded her. Desperation did that. It was life or death now, and she was making a very risky bid for life.

Vantos hesitated as if her offer had caught him completely by surprise. "There's more where this came from," she said.

"More than that bounty?"

Her heart almost stopped. He wanted the bounty. Of course he did. Everybody did.

"More," she said, "than that."

"It's fifty million queens."

"Pocket credits compared to what I can give you if you get me out of here." She hoped she was right. She honestly didn't know what kind or how much treasure waited to be unlocked, or where she'd find the mysterious Ara Ana.

"Go on," he said. "I'm listening."

Her spirits leaped. Dangling her bait, she'd appealed to his greedy side and caught him. Now all she had to do was reel him in by convincing him that her offer trumped the Triad's. "I have a key to a treasure. I need transportation there. In exchange, you'll get a percentage."

"You still haven't told me how much."

"Riches beyond your imagination."

"You don't know my imagination. It's pretty big. Where is this treasure?"

"No more answers until I'm safely on your ship. And don't think you can steal the key and keep the treasure for yourself. I have to be present to open it."

"You'd better be telling the truth. When we get to the treasure and there's nothing for me, it won't go well for you, sweetheart. I guarantee that."

*When.* He'd said when. "So, you're in."

"Hells, yeah, I'm in. I know a win-win situation when I see it. Let me see that key."

"I'll show you on your ship. Not a moment before." Fates, she thought, growing light-headed from the heat and nerves. What had happened to the quiet mouse?

*She disappeared weeks ago.*

Whatever doubts he'd had earlier, he'd conquered them. "Let's go." He started walking her away.

"Vantos! Where are you going?"

"To complete a business transaction."

"What about her eyes?"

"Give me her data square back. They won't see her without it."

"No can do."

Wren sensed tension ratchet up in Vantos. It put her on alert. She was desperate, but she'd make blasted sure her instincts were right about him before she set foot on his vessel. Why was he suddenly her champion? He'd jumped in to help her even before she'd brought up money.

"My job's to keep you and everyone else in this camp from obstructing justice. I can't make exceptions, even for you, Vantos."

"Come on. This isn't justice."

"How do you know? This camp is crawling with

criminals. We just haven't the time or resources to find them all. Not that you're one of them, sister," she assured Wren. "But we have to be cautious."

It didn't matter. If the guard put enough doubt in the trader's mind, he'd never consider her proposal.

"Don't do anything stupid, Vantos. I've got agents on the way. They're armed." Ellie paused. "And I'm armed."

He choked out a laugh. "You'd shoot me, Ellie?"

"I swear, Vantos, you are going to spend the night in the brig if you don't stop interfering."

"It's me, Ellie." He banged his fingers against the center of his chest. "Me."

"That's the only reason your ass isn't already in jail, you crazy runner. In fact, I'm inclined to throw you in one cell and her in the other when I bring her in."

*Jail.* Wren imagined a cell with no way out but the executioner. Suddenly she felt weak in the knees. The black spots floating in her vision ballooned and she wobbled on her feet.

The heat and terror had finally caught up to her. Her skin went cold despite the sun baking down. The scene spun, her ears whooshing.

"I've got you," an unfamiliar voice said. Strong arms catching her was the last thing she remembered before she became aware of sitting on the ground in the shade with her head lowered between her knees. She heard Vantos some distance away, arguing with the guard. Several pairs of boots kicked up dust next to her.

She was so parched and hot that all she wanted to do was to lie down and go to sleep. It was too dangerous. She might not ever wake up, but the temptation to give in was strong. Only the need to get out of Zorabeta alive kept her conscious.

A straw snicked between her lips. "Drink." Cold water squirted in her mouth. She choked and managed to get some down her dry throat. "More."

She shook her head, but he didn't take no for an answer. At his insistence, she drank her fill. Thankfully it stayed down.

The man crouched behind her. The smells of leather, dust and faint tang of sweat filled her nostrils. "Listen closely. You are not under arrest. This is a rescue operation. A raid." He spoke close enough now for her to feel the warmth of his breath on her ear. Her body reacted with equal parts interest and alarm. "Obey my orders and you'll get out safely."

"Out of the camp?" she asked, not believing it could be true. Vantos had helped her, but how could she be sure about him? How could she be sure of this man? Suddenly everyone wanted to help her. Something was wrong. On the ground she was vulnerable. Blind and cornered, she wouldn't let it end this way. As it ended for her father—blind to his enemies, a prisoner on his own ship. An inner voice urged her to run. She dragged her boots under her and pushed.

Hands heavy on her shoulders kept her in place.

"Let me up."

"Do not fight me. For one, you won't best me. Second, I'm not the enemy here. *They* are."

*They are.* Since Sabra had died, she'd been a solitary player in a terrifying game. No one had been on her side. She tried to wrest free.

"Awrenkka," he warned low and soft in her ear.

She froze. He knew her name. Her real name. It startled her out of her daze. She blinked, swinging her gaze around. For all the good it did her. She couldn't see. But she could hear and finally noticed what she should have before: the hint of the inflection characteristic of a noble-born Drakken in his voice. "You're a loyalist," she hissed. They'd finally found her. He claimed he was on her side. The words were seductive, all right. He knew just what to say. But this man was no rescuer, no savior. He was a self-absorbed, power-hungry crony of her father's, the kind of man to whom her spirit, her feelings, meant nothing. She wanted nothing to do with the spoiled rich of the Hordish nobility, their rampant snobbery and class-awareness, their grating, suffocating attitudes on the subject of monogamy and commit-ment—one-sided, of course, to be obeyed only by the woman forced to marry them—which she'd decided long ago was a dangerous proposition for any sane-minded female. Growing up, she knew that marrying a battlelord was as inevitable as death; it would eventually claim her. Avoidance was futile. Had she found freedom only to stumble back into this trap: an ur-wolf dressed in trader clothing? Part of her wanted to throw herself on the mercy of the camp guard and plead for help. The other part of her knew it was too dangerous. Publicly making a connection with her and this loyalist could very well expose her true identity.

"A loyalist?" The man's soft laugh was as weary as it was bitter. "I have no allegiance to the empire. I never did. I did however do what I had to do for us to be together."

*Us?* He was delusional. She felt faint all over again.

His voice was low, too low for others to hear, and close enough to tickle the tiny hairs on the nape of her neck. It raised bumps on her flesh. "The entire galaxy's searching for you. We'll find a way out. I am going to save us both."

*We'll find a way out.*

She twisted in his arms, her heart slamming hard against her ribs as she thrust a hand at his face. He didn't flinch, didn't fight her as she used her fingertips to "see," tracing with no gentleness whatsoever the length of his nose, the jut of his cheekbones, the hard line of his jaw. The dimple denting the very center of his square chin stopped her. Her fingertips hesitated, an unintentional caress. Aral… "Aral Mawndarr." Her lost boy.

"Your legal husband."

# CHAPTER TEN

"HUSBAND?" Awrenkka spat out the word as if it were a bad piece of meat. She scrambled to her feet, shoving away his attempt to help. Disbelief blazed in her eyes, her chest heaving. "There was no decree. There was no joining ceremony in absentia. There is *no marriage.*"

"There is a provision in Hordish law that allows for a marriage-by-proxy in the event of the warlord's death. I was your father's choice."

"A handshake between the warlord and his crony?" Her hands were balled into fists. She'd squeezed all the blood out of her knuckles. "He's dead. The war is over. The arrangement is void."

Aral drove a frustrated hand through his hair. He'd assumed that shocking her with the news would work in his favor. She'd accompany him to his ship if not meekly then at least out of tradition and respect. She argued every one of his points. He missed his battlelord days on the bridge, when everyone in his sight was required to follow his orders or else. It had become apparent quite quickly that his best-laid plans were laughably insufficient. He'd acted true to the battlelord he once was and as if Awrenkka were the obedient daughter she once was. The old molds no longer fit.

They never did, he thought. That was why they were here.

"Peace alone doesn't void the agreement. Else you'd have marriages dissolving across the galaxy with the end of this war."

"A victory for all Drakken women in that case. Marriage is a man's invention. Another word for *life sentence*."

"Some people marry for love, Awrenkka."

The note of candor, of hope, he knew slipped into his tone caused a deep and telling blush in her. It wasn't he that she despised, he realized, but the concept of their marriage—and that it had been done without her consent. He'd never considered her consent. It was *implied*. Apparently not.

What did he know about women? Other than Kaz, that was. Awrenkka was in a different category entirely. She was a wife. This marriage business was far more complicated than he'd ever imagined.

"I have choices now," she railed at him. "I will not go anywhere or with anyone unless it is of my own free will. I'm a free woman."

"*Free?* Is that what you think you are?" Her misguided sense of independence nearly stole the last of his patience. He redoubled his efforts to hold onto his temper. "You aren't free. Nor am I. No Drakken is. Peace is the word bandied about nowadays, but the war lasted a thousand years. That's an eternity. The rancor, the distrust—on both sides—will be with us for some time to come. The Triad, for all their good intentions when it comes to unification, intends to keep us Drakken confined to our home planets or in these camps for a good long time."

"Not me. I'll live on the run if I have to."

"Living on the run isn't freedom by any means." He heard the weariness in his voice. He was tired of running, and it damn well showed.

"I'll be the judge of that." Her mouth was firm, her eyes determined. Then she seemed to crumble. "Fates, I'm *married*." She cast her gaze around with the desperateness of a trapped animal. Her dread yanked at his heart, and made his skin crawl at the same time.

*You're imposing your will on this woman.* Blast it. He was not a monster like his father. Or like her father. They were different.

Weren't they?

A believer's cheery voice shattered the tension between them. "Good day to you, priestess." A small child accompanied him, thin and hollow-eyed. "Sister, please bless my daughter. She's been ill. The camp medics have given her nano...nano..."

"Nanomeds," Aral supplied.

"Aye, a miracle. She's already improved. But the blessing of the goddesses is what she needs most."

Awrenkka's smile was genuine as she circled her thumb over her heart. "May the goddess heal your child."

"Thank you. Thank you. May the goddess be with you, sister."

"And also with you."

The man returned the sign of the goddess and departed. Awrenkka was incredibly convincing. The robe looked as if it belonged to her, as if the calling came naturally. If they remained in the camp any longer, he might very well have a full-fledged priestess on his hands.

When he'd rather have a wife *in* his hands.

Her cheeks were streaked with dust and perspiration, not tears. A lesser woman would have wept by now. Awrenkka was made of stronger stuff. That strength only intensified his desire to protect her, to care for her. To make her his. The look on her face when she recognized him revealed all he needed to know. Mixed in with her qualms about him and his intentions and her well-founded abhorrence of loyalists had been a bright spark of relief and joy. Seeing her reaction, feeling her warm hand on his face, he'd nearly lost control, something he'd held to without fail all these years. It had taken everything he had not to sink his fingers into her flame-dark hair and pull her close. He wanted to do so now. If not for being toughened by denial and self-discipline, and the indisputable fact he was in the middle of Zorabeta refugee camp with a woman who looked as if she wanted him dead, he'd have done it.

"Ten years, Aral," she said. "Ten years since all those old men, rubbing their hands together at the prospect of me as their wife, their trophy for their good service to the warlord. Then I saw you." A gentler note crept into her tone. "You looked so sad. So alone. I knew just how you felt. I thought I'd finally found someone like me. The next minute, you were just like the rest of them, dismissive and stuck up."

"I wanted to keep you safe from my family."

"By humiliating me? By making me feel stupid and plain and clumsy?"

"I thought none of those things."

"I saw it in your eyes, Aral."

"What you saw was a young, inexperienced man whose breath was taken away by a beautiful girl."

Awrenkka went still, her voice softer. "Beautiful?"

Real feelings for him glowed in her eyes before she lowered her lashes and retreated behind their thick veil. "You acted like you despised me."

"To protect you. To keep you far away from my family. If Karbon had seen any interest in you at all, he'd have competed for your hand until he won it."

"I wouldn't have given it to him."

"It wouldn't have been your choice. It would have been the warlord's choice. I would not have been able to bear your suffering at my father's hands. You have no idea what he'd do to others. No idea." Old, dark memories screamed. Aral stopped himself. He needed to reassure her, and he couldn't be doing a more piss-poor job.

"They're ruined, I'm afraid." He rested the mangled remains of her eyeglasses in her hands. "I bent them into shape as best I could." The right lens was gone. The left was cracked but seemed to be intact enough to allow her to see. He slipped them onto her face. Almost shyly he adjusted her glasses until she took over, pushing the crooked frames higher.

She squinted up at him as if she found the awkward tenderness of his gesture strangely endearing. Him *endearing?* Bah. His wife was bringing out many attributes he never knew he had. Negotiation, for one. Years of being a battlelord had acclimated him to having his way, being in control. He hadn't felt in control for one blasted moment since reuniting with her.

Kaz strode up to them. Concern tightened the edges of her mouth, a sign of anxiety he wasn't use to seeing. She showed her fears only rarely since Bolivarr's death. His relief at Awrenkka's fractional softening toward him evaporated with the certainty she bore bad news. He'd sent her to process Awrenkka's booking at the port authority office to speed up their departure. It should have been a simple task. Her appearance told him it had been anything but. "Rumors are flying about the fight. It's all over the camp. They're calling her the boxing priestess. The head sister is going through the ranks, trying to find out who it is."

Without hesitation, Awrenkka pulled the priestess robe over her head. She balled up the fabric and shoved it under her cloak. "If they try to find her, they won't find me."

"Unless they are looking for a pregnant woman."

The disguise was brilliant, if unintentional, Aral thought. "I have your data square. Do not show it for any reason unless we agree."

"And no more gladiator matches." Kaz observed Awrenkka, her hands folded at the small of her back. "You can kick some serious ass. I'm just glad it wasn't mine. Were you trained in martial arts? Or do you come by beating a man to an inch of his life with a food tray naturally? They say the gornut never falls very far from the tree."

Shame sparked in Awrenkka's eyes at Kaz's goading. Fury, too. As much as the warlord's daughter wanted to distance herself from her sire, she had her pride, and perhaps more than a touch of his temper. She was, after all, her father's daughter, whether she liked it or not.

Just as he was his father's son. It seemed they both despised their genetics: both wanted to escape it, and yet found themselves trapped by their ancestry more often than not.

"Perhaps I am more like my father than I want to be,

but I offer you my genuine apology for calling attention to you, as well as to me. Take it. That's more than the warlord ever gave me or anyone else."

Kaz nodded. He suspected her respect for Awrenkka had grown from her original impression of a spoiled, sheltered girl. She turned to him. "There's more, Aral. They're looking for a battlelord. The warrant was generated by outside authorities. High up, judging by the buzz going on in there. What I know, I only overheard, but it came from the Ring."

Zaafran, Aral thought. Was he trying to track down Aral in the wake of his "disappearance?" Quite possibly. Finding him would be like picking a microbe out of a mud puddle, but not impossible, especially if he cast a large enough net, like stopping each ship in and out to see who was flying it.

He'd long had doubts about the sentiments of the high command about his role in their victory. Giving credit to a Drakken, a battlelord, no less, would only weaken their image as the stronger power in this conflict, and the *rightful* power. The resistance movement would exploit that weakness. Aral coming and going as he pleased was a dangerous proposition for the new government. Zaafran must see it, as well. Why else had he never revealed Aral's role publicly? It was telling indeed. Maybe now the man had developed second thoughts on letting him go free. He didn't think Zaafran would go that route. They'd built a trust over the years, an understanding. But the man was under a tremendous amount of pressure, faced with regrouping loyalists and the discovery of the existence of a surviving child of the warlord. Desperate measures would not be unexpected.

Putting Awrenkka at even greater risk.

And nothing Kaz herself didn't already suspect.

He scanned the immediate area for any sign of the meddling trader and his guard friend. He hoped she'd tied him up with fines or paperwork for interfering. "To the ship," he said.

"Guards," Kaz warned.

Four camp guards were pushing through the crowd, stopping refugees and demanding what they knew or had seen. At least one priestess was being questioned. Wren cast her gaze around, looking for a way out as the sensation of being trapped, of being tracked, returned. Then Aral was at her side, strong, reassuring. "Split up," he told Kaz. "Meet me at the ship, ready to depart."

Kaz hurried away.

He undid the fasteners of the shirt sticking damply to his torso, revealing a hard, muscled body and bronzed skin. He'd camouflaged his tattoos. Their faint outline was visible in the blinding, yellowish sunlight. He did have another shirt on underneath, but it was a tank, nothing more than a black scrap of fabric. He draped the shirt over her shoulders and urged her in the opposite direction from Kaz. She hoisted the wadded-up robe higher to keep it from slipping out of her blouse. It won her a few smiles from passing refugees. "Many blessings," an old woman said, patting her on the arm.

"Good to see new life after so much death," another refugee told them, tattooed and toothless. A veteran. Warily she glanced around for the ex-soldier she'd knocked out, and hoped he and his friends weren't searching for her.

Their boots hunted for traction on the gritty street.

Gravel shifted under his heels, turning to smoky clouds of dust with each stride. Something hollow and metallic collided with her toe. Aral caught her before she took a nosedive. "Why didn't he ever see to your eyes? It was outright neglect."

No one other than Sabra had ever gotten angry on her behalf. "Kidnapping, murder, genocide, plus the proper training of my half-brother—it took time. The warlord was a busy man."

He made a derisive sound in his throat. "We'll see to your eyes first thing, Awrenkka."

"Wren," she said. "Awrenkka is the warlord's daughter, the woman whose value was in who she'd be bred to. Wren is *me*."

"Breeding. Is that how you see marriage? No wonder you despise the concept."

"That's the real reason he never had my vision repaired, I suspect." She pushed on her glasses. "He wanted to keep his prize racehorse hobbled so she couldn't run away. If I couldn't see, I couldn't very well escape, could I?"

"Would you have?"

"If I'd known what I know now—about my father, about his battlelords, and what crimes they committed— yes." She felt his hands tense. "You, I wanted to run away *with,* not from."

"But not marry me."

"I have no issue with the trappings of marriage. I don't want the trap."

"The *trappings?*" She met his dark eyes, saw the desire there. It made her skin warm all over.

He turned a corner. The tents were closer here. Ahead was a knot of guards ordering around a few refugees. He spun her so fast in an about-face that she almost lost the robe.

Gasping, she clutched at her stomach, hoisting it higher. It won her several concerned glances from those passing by. He had her up against a tent. "Put your arms around me. Do it," he demanded at her hesitation. Then, lower, he whispered in her ear. "They're watching, talking about us." He flattened his hand on her fabric-stuffed belly, tenderly, as if she carried a real child—theirs. His breath tickled her ear. "Pretend we're lovers. People, even the guards, give lovers privacy. In both our cultures the natural inclination is not to stare at kissing people but to look away."

Kissing? His explanation was ever so scientific, but she was too aware of his heat. His intensity. He was close enough now for her to study the tiny nubs of his beard on his golden skin. She'd never viewed a man so close. Never smelled anything as good.

Unfamiliar voices in Coalition accents came closer. He tucked her close again, one hand brushing over her hair, his parted lips pressed to her jaw. She'd stopped breathing—equally because of the guards and Aral's caresses. They stayed close, Aral's lips touching her cheek. She began to lean into the embrace. His mouth dragged to her ear, his hand sliding up her back. "Wren," he whispered. His soft lips grazed hers. A tremendous shudder ran through his body. Their embrace was no longer a ruse, she thought. It was real.

# CHAPTER ELEVEN

THE GUARDS PASSED BY. "Nah, leave 'em alone," one said. "She's got one in the oven."

"They breed like mar-mice, even in the camps."

Aral squashed his anger at their comments. It cheapened what he'd felt with Awrenkka.

Worse, from inside the tent next to them came giggling and a deeper, throaty laugh, followed by the very distinct sound of a hand slapping against a bare rump. There were three or even four people in there, and all in bed, Aral realized. Awrenkka appeared oblivious. It was he who was ready to turn red, if he were even capable of such a feat.

A girl who looked no more than half his and Awrenkka's ages appeared from behind the tent. Her blouse was unbuttoned. Underneath tiny, tattooed breasts peeked out. They were splotched with pink marks and a fading bruise. Sex for money. Few females had the opportunity to bring valuables with them as Wren had. This woman's value was in her body. The scarcity of young, pretty women in this camp no doubt allowed her to charge high fees for sexual services.

"A little fun, fine sir and lady?"

He turned her down with a scowl. She disappeared

into a warren of pathways winding deeper into a make-shift city of tents. He wished to the very core of his being that they were anywhere else but this heat-soaked, dust-ball of a planet. Little wonder it was being used to house Drakken refugees. No sane person would live here voluntarily.

He snatched Wren's hand. They were almost at the docks. The sky had taken on a sickly yellow cast. It had all the look of an approaching dust storm. Grit in his teeth confirmed it.

His PCD was still lying on the console where he'd left it.

It sat there, a challenge. As much as he liked Zaafran, he'd wanted no more ties with the Triad. They were looking for a battlelord. Him. If it made Zaafran feel better, he'd check in. The missing battlelord. He hooked the unit on his ear. "Call Z," he said to initiate authentication that could not be traced to his ship.

"Stand by…" the artificial voice said.

"Oh, I am," he said under his breath. "Nothing more I can do but stand by." He paced, anxious to leave.

"Authentication completed."

"M?" The prime-admiral sounded downright stunned. Something else was in his tone, something off. "Still taking care of your private matter?"

"Yes. And for some time to come."

There was silence on the line. Then, "We lost him. Karbon Mawndarr is missing."

Aral halted as if he'd been flash frozen. As Zaafran offered the excuses as to how Karbon slipped away, Aral met eyes with Wren and couldn't help wondering if his hope of escaping with her and finding a new life had been nothing more than a pipe dream.

Incompetents. The entire Triad. No wonder he'd had to hand them their victory; they could not have done it themselves. Their idiocy made a mockery of his efforts to see Karbon executed. Now he was free. Watching him. Knowing who sold him out. There was no doubt in Aral's mind.

He took full blame. In wanting to keep his hands clean of the actual killing, in wanting to be something better than his father, he'd brought danger to everyone around him. He should have been there for the execution, seen it through to the end. But he'd been afraid of hearing his father's caustic words. Words that deep down Aral feared were true. Words he'd fled from, words that had driven him to this point in time.

A dead end.

He'd never been able to escape the man before. What made him think he could now?

"M, I'm under pressure to bring you in for questioning on the matter."

"For Karbon's escape? After everything, Z, you think I'd help that bastard?" Because he was Drakken, and to many on the other side, they were all monsters. "I'm afraid that's impossible, Z. I cannot assist you."

He ended the call before Zaafran could anger him more.

He dashed the back of his hand across his mouth. "Karbon escaped, and some want to blame me."

Kaz was white. Wren watched him with compassion, or something close to it. There was so much about him that she didn't know. To have any hope of a normal life with her, something he wanted desperately, he would have to allow her a window into his dark soul. He hoped what she saw there didn't send her running.

As part of his carefully crafted and so far flawlessly executed grand plan, Karbon was to be dead or at least in custody before Awrenkka was evacuated from Barokk. But it hadn't worked out that way, and he'd have to accept the fact. If anyone knew that life wasn't always neat and tidy, that loose ends weren't always tied up, that scars remained open and bleeding years after they were gouged open, it was Aral.

"Zaafran helped me obtain fake transponder codes for the ship. The minute we take off, we'll be traced."

"We'll fly with the transponder off," Kaz said. "We've done it before."

"And raise a red flag in the middle of the space lanes? It's doable, but I don't like it. We need to ditch the ship and find another."

"We can go with Vantos," Awrenkka said. "He's a freelancer. He has no loyalties. He was willing to take me out of the camp for a price."

"No. Not Vantos. He's already curious. This will confirm everything he already suspects."

"If he does, he cares not for the morality of turning me in so long as he gets the money."

"A guess? Intuition? I will not hand you over to the executioner on a hunch, Awrenkka."

"I offered him more—more than the bounty. He agreed."

"Your dowry was lost in the fall of the palace." Even the vast Mawndarr fortune and assets had been frozen by the Triad. He wasn't a pauper by any means—he'd hidden away money on several different worlds, and on his ship—but she'd have nothing except what she could have stuffed into her pockets. Some jewelry or gems, a little money, that was all.

"This isn't a dowry. It's tied to no marriage. It's treasure. Priceless. And it's mine."

ON THE BRINK OF ASSUMING her first command, Hadley stood outside the entrance to the bridge of the *Cloud Shadow*. In view of the bridge but behind a glass privacy wall, she was able to steal a few moments of privacy before making her grand entrance, an entrance that would help set the stage for the entire voyage.

Suddenly Bolivarr was at her side, steadying her with his quiet strength. That was his way. Tall, dark and intense, he could appear and disappear like cloud shadows on a summer day, sliding silently in and out of sight. She'd often told others of the vast sky on her home-world, and how clouds raced across sun, casting fleeting shadows over the farmland. Admiral Bandar thought the name would fit a small, swift vessel. And thus the *Cloud Shadow* was born.

Within minutes she'd step onto its bridge. "I spent so many years an executive officer, a glorified assistant, really, to my personal hero, that it's hard to wrap my mind around the concept of commanding my own ship and crew," she confessed. "Especially knowing how I got here." Saving Admiral Bandar's life earned her the promotion ahead of so many others. Now she'd have to bear the burden of proving that she deserved it. She didn't like that fact, but there was no way around it. It was the way the military viewed outsiders. She was an outsider, just a farm girl from Talo. She pictured offspring from families that had produced generations of officers waiting in line for her to fail so they could step in and take her place.

"Your bravery won you this command, Hadley. And your quick thinking. Your out-of-the-box thinking. If the Triad wanted robots to command ships, they would do so. They want leaders. Leaders think outside the box when required. Leaders make brilliant decisions, and mistakes. Leaders are human."

At the faint change in his voice, she glanced up at him. There were times he despaired that he was not fully human, though she knew otherwise, because of the alterations the empire had made to his brain to allow him to function as a wraith. Alterations that allowed them to erase his memories, and his sense of identity along with it.

"You're going to do great. This is just the beginning of a long and distinguished career." He brushed his knuckles against hers, a reassuring warm caress. "If I didn't feel that way, I'd have already begged for reassignment."

She laughed. "No, you wouldn't have. That would have landed you back in the hospital. More tests, more meds."

Leaning on his cane, he cringed. "I'll take the risk and serve with you, then," he teased.

From a portside briefing room came laughter then a few whoops. Then something thudded against the wall. A body? What were the cadets doing in there? "Dear goddess."

Bolivarr tipped his head to listen along with her. "Almost sounds like a Drakken crew."

Her second-in-command walked up to them, looking nervous. "Gods forbid." The mere mention of their former enemy made him turn pale—paler than usual. Clearly out of his element, Garwin Tadlock was an aging star-lieutenant on his last mission before retirement. He was a scientist not a soldier. He had little charisma that Hadley could discern and almost no battle experience. It doubly assured her there would be no action on this mission. Her only hope was that he wouldn't panic if they encountered pirates, a definite possibility across the Borderlands. But he'd be invaluable once they reached their destination. For that reason, she was glad he was aboard, as well as Sister Chara, their resident priestess, a wiry, athletic woman who'd already inspected—and blessed—the facilities in the ship's gym.

The cadets grew quieter as they filed into the bridge in anticipation of her entrance. It was more of a low-level hum of energy now. She remembered well her exuberance for her first summer voyage as a cadet at the Royal Galactic Military Academy. Rooks ranged from fifteen and a half to nineteen years old. Someday one of them could very well rise to the top leadership spot in the Triad Alliance and lead them into the future, as Admiral Bandar did, and Prime-Admiral Zaafran.

"Shall we?" With a soft smile at Bolivarr, and a nod to her first officer, she squared her shoulders with their shiny new epaulets, pausing for a brief moment to take in the sight of the brand-new pilot and weapons stations and a state-of-the-art command array, the banks of viewports with the graceful arc of the Ring rotating slowly against the icy backdrop of Sakka. She took that extra moment to ponder her good fortune for good reason. The war may have ended, but her life was just beginning. With one last tug on the hem of her uniform jacket, she stepped across the imaginary border of her life before and the rest of her life.

"Attention—Captain on the bridge!" Garwin called out.

Hadley strode across the bridge, back ramrod straight, her hands clasped at the small of her back the way Admiral Bandar used to do when addressing her crew. In fact, the admiral affected that stance almost all hours of the day. Hadley used to wonder if she slept that way—with perfect military bearing. Hadley imagined she'd settle in to a more casual leadership style, but for now she felt a little unsure—okay, a lot unsure—and certainly in need of building respect. Whatever she could borrow from her mentor and hero she would.

"Greetings, ladies and gentlemen. And rooks." The rambunctious group of first-year cadets—rooks— immediately became serious. Dressed in their crisp cadet uniforms in the new Triad colors—red and blue on a mostly black background—they stood at attention.

As Garwin read out their names, she stopped to straighten the epaulet of one young man. He turned white, then red. "Cadet Tenru," she said.

"Yes, ma'am."

"Your father is Baru Tenru. One of the best fighter pilots we have." And one of the most annoyingly egotistical. Though his ego didn't come close to Tango's. "I'll expect great things of you."

"I'll try, ma'am." *Try?* Had the ego gene not made it into Tenru, Jr.? He certainly shared the fighter pilot's cocky good looks. "I'll just have to be careful not to show up my fellow cadets here."

That elicited a quiet snort from one of them. I stand

corrected, Hadley thought. Apparently he was indeed a chip off the ol' block.

Garwin read off the names of the other cadets—Holster, also Coalition, and the twins Arran and Arrak of mixed heritage. The twins' mother was a Drakken healer who somehow had managed to stow away on a ship where she'd met their father, a Coalition physician. It was rare to see half Hordish, half Coalition offspring that weren't the result of rape. Regardless, they were never really accepted in either society, something she hoped would now begin to change.

Hadley stopped in front of the two young girls. "Who snorted?"

They were instantly contrite.

The taller of the two stepped forward, snapping her heels together and bringing her hand up for a salute. She was slender with a long, Earthling-style hank of hair swinging around her graceful neck that added to the impression of a dancer. "I did, Captain, ma'am. Cadet Holloway."

Holloway, as in Ellen Jasper Holloway, Hadley thought. A prebriefing on the girl's presence had prepared Hadley for having the queen's consort's niece assigned to her ship. Admittedly it had made her nervous having the queen's family on board. Partly for this very reason—what if she felt she was above shipboard rules?

"Do you see anyone else here showing disrespect to the captain?" Bolivarr asked.

"No, sir." Ellen pressed her lips together, staring straight ahead. She'd screwed up and she knew it. Hadley liked that she didn't try to justify her small breach of decorum. "Sorry, ma'am."

Hadley shifted her attention to the rest of them. "It's going to be a long voyage on a relatively small ship. There will be people aboard who will drive you crazy. Some of *you* will drive me crazy. What separates military professionals from the rest is that we do not reveal our less than positive personal opinions of fellow crew members."

"Yes, ma'am," the six rooks responded.

"Yes, ma'am." Ellen said, a little more forcefully than the others.

Garwin concluded the roll call with the final rook. "Last we have Cadet Meith…Meitheera…"

"Meitheeratanaphipat, sir." The correction came from a small girl with lovely dark hair and eyes standing next to Cadet Holloway.

"Mee…theera," Hadley tried. "Tana…" She gave up trying to read the name badge.

"That's okay, Captain." The rook accepted her attempts at pronunciation with a shy, wry smile that told Hadley this was nothing new. "My ancestors are from a place on Earth called Laos. We have long last names."

One of the twins said, "We call her M-19, Captain."

"Is that what you prefer?" Hadley asked the girl.

"Yes, ma'am."

"M-19, it is." It would have to be. Hadley shared an amused glance with Bolivarr. Though he'd give anything to know what his last name was. Long or short, any name was better than having no name.

They ran through the rest of the introductions quickly—the pilots, mechanic, engineer and the ship's surgeon. "Battle-Lieutenant Bolivarr will now brief us on our mission." She refused to call it an expedition. He took center stage and ran through the briefing that Zaafran had given to her.

Through it all, Bolivarr's eyes were unreadable. So much hinged on this mission. If he couldn't recover his memory soon then he was likely doomed to live out his life without knowing who he was.

As she'd suspected, there was quite a bit of excitement at the prospect of exploring an uncharted world at the farthest edge of civilized space. Civilized? Hardly. The planet they'd fancifully dubbed Ara Ana had existed, forgotten, in the mostly lawless Hordish frontier for generations. Who knew what they'd find there? Prime-admiral Zaafran had high hopes for a windfall of religious relics. Hadley was certain anything of value to be found had been plundered long ago. But it was supposed to be a mission of hope, and hope she'd have.

The cadets chattered excitedly about the uncharted, possibly unstable wormholes they'd have to traverse and pirate attacks, but in truth, they'd be hard pressed to see any real action on this ride. Their parents would probably be relieved. The academy didn't believe in coddling cadets, still, no one wanted to see teens placed in harm's way.

Bolivarr stepped down and the crew reported to their stations to get ready for launch.

"Captain Keyren—Cadet Holloway requests permission to speak."

Hadley turned. Ellen was standing in front of her. Her military bearing was perfect but she was clearly nervous.

"Go ahead," Hadley said.

"I wanted to apologize again. I didn't mean any disrespect. And I wanted you to know that I don't want or expect special treatment. I want to succeed on my own terms. I want it more than anything." She lifted luminous, determined eyes to Hadley, as if willing her to understand.

Hadley did understand. Very much so. She, too, wanted to succeed outside the bright light of her famous mentor. She nodded. "Then I expect great things of you this trip, Holloway."

"Yes, ma'am! You're my hero, ma'am."

Her hero?

"Admiral Bandar was abducted. You took a shuttle without permission and—"

Bolivarr cleared his throat to stop Ellen as Hadley thought, *Oh, dear.* Unfortunately, one of the twins finished for Ellen. "You went around orders in order to save your captain."

Yes, and won her promotion for that act. So had Rakkelle, the feisty Drakken pilot-cadet-ex-pirate who'd flown the shuttle in question and who was still serving on the *Unity,* Hadley's former ship. But that was bar talk. She didn't want the cadets worshiping her for a mission that could have easily blown up in her face. The ramming during the checkride notwithstanding, she was determined to be more conservative, to play by the rules. "The lesson *not* to be learned is that it's okay to disobey orders and do what you want. The situation was unique." She frowned at them, her best captain's scowl. No one laughed, so that was good.

Back in her office, Bolivarr leaned heavily on his cane, seemingly amused by the cadets' idolization of the incident she'd most like to bury in her past. After weeks of improvement, physically he appeared to have taken a turn for the worse the past few days—no seizures, just an overall fatigue. He'd not wanted her to say anything, lest he be pulled from the mission.

Maybe she was asking too much of him. "Bo, are you sure you feel up to this?"

"Hadley, even if I were on my deathbed I'd go." He paused. "I have to go. It's my best chance at remembering who I am. My last resort before surgery," his mouth thinned, "that I really don't want to have. In fact, I've decided I won't go under the laser-knife, Hadley. My brain has been damaged enough, and some things even nanomeds can't fix. If this doesn't work, if Ara Ana doesn't release my memory, I'm done trying. I'll just start fresh. What happened in my past will stay in my past."

"You're still having the dreams, right? You're still seeing the five marks?"

"And writing gibberish in runes that I know I once knew how to translate. Why, Hadley? What would I be doing with knowledge of an ancient language that only a few priestesses know? What did I do in my past that gained those secrets?" His jaw tightened. "What did I do?"

Silent, she moved beside him, slipping her arms around his waist. "Good things. I know you."

"But *I* don't know me."

She held him tighter. The quiet sadness that was always a part of him seemed more pronounced as he turned his dark, narrowed eyes to a view of the Ring they'd soon trade for the unknown.

She reckoned that Bolivarr's memory was as ripe for discovery as the uncharted space they'd soon explore. As much as she looked forward to beginning the mission, she couldn't shake the sense that it would soon change everything she thought she knew about herself—and him.

BLOWING DUST turned Zorabeta's sun into a bloated yellow orb bearing an uncanny resemblance to a decaying sun-melon. The wind whistled as Keir pulled out a fresh nanopick and faced down the three Drakken who'd showed up at his ship.

A fancy weapon glinted in the battlelord's hand. It looked like it could do some damage, too. Keir reached for his pistol before he remembered it was on his ship. He'd been disarmed upon arrival like everyone else visiting the camps for commerce and otherwise, but both blue-bloods were posing as law enforcement.

As for Wren, she looked like the girl next door, and here he was, acting as if sending her to the executioner was as routine as ordering a drink in the bar. He *was* a jerk. She must know by now that he'd fully intended to use her. The way he saw it, he had nothing to apologize for. It was high time she got to know him the way every other woman knew him. He was in this game for himself.

"So, it sounds like our deal is still on," he told her. "Riches beyond my imagination. Right, sweetheart?"

Mawndarr frowned at the endearment.

"Don't worry, battlelord. Nothing happened and nothing will. Ours was a financial relationship." Nipped in the bud before it had the chance to bloom.

Bloom, hells. Fifty million queens were still his if he turned Wren in. A life of comfort (and no more chem-toilet running) would be his future. He ought to call Ellie back for reinforcements right now, land Mawndarr's ass in the brig and turn his wife in. All he needed to do was deliver her to the camp commissar's office in person and claim the bounty. One bellow and the curtain would come crashing down on the little Drakken right here, right now. Except his potential-profit meter was pegged. This gig reeked of money. The company could be dangerous, yeah, but in his experience, a little extra risk reaped a larger reward.

As ochre dust swirled, Mawndarr studied him as if trying to get his bearings with an unexpected adversary. He wasn't the first battlelord Keir had faced. Battlelords were the opposite of a good runner: they were thinkers and planners. Right now he was thinking this through. Finally he said, "I see we have three options, Vantos."

"I'll love them all, I assume."

"One—I can take your ship and leave you in Zorabeta, maybe even bribe you to stay quiet."

"Bribes are nice. What's two?"

"Rather than risk leaving you behind to tell everyone what you know, I can kill you where you stand."

"I think that if you'd wanted to kill me, you'd have done it already."

"What I want is irrelevant. I'd actually prefer to have you shock-cuffed—or dead—in the hold of your ship. But I can use you. Your so-called unmatched talent as a runner."

"So you know a good runner when you see one, eh, Mawndarr? You made the right choice. I'm the best there is. Six years and barely a scratch. Don't worry about a thing. Keir Vantos is behind the wheel. I'll get us across the Borderlands so fast, no one will ever know you were there."

"You're not that good, Vantos. I let you pass all those times because it served my purposes."

"Bull flarg. We've never crossed paths before."

"Victory day. You were coming across the backside of the Inelglio dust cloud. You passed close enough to my battle-cruiser to shake hands."

Holy hells. "That was you?" The sight of that battle-cruiser bearing down on him was burned into his memory. He'd been sure he was dead meat. He'd actually muttered his goodbyes to this world. It wasn't something he cared to share with Mawndarr. "Do you have any idea how much repairing that warning shot cost me? What were you doing out there on victory day, eh, Mawndarr? Trying to save your ass?"

"You could say that."

Rumor was that insiders had let the queen's consort through the perimeter around the warlord's flotilla. Gods, was Mawndarr involved in that? He could very well be in the company of one of the biggest traitors in Empire history.

"I watched you cross the blockade more times than I care to count," Mawndarr said. "You were good, Vantos. Smart. Probably the best I saw out there, but you didn't live this long without my help."

"Yeah. I get the point. No need to rub my nose in it. I got around you a few times, too, you know."

"I do. And that's exactly why you're hired."

# CHAPTER TWELVE

*BORROWED TIME.* A better name these days was borrowed money. That's what it would take Keir to see to all the repairs he had pending. His new gig couldn't have come at a better time.

This was what he'd missed: the adrenaline rush. It was like the old days when he'd say to hells with it all and let instinct carry him through to the finish line. Like he planned to do now, because logically he had no damn clue what he was going to do tomorrow or even five minutes from now. He'd just do what he did best—run. Full-bore and without fear, just like always. His goal: only to get to the other side. He'd check out those riches Wren had tantalized him with, and if they didn't pan out, well, sorry sweetheart, she was getting turned in. Talk about a money-back guarantee.

Meanwhile they needed him. The battlelord recognized the danger, and didn't let his ego get in the way. He was used to command, and obviously used to surrounding himself with the right people. Keir liked being the right person in this case. It was going to make him a rich man.

He climbed up the gangway and pulled on the hatch to let them in. A warning blipped. "Flarg." He'd put the blasted security hand reader on, thinking he might have to leave the ship unattended for longer than he'd like. He thrust his hand in the slot.

*"Access denied,"* said an artificial voice.

Denied? "Bite me."

*"Command not understood."*

Mawndarr's assistant let out one of her trademark husky chuckles. He opened his mouth to elaborate a few of his inner thoughts, then clamped it closed. A tense hand would only baffle the reader even more. He stuck his fingers back in the slot.

*"Stand by."* An amber light blinked while the unit attempted to read and reconcile the image of his sweaty, tense palm with his usual cool, dry hand.

"Your ship doesn't seem to like you," Kaz said. He didn't need to see her dark eyes to see the spark of amusement there. He could hear it in her condescending tone. As if it wasn't bad enough having his reputation as a runner decimated in front of her, now his ship wouldn't cooperate.

He could lose this gig unless he got in soon, real soon, and he'd be back to shuttling toilets instead of Drakken renegades. No, he'd be marching little Wren Senderin down to the commandant's office for collection. And her husband, too. The thought sat like acid in his gut.

They were the enemy.

Or were they? Mawndarr had had the chance to kill him plenty of times, but chose not to, and the warlord's daughter trusted him. No one ever trusted him.

And for good reason.

*"Saving…saving…"*

He knew he should have gotten the balky thing repaired the last time he was at the depot. It'd been nothing but trouble. The reader had been on sale when he bought it—second hand. He wasn't a rich man. But he would be.

*"Identification verified."*

Thank the gods. "Get in, get in."

With a hiss, the hatch closed behind them.

VANTOS'S SHIP WAS a patchwork of rivets, sheets of metal and scattered personal items that defined a man Wren didn't know but about whom she hoped her trust was warranted. Good instincts had kept her warlord ancestors in power for millennia...until her father made his one, fatal miscalculation. Under the warlords' rule, countless people had died in the name of war. On the other hand, if *she* miscalculated, how many more would die in the name of peace?

Aral caught her by the arm before she got to the bridge. "This is yours." In the shadows of an alcove half filled with discarded equipment, Aral thrust a heavy pistol at her. Black, cold, deadly, the weapon sat in her hands.

She shoved it back. Deadly force. The beast inside her slumbered now. What if it was roused by fear or anger? The last thing she needed was a gun within reach. She didn't want the temptation. "I can't see."

"You see enough." He took the gun from her and aimed into the ship to demonstrate. "Point and fire."

Aral filled the small space. His body heat carried his scent, that unfamiliar spice and the faint tang of sweat. Their bodies brushed together. She pressed back against the wall, to place a sliver of space between them. Aral appeared to be just as aware of her, his throat moving, his gaze diverted to the weapon between them. "In this, I won't let you fight me. You must be able to defend yourself if something happens to me. You were sheltered long enough. Your unfamiliarity with weapons will fade as you learn."

"Unfamiliarity?" Fates, if he only knew. "The last time I had a dagger in my hand, I used it to kill the woman who poisoned my guardian. Sabra was like a mother to me."

"Bloody hells," he muttered.

"Ilkka did it to gain control over me, to hand me over to loyalists. She knew about the treasure, too. Everyone did except me."

"I've heard nothing of it, and of all the hours I spent with the warlord, even after he gave me your hand, he never mentioned it."

"If it wasn't his, then...perhaps it was my mother's. It was an unhappy marriage. She may have kept it secret."

"If it's not there, Vantos won't be happy."

"We have to find Ara Ana. She pulled the pendant from her robes. It dangled from the chain, seeming to glow from within. The five tiny dots twinkled like miniature stars. "My guardian gave me this."

Aral made a small sound of disbelief. He reached for the pendant, bringing it closer. Thrusters roared to life. Swallowing, she turned her head. "We'd better go sit down." They were about to launch, and Aral was mesmerized, and in a different way, so was she.

"I know this pattern," he said gruffly. "My brother Bolivarr was killed after discovering it." Grief wasn't so far in Wren's past that she'd forgotten what it looked like.

"He was a wraith," he said. "He was serving under-cover across the border during the war. He transmitted a page from a religious text. This pattern was centered on that page. He told me to hold on to it for safekeeping. I never heard from him again."

Suddenly her key to freedom, to atonement, felt like a noose. "Did the page say anything about Ara Ana? Or the treasure itself?"

Aral shook his head. "It was all in runes. Untranslatable. All he mentioned was that he'd found a key to a secret with the potential to destroy us all."

"Fates." She stared at the pendant glinting innocently in his hand. "This is the key."

HADLEY LEFT the noisy dining hall, walking with businesslike purpose. Bolivarr walked with her, equally professional. They'd left the meal without eating dessert.

He unlocked his door and let them in. "Close," he told the door.

"And lock," she added.

The door had barely closed when he swept her into his arms, kissing her laughter away. "First order of business," he murmured, kissing her breathless. She sighed as his fingers sifted through her hair. "They're going to think this is one secure ship with the amount of meetings we've been having." Where they ended up in bed.

She'd taken a careful look up and down the corridor before slipping inside his quarters. It was probably not a secret that they'd hooked up, but as the captain she felt obligated to keep their relationship out of sight of the crew.

His dark eyes twinkled. He lowered his head to kiss

her again. His cane clattered to the floor. Smiling he said, "We won't need that in bed," and resumed their kiss.

Bolivarr had been her first lover. He considered himself a virgin-in-spirit, as he couldn't remember any previous lovers. She hoped it meant there were none. His amazing mouth was on hers again, erasing all her doubts. Well, except for a few. They kissed until she was absolutely feverish.

Equally breathless, he tore his lips from hers, smoothing his hands over her body, and the layer of her uniform between those hands and her skin before he brought his hands to her face to cradle her cheeks. "I want this to last forever, Hadley. I want us to last forever." He seemed so happy. For once the eternal sadness in his eyes was absent. Maybe this was what he needed—what they both needed. She was glad she could be a ray of light in his life. Goddess knew he'd suffered. And he had no one else but her.

He laced his fingers with hers and led her to his sleeping area. Anticipation swelled. Then he stopped so abruptly that she collided with him. Sliding her arms around his waist, she peeked around his body. "What's wrong? Didn't you make your bed this morning—?"

The sight before her stunned her into silence. There were papers everywhere—from large sheets to mere scraps. Some were crushed into balls, others scratched out. A few could be considered works of art. He'd even scribbled digitally on his wall datapad. It was all the same pattern, some filled in, others accompanied by runes. "The five marks," she murmured, taking in the disarray with concern. It obsessed him.

She spun around. "When did you do all this?"

"I'm not sure." Clearly agonized, he dragged an unsteady hand over his hair. Inky black, it stuck up in little spikes. "I don't remember. I have no memory of drawing all this. None." His hands shook.

"Bolivarr!" She reached for him.

He blocked her, sitting down hard on the edge of the bed, one hand raised to keep her away. "It's not a seizure."

"Then what?"

"It's…" He let his head fall into his hands, curling his fingers in his hair as if in pain. "I don't know. Memories. People. Things I can see, yet can't."

She struggled to understand, then realized she couldn't. It was a gulf between them—his suffering and her inability to make it better. "I want to help you, Bolivarr. I don't know how."

She stood there awkwardly. Obviously their plans for tonight were off. More important was his health, especially in light of the fact she'd lobbied to have him on this mission. If she had to turn around to deliver him to a hospital, word would reach Zaafran. With the prince's niece onboard, the incident would get too much notice. She pushed aside the worries. She was a captain, yes, but she was also a friend. A girlfriend. If he needed her, she'd stay.

He seemed to have to climb out of a dark place before he spoke. "I'm sorry. I didn't mean to push you away." He shoved to his feet and limped to her, drawing her into an embrace that felt surprisingly rock-solid despite his condition. His voice rumbled in his chest. "I love you, Hadley. You're the most important thing in my life. I don't want to lose you."

"You won't lose me. How can you think that?"

His silence was more troubling than his words.

# CHAPTER THIRTEEN

WREN'S TREASURE WAS suddenly much more than riches.
It was a lure—a fatal one. The muscles in Aral's jaw
moved, hinting at the tremendous turmoil inside him at
the sight of the pendant. In his large hand it seemed little
more than a unique, pretty piece. It was now, to him, a
threat. "How long have you had this?"

"Since I left Barokk. My guardian took it out of a
chest in the floor of our shed the day we evacuated. She
gave it to me only after she knew she was dying."

"She knew it was dangerous," Kaz warned. "Bolivarr
didn't. The mistake killed him."

A concept Kaz struggled with still, Wren realized.
"Sabra was a believer, more devout than I ever knew.
She kept that from me, she kept every secret imaginable
from me, including this pendant. It was her dying wish
that I find the treasure. She said it was my destiny to
make the galaxy whole again." She was no closer to
understanding the cryptic request now than she was
then, but she had to go. "It's my duty to go."

Aral rubbed a frustrated hand over his face. "A
dying wish. You'll want to fulfill it. And I won't be able
to stop you."

"No." Since discovering her father's true legacy,

Wren had spent days wondering how she could make it up to the worlds. The last in a line that perpetuated war, she'd make amends by ensuring peace. *That* was her destiny. Not riches. Not a battlelord's docile wife.

Did she have the guts to do all she intended?

She'd find out soon enough. "If there truly is a treasure, I'd rather it be in my hands than have it left for people to fight over. I'll see the riches to those who need it."

*"Anonymously."*

"In whatever way causes the least harm to everyone else," she argued. "The decision is mine to make." The long and terrible day had proved it was time she took charge of her destiny. She'd already taken steps. She'd procured this ride, for one, their escape out of the camp. Next, she'd make sure they got to where they needed to go—Ara Ana. From there, who knew? Away. Far away. It was a plan—*her* plan. She'd left control to others for too long, allowing them to take responsibility of what she needed to do for herself. It usually ended with them dead.

She gripped the gun in cold hands, knowing that with it she could dispense death. Torn, she wanted to fling it away, but if it kept her from falling into the hands of those that would use her for their goals and their power, *their evil,* she'd use it. And if they tried to hurt Aral or any of the people helping her, by the fates, she'd stop them dead. The beast stirred, and she immediately struggled to quench the anger. Somehow she had to control it, just as she had to take charge of her future—if there was one. What precious little time she had left she'd not hand over to others to dictate. She knew her fate if the loyalists like Karbon Mawndarr got hold of her. If she fell into Triad hands, some might want to spare her life, but the tide of sentiment was against it. Too many people needed an outlet for their blame. Closure, the leaders would call her execution. The first step in healing. Bah. She wouldn't give the loyalists or the new government the pleasure of using her.

The thunder of *Borrowed Time*'s thrusters starting up shook the floor. It was time to launch. Aral caught her arm. "Then we'll find Ara Ana. But know this—knowledge of those five lights killed my brother. By the fates, I won't let it kill you, too."

Her heart gave a twist at the fervent sincerity in his eyes. He was, again, the young man she'd glimpsed a decade ago, just as determined now as then to protect her. He was equally a battlelord, the man no one dared disobey. A man smart enough and determined enough to find her in a refugee camp in the middle of the Borderlands. Even the news that Karbon Mawndarr roamed free didn't distract him from his vow to see her to safety. She'd let him—as long as she could continue her search for Ara Ana. If anyone could unravel the mystery, Aral was the man to do it.

They headed for the front of the ship, their boots clanging against the bumpy metal floor. The noise and the smells of spacecraft would forever remind her of her trip to see the warlord. Kaz's posture was erect as she crossed to where Vantos sat at the pilot station, her shoulders squared, her hands swinging just so against her sides. The softness she'd revealed when talking about Bolivarr was gone again, buried.

Wren followed the lead of the others, finding the harnesses in her seat and fumbling to get them closed.

Her broken glasses required trying to see through a web of cracks. Now, getting her eyes repaired was less a matter of disguise than it was sheer survival.

Aral helped her fasten her harnesses. He had strong, long fingers and sturdy wrists. And no marriage tattoo. She hadn't noticed its absence before. He'd assured they were legally bound, but had taken no steps to personalize the union, or show it to the world.

He had married her only to prevent anyone else from doing it.

He was equally silent as he secured her into the seat for launch. Up close he was larger and stronger than she'd realized. His shoulders were thick, his biceps full and rounded. As he pulled the straps over her shoulders, warm knuckles brushed the side of her neck. The memory of his caress in the crowded streets of the camp left her curious and wanting.

In his haste, or in reaction to their awareness of each other, Aral yanked the harnesses tight, then realized he'd made her wince. "Did I hurt you?" he said all too quickly.

He thought her frail. Fragile. *The warlord's runt.* "I'm stronger than I look."

"Your strength causes complications I didn't anticipate." He softened his voice. "But it's also one of the things I know I will grow to love about you."

Love? She met his dark eyes, saw the desire there, and glanced down, suddenly shy. Would he expect her to be with him tonight? They were married after all. The idea didn't repulse her. In fact, it made her skin warm all over. Was being with him one more decision she'd make?

He swore under his breath. "I did not mean to talk of love so soon, Wren. Not yet. Perhaps—we—I… Ah."

He made a frustrated sound and focused on her with those dark and tortured eyes. Eyes that also glinted with hope. It took her breath away.

For the first time a hint of a smile, a very male one, played round his lips. *He sees you as a woman—his woman—not as the warlord's daughter.* Something inside her leaped at the thought. All her long existence had she not fantasized about being a woman like any other? A female free to choose her mate? Not a possession to be married off to a stranger.

*"What do you know about romance?"* Sabra was right. Admittedly, it was exhilarating to imagine Aral having feelings for her, and her for him, but allowing herself to get involved for real was another thing entirely. The vulnerability would be breathtaking. Terrifying. And most certainly life-threatening for the unlucky man. She was dangerous company. Even for Aral Mawndarr.

Vantos swore and slammed down his hands. "Port Control's put a hold on us. They won't release us for departure."

"They won't let us launch?" Aral sat in the seat next to Vantos and pulled his harnesses over his shoulders. "For what reason?"

"Yellow alert. It means they're probably acting on your warrant. They won't let us go until they check my manifest and history."

Wren's hand closed over the pistol. She stared straight ahead as Vantos fielded communications calls with the people who'd allow them to leave—or not. They wanted Aral. If they found Aral, they'd find her. Unless he gave himself up. She wouldn't let him. She'd never abandon him to the same fate she faced.

Vantos tried again. "This is *Borrowed Time.* It's just me and some toilets. Come on, lift the delay."

"No delay, sir. It's cancelled. You can come back inside with everyone else and wait it out."

The massive thrusters roared, rocking the ship.

*"Borrowed Time,"* the port control yelled. "Cut your power."

The craft shuddered as it turned within the confines of the docking bay.

"I repeat—you are not cleared for departure!"

"The airspace won't be cleared for us," Vantos said. "Keep an eye out for other ships." Clearing the bay, he aimed the ship's nose at the sky.

Violent turbulence bounced them in their seats. Wren held on for dear life. The nanomeds in her system staved off space sickness, but did little to ease her fear of flying.

To the protests and demands of Zorabeta's traffic controllers, Vantos merged into arriving space traffic, most of it coming right at them.

Aral leaned forward, his hands guarding the yoke, as if he were contemplating taking control of the ship away from the runner. Wren would not have complained. The front display swarmed with colored symbols denoting other vessels. She lost count of how many times the onboard siren wailed of oncoming traffic.

"How did you ever run the blockade in this?" Aral said. "I can't see a freepin' thing."

"Sometimes it was better not to see. Now hold on." Vantos pulled hard on the controls. Forces pressed her into the seat. If she hadn't strapped in, she'd have been on the floor. To her horror, Vantos breathed in deeply, savoring the moment. "I missed this, I really did."

"Don't kill us, Vantos," Kaz said.

"Don't worry. I'd rather be rich than dead any day. And just to give you a heads-up, expect a rough ride. We've got wormhole transit coming up right after we clear the space lanes."

"That's illegal," Kaz mentioned. "Rules of proximity."

"Rules." The ghost of a smile curved the runner's mouth. "After that one, the next transit's, well, let's just say a little dicey. It's closed."

*"Closed?"* Kaz looked ready to come out of her seat. "What the hells, Vantos."

"And the next one's uncharted. Look, they're scrambling fighters to come after us. This is how to lose them. If you wanted to take a cruise, then you wouldn't have hired a blockade runner."

"Do it." Grim, Aral seemed to have no qualms about taking a hazardous circuitous route. It drove home the precarious magnitude of her situation—and the risk Aral had taken in rescuing her. He'd commanded a battle-cruiser, a leviathan, Wren thought. Yet he kept his ego in check, letting Vantos do what they'd hired him to do.

"Aw, flarg. Here they are. Fighters." Vantos magnified the images on the screen. "In our six—locked on and tracking us. Ah. Here's a message now. They want us to pull over."

"No." Wren flew forward in her seat. The harnesses pulled her back. The beast inside her growled. She took an extra moment to calm herself. "Run," she said at the same time Aral did. They exchanged a glance. They might not be in agreement on the subject of their marriage, but when it came to running, they saw eye to eye.

Vantos grinned. "I was hoping you'd say that. Hang on." He accelerated until the ship shook. Chimes and then turbulence told that they'd entered a wormhole. The stars stretched into thin lines. Then, as quickly as they'd entered, they roared out the other side. It was like being shot out of a slingshot.

Wren saw no blinking ship symbols on the big screen.

"They're gone," the runner said. "But I want to make extra sure they stay gone. Here we go. Ready everyone?"

Vantos blew through the wormholes one after the other. He was an incredible pilot. And, Wren feared, crazy. From what she could gather from Aral's and Kaz's swearing, he ignored regulations and didn't give the ship a chance to recover before making another jump.

Finally he said, "We shook them loose."

"We probably shook them loose four transits ago," Kaz said dryly.

"Better to be safe."

"Safe. We're not safe. Not even close." Wren threw off the straps on her seat as if she were throwing off the shackles of her previously sheltered life. "As long as you're in my company, you're not safe. No one is. That's how we go forward from here. Knowing that. I don't want to lead anyone on."

Vantos pulled a nanopick out of his pocket as Wren pushed on her glasses. "I'll take the danger over hauling soap and toilets any day. Remember, I'm in this to get rich."

"I don't know how long that's going to take."

"If you've got the money, I've got the time."

"How are you set for provisions, Vantos?" Aral asked.

"Not good. I wasn't expecting a long trip—or

company. I've got enough for a few days—maybe. Your situation's gonna limit our shopping options."

"If you know a place, I have funds."

"I know where to go," Vantos said. "No one cares who you are, or where you're from. First time I showed up, I had no place else to go. They took me in for a while." The runner seemed to shake off old memories that weren't necessarily good ones. "Blast it all. I said I'd never go back. It's not a period in my life I feel like revisiting."

"Will they fix my eyes?" Wren asked.

"No questions asked. It's a sanctuary—religious. They're goddess worshippers, but an old sect. They mind their own business, keep to themselves. Issenda Cross-roads—that's the unofficial name. No one knows the real one. Crossroads. Yeah, a crossroads for lost souls."

"If it's a crossroads, they may know of Ara Ana," Wren said.

Aral exhaled as he met her gaze. She could tell by the mix of dread and hope in his face that he agreed.

Of all the trillions of people in the galaxy, Ara Ana was but one. Now they had to find her.

"ARA ANA—ONSCREEN." Garwin, Hadley's first officer, waved a proud hand at the holovis. "There she is."

The crew of the *Cloud Shadow* gathered around the holovis for their first glimpse of the planet at the far edge of settled space.

A virtual journalist was along to capture the moment. Her real person was located in a studio countless light years away. "Mission Origins—the quest to find the birthplace of the goddesses," the wavering image said.

"And now the challenge remains to find out what lies on the planet's surface. The discovery of a lifetime, or the remains of Hordish pillaging?"

At a desk nearby, Ellen Holloway sat hunched over an ancient religious volume with another cadet, Arrak, one of the half-blood twins. As part of their special project, they'd chosen to attempt to decipher Bolivarr's scrawled runes, guided by Sister Chara, a pious woman who'd dedicated her life to the study of ancient Sakkaran. At the derogatory term "Hordish pillaging" Ellen glanced up with narrowed eyes. Was it a budding romance? Or was Ellen merely being protective?

Hadley could relate to both. Her focus shifted to Bolivarr studying the holo-image. If he broke down or had a seizure, she would cut off the transmission immediately. It would take time before Drakken were seen as entirely human. Too many monstrous acts during the war had given them the reputation of being soulless mercenaries. She didn't need more negative press. Hadley switched off the broadcast feature and used a private channel to speak to the journalist. "Whether or not Drakken are responsible for any acts of looting, this mission wasn't launched to place blame. It's to bring us together and give us hope." Disgusted, she let the interview resume. "Star-Lieutenant Tadlock is mapping the surface," she said. "Using the most sophisticated equipment we have, we're examining every square inch of the surface, and under every rock. If there's a single relic left, we'll find it. Even the smallest piece will be significant."

"What are your concerns, Captain, in sending an advance team down to the surface?"

"That they'll be able to see the wonders of a discovery before I will," Hadley replied, all while keeping a wary eye on Bolivarr, who was now making a circuit of the holovis, his focus intense. "And, yes, there is the concern that others will have beaten us to the site. The planet's been forgotten for generations. No telling who's been here first. There is the threat of treasure hunters and pirates. I and my crew have full authority to arrest or deter any interference with our exploration." She sounded firm enough, but knowing how green her crew was, an encounter with either treasure hunters or pirates would have her hands full. Hers and Bolivarr's.

Hadley returned to the holovis and Bolivarr. He shook his head. "The planet itself means nothing to me," he said, his hands flat on the table. "Nothing." Somewhere inside he held the secret to finding the location of a significant artifact. Hadley was certain. But it remained locked inside him with the rest of his memories.

*"It's something from my life before."*

*"Something bad?"*

*"Something I'm supposed to know."*

A wraith obsessed with the religion of his enemy, she thought. She hoped it reflected an epiphany he'd had before he was attacked and lost his memory, and not acts of genocide, ferreting out believers and turning them in. His bitter hatred of the warlord gave her hope.

His fingers brushed furtively along the line of her uniform pants. He motioned with his chin in the direction of her office. She followed him in and closed the privacy door.

"I've briefed the crew on the security warning," he said. There were now three Drakken fugitives on the loose, two former battlelords and the warlord's daughter.

Big trouble for the Triad. They were to be detained on sight. "We got out of the Ring just in time. Things must be chaos right now."

"It's humiliating for Zaafran. He trusted the younger Mawndarr and he turned on him."

"What if he didn't?"

She stopped in the middle of neatening her desk. "I...don't know. I never considered doubting what Zaafran said."

"I'm not saying we should doubt him. It just seems premature to assume the son freed the father. It's too easy."

She considered Bolivarr as she pondered his opinion. "It's easy because it's obvious."

Bolivarr's brow lifted. "Is it?"

"If Aral Mawndarr didn't free his father, then who did?"

"They'd better be looking down that path, Hadley. That's my point. Otherwise, all we've got is a witch hunt, and that might be exactly what the resistance wants."

He seemed to be leaning more heavily on his cane than usual. Meds had kept him from obsessing over the five points to the point of losing sleep, but she wasn't so sure they were working. "On a lighter note, I wanted to let you know I'm looking forward to our dinner tonight. I can't remember the last time I had a home-cooked meal." He pretended to concentrate. "Hmm. I can't remember anything at all, in fact."

She pretended to frown at him. "Stop that."

He smiled.

"Mother's package arrived before we left the Ring. I've got most of the ingredients I need. The rest I'll procure from the galley. Talo cuisine is so good it's rumored to be an aphrodisiac."

He said in her ear, "As if we need one."

She almost kissed him, then remembered where she was. She sat in her desk chair. It was the safest spot in the room, and the only place she could keep her hands to herself.

"I'd like to be able to eat Talo home-cooking the rest of my life. But only if you come with it." He sat on the edge of the desk, his hand tight on his cane. "I don't want to wait anymore, Hadley. I've been thinking about this a lot. We've been together for a while now. Waiting on my memories to come back to make us official isn't something I want to do anymore."

Was he revealing his intentions to marry her? Her heart couldn't be beating any faster than when she'd been facing down the missiles of that Drakken battle-cruiser.

He rooted in his uniform pocket. "It's just a little surprise. Something I hoped you'd wear tonight."

"Wear? Ooh."

He handed her a box that fit in the palm of her hand. As she lifted the lid, he watched her with a sweet, boyish smile and those dark, soulful eyes. Two tiny earrings sat on a square of silk. Each was set with a perfectly cut, red ruby stone. His choice surprised her because she'd never mentioned an affinity for rubies or even red. She'd just never considered herself a red girl. Pink maybe. Or powder blue. But they were lovely and maybe it was time to start being more "red" and daring. "Ah, Bo. They're beautiful. Thank you." Hurriedly she put them on, angling her head so he could admire them.

Watching her, he went still. A strange, almost confused look took over for a split second. "Memory?" she asked. "What? Get it out before you forget it."

"It's gone. Whatever it was."

The earrings, she thought. "Where did you find them?"

"I was wandering around that indie market in the basement of the Ring before we left. I didn't even mean to stop at that jewelry merchant. These just jumped out at me, stopped me right in my tracks." He cracked a soft smile. "I actually didn't buy them at first, but I kept thinking about them. Seeing them. It developed into quite a little obsession. That was it, I thought. I'm going to buy them for Hadley. So I did. I'm glad you like them." He hopped off the desk, suddenly energized. "Dinner. Later." He lowered his voice. "You'll look great wearing red."

Red. Blood. Drakken. She didn't let her doubts appear in her face. She smiled instead as Bolivarr walked from the office, and reminded herself that red also meant love.


VANTOS RETURNED to the bridge after seeing to some repairs caused by the repeated transits. "We're in good shape, all things considered. Now, for practical matters. We've got four people aboard and one bunkroom— mine. Who's sleeping with whom? I've got no problem doubling up." He aimed a wicked grin at Kaz, who maintained her perfect military bearing and paid him no mind at all.

"The women will share your quarters," Aral said. "I'll take a mat on the floor." And as far from Wren as possible.

The nightmares necessitated it. He would not risk her seeing the insanity tickling the edges of his mind. Karbon's legacy.

She was searching his face even as he formed the thought. Her eyes missed nothing when it came to him.

She saw the signs of exhaustion, gut-deep and inescapable. Too many interrupted nights. In all his careful planning, he'd not planned for that eventual aspect of their marriage. Sleeping together. She'd never be able to spend the night with him. His shattered sleep would rob him of her in his arms.

Vantos gestured down the dim, narrow corridor with a flourish. "Hydroshower's in my quarters. The bio-cleaner's over there by the second lavatory. See? What service. When you feel the need to travel again, I want you to remember Vantos airways." Chuckling, Vantos rubbed his stomach. "Running sure gives me an appetite. Anyone else famished?"

Wren stifled a moan. She was pale, her hair messy.

"Why, I thought you'd have your space legs by now," Vantos said.

"I loathe flying. I abhor it. I want to find somewhere to live that doesn't move—and stay there."

"Not me. I can't be still."

"Neither can I," Kaz admitted, and made a quick exit to use the hydroshower.

Aral wasn't surprised to hear the runner wanted to keep running, but as close as he was to Kaz, her answer came as a surprise. Perhaps it was because her best memories were on board a ship. Oddly, his own were the narrow windows of time growing up on the Mawndarr estate when his father was away on duty. Bliss, those days were.

"And you, Aral?" Wren watched him with curious, appraising eyes. "Would you miss being on a ship?"

"Being in another ship's missile sights, sending my best-trained pilots out only to see three-quarters of them return, seeing lush worlds blackened to cinders. No. I won't miss ships, and I won't miss war."

Vantos observed Aral for a pensive moment before nodding and walking away to the galley.

*Nevermore* had been stocked and ready for a prolonged journey. Vantos's situation was the exact opposite. The man lived day to day. Aral planned years in advance. For what good it had done him, he thought. Nothing had turned out as expected.

From down below, cookware clanked and rattled. "Go with Vantos," Aral told Kaz when she emerged clean from a quick and efficient sailor's shower a few moments later. "Keep an eye on him."

Kaz looked as if she wanted to do anything else as she turned toward the galley.

Next, he looked for his wife. They were finally under the same roof. He could hardly believe it.

Wren held the soiled priestess robes in her arms, about to deposit the bundle in the bio-cleaner.

"Careful," he said. "We can't afford to risk angering the gods. If there are any, I want them on our side."

"That's what I'm thinking." With as much respect as possible, she lowered the garment into the cleaner. It was a disguise they may well need in the future. "This technology is a marvel. We had nothing like this on Barokk."

Quieter, he asked, "How are you faring?"

"I'm exhausted."

"I hope Vantos's quarters are to your liking. On *Nevermore* I had quarters specially made for you." He'd taken pride in its construction. It had sat empty for months waiting for Wren to finally sleep in it.

"You planned for us to always sleep apart?" She

seemed confused. "Is the marriage only out of duty then? To protect me? I know I'm small…and plain, but…" Her voice turned a little husky. "You called me beautiful—"

"You *are*." She had no idea what she did to him. What was beautiful about her went straight through to the soul.

"So you have no expectation of this marriage ever working?"

"Nor is that the case." He scowled. His tone was sharp. "Sometimes I don't sleep well."

"It's like that for everyone."

"No. Not like this." He turned to look out at the stars when all he wanted to do was tuck her into his arms. She'd probably crack him over the head with the pistol he'd given her, unless he concocted an excuse like he did in the camp, telling her they had to disguise themselves as lovers.

"I went through great pains to create a comfortable living space for you. It's a sanctuary where you'll feel safe. A place you can call your own."

"You made a nesting spot one might put together for a new pet."

"A pet!" Had he? Blast. "You will know the difference between being my wife and being my pet. I'll make sure of it."

Wren's head tipped back as she adjusted her glasses. Her long, exploratory gaze started at his mouth and ended up somewhere near his belt. He didn't think it possible, but he turned red.

Blast. Not again. Wren's glorious eyes flickered with a hint of amusement. "What might that entail, Aral Mawndarr?"

"You wouldn't know about such matters." She was an

innocent, a quality held in high esteem for the typical battlelord husband. And why he probably didn't place importance on the issue, aside from knowing he'd have to take care their first time. *If* there was a first time. Undefeated in battle, his record with Wren was laughably poor.

"I know more than you think," she said. "I read a lot of books on Barokk."

"I'm not talking about folk tales."

"Neither am I. My guardian had several volumes of erotic literature. Dog-eared." That seemed to strike her funny. It hit him that it was the first time he'd heard her giggle outside his fantasies. It got to him, too. His cold rock of a heart went out to her. Not in pity, but in stark admiration. After being pulled out of her sheltered bubble of an existence and threatened with an executioner's chambers, if she'd curled up into a fetal position and given up, no one would have blamed her. Yet here she was, leading him in circles.

Leading him into bed with her.

She had already made it clear she didn't mind the trappings of marriage. She just didn't want the trap.

By the time he turned back to her, she was striding away in the direction of the hydroshower. It took a mighty effort, but he tore his mind from thoughts of his naked wife standing in the shower, water sluicing over her body, and how he'd like to chase the rivulets with his tongue. Then again, he'd always been able to express himself better physically than with mere words. If he could be with her the way he wanted to be with her, she'd understand his intentions, and perhaps even trust them. He wanted her as neither a slave nor a pet, but, blasted fates, he'd certainly not been very convincing.

He scrubbed a hand over his face. His head ached with fatigue. *Bed her.*

Kaz was wrong. He couldn't just launch ahead without laying the groundwork. After all, one didn't take off without a flight plan and checking the route. There was work to be done first. Oh, he'd planned her rescue from every angle and in every conceivable detail—except for Vantos and the treasure—but he hadn't thought any further along than a vague understanding that they'd settle down far from the central galaxy, perhaps in the wild fringes near the Uncharted Territories.

Hells. Awrenkka e'Rakkuu was his uncharted territory.

## *CHAPTER FOURTEEN*

KEIR'S BLOOD STILL PULSED with the thrill of the run. He'd never dreamed he'd be back trying to outrun Drakken when only days ago he was trapped in a boring dead-end job supplying sanitation supplies to refugee camps. Yep, he was running again, thanks to a little girl with a big bad temper and guts that surprised him. She also happened to be an uncashed fifty-million-queen check, a check that anyone else in the galaxy would cash in a heartbeat. He'd wait to see what happened with the treasure. Hunting for it—and being paid to do it— appealed to a certain part of him. He'd heard rumors of treasure left behind by fleeing priestesses in the time of the Great Schism. Wren's claim that she was bequeathed something hidden in the UT wasn't that farfetched. It was a matter of finding it. As he'd told her and the battlelord, he had the time.

And if there wasn't any treasure? That's where he wasn't sure how the story would end.

Keir tore off another bite of the snack he'd grabbed while looking for fixings for dinner. The protein stalk tasted like a water hose. He swore, tossing it in the trash. Money wasn't so tight that he couldn't cook real meals more often. He'd blasted well better for the

Drakken. The warlord's daughter was aboard. Imagine that. Royalty. Even if it was the wrong kind.

He opened empty locker after locker, hoping he'd get lucky and find something to prepare that didn't begin with protein and end with stalk. Quiet footsteps interrupted his concentration. He turned around. "I was sent to offer assistance," Kaz said.

*Sent.* She said it as if she'd been told to pitch herself off a cliff. "You in the kitchen?"

"It's unfamiliar territory, yes."

"You used my shower. You smell good."

At the compliment, she went rigid. "Where are your supplies, Vantos?"

"I pulled out what I could find. It's all there on the counter."

Silent, she began sorting through the items, setting aside what could be combined to make a meal. Folding his arms over his chest, Vantos simply watched. It was a sight he'd never thought he'd see—a woman in his galley. Whether it was blockade running or carrying toilets across sector lines, it was him, his ship and what bar he'd frequent next—that was it. Though he had to say, the thought of Kaz sitting at his table wasn't too hard to swallow—her, waiting for him to make dinner, that long elegant body curled up in the chair and, later, around him. A surge of lust ran through him.

Sleeping with a Drakken. Blasted hells.

Kaz tore the seal off a pouch of vegetable soup with all the enthusiasm of preparing a funeral meal. "Take a seat," he said. "Pour a drink. I can handle this."

"I have my orders," she said coldly.

"Your orders? You had to be forced to come down here and help?"

"It was to keep an eye on you, Vantos, if you want to know."

"Ah. Well. That makes more sense."

She took the pouch of vegetable soup she'd unsealed and placed it in the heater. Then she sorted through the other items he'd set out, picking and choosing from the limited selection. Keir folded his arms across his chest. In manner, Kaz was unlike any woman he'd ever encountered. Like a gorgeous doll in a glass case, she was remote, untouchable. Off limits.

And it roused his curiosity.

"All right, doll face, what is it about me or maybe men in general that you find so blasted distasteful? Is it that you like girls better and I'm just misreading the signs? If so, tell me now and put me out of my misery."

"Girls?" For the first time her lush red lips formed what could almost be termed a smile. Almost. It was more a wry indication that she thought him a complete idiot. All right, he'd give her that because around her he felt like one. "No. I like boys." She glanced up from the soup. "Men, actually. Maybe that's the problem. I like men, not boys."

"Ouch." He spread a hand over his chest. "I'm not man enough for you."

She made a fist on the countertop. "It may be hard for you to grasp, but I don't want you. Or anyone right now." A spark of anger flickered in her dark eyes. She was becoming more animated by the minute. He was definitely thawing her out, but he wasn't too sure if it was in a good way. Well, he'd take it however he could get it. She was a challenge too good to pass up.

"Broken heart," he guessed.

Her proud stance faltered almost imperceptibly. But as a runner, he'd learned how to pick up subtle clues. He was about to give her hells for loving and leaving some poor sot, but seeing her sudden awkwardness, he ditched the idea.

"Mawndarr?" he asked, gentler, knowing the battle-lord was a fool for the warlord's little daughter who had him wrapped around her finger.

She recoiled from the idea. "Aral and I? There was never anything like that. I loved his younger brother. Why are we even having this conversation?"

"I don't know. I kind of like it, though."

"I don't. I don't like any of it."

"Not part of your *orders?*"

She glared at him.

"Sorry, doll face. Didn't mean to rub salt in a wound I didn't know about."

"It's a wound that's not even supposed to be there. It's old. It should have healed up and scarred over years ago."

Kaz tucked her short black hair behind a pretty little ear. Unlike other Drakken he'd seen, she wore only one red earring in each lobe. They reminded him of drops of fresh blood. Must have matched her blood red Imperial Navy uniform. "He died," she said. "In the war."

"So did my parents. They were soldiers."

She glanced up, her eyes suddenly wide, allowing him to see the person who lived behind them for the first time. "But you're helping us."

"Selfishly."

"For an unnamed treasure."

"Don't mistake it for anything more."

Gods. He'd dumped about his parents. He hadn't thought of his mother or father in so long it took a moment to conjure their faces. He'd started it, so he might as well finish it. Pouring two glasses of whiskey, he offered Kaz one. With the tip of a manicured index finger she politely pushed it away. "They crossed paths on a troop carrier ship inbound from one of the bloodiest attacks of the war, both of them young soldiers with no business falling in love. Except they did. I was the result. They married the year after I was born, something they had no business doing, either." But at Onsara Barracks, they made it work somehow. The glue that held the family together was their love for Keir and each other, and their hatred of the Drakken Horde, both of which they did their best to instill in Keir.

In his datapad was an old picture of him as a small boy, dressed up as a soldier. He opened it up. The glow lit up Kaz's perfect skin and her eyes as she absorbed the image. "How cute," she said.

"Yeah. How cute my parents must have thought I was, a little hero-to-be pretending to blast away Imperial soldiers with a toy plasma rifle." He must have been no more than six cycles. Less than ten cycles later, both his parents were dead and he was out on his own, running as far from their futile heroism as he could. Spending those few months at Issenda Crossroads because he didn't know where else to run.

*"Son, this is my proudest moment, seeing you in uniform."* His father's voice rang in his memory. Keir wore his dress blacks with his rook stripe on the sleeve, symbolic of a first-year academy cadet. Even now he

could hear the gruffness in his father's voice, could feel how tight he gripped him in his embrace.

Happy, bashful, Keir had insisted, "I'm just a cadet."

"An *officer* cadet." It was the only time he'd ever seen tears in his father's eyes.

A few short months later it was a different story.

"I'm out of here," he'd told the commandant of the prestigious Royal Galactic Military Academy after word came that his parents had been killed in action.

"Your father wouldn't want you to take off that uniform," the commandant of the prestigious Royal Galactic Military Academy said when Keir handed in his papers to resign. "Take time to grieve, son. Then come back."

Keir shook his head at that. "No flargen thanks." He'd acted disrespectfully to the commandant, but didn't care.

He told Kaz, "My mother and father were considered heroes—and all it got them was this." He reached above their heads and gave the small box that contained their wedding rings and various commendations for bravery a shake. "Hear that? A few small rattles."

Kaz studied her hands, flat on the countertop—slender fingers, neat glossed nails. Here he was, telling a Drakken his sob story. Talk about times changing.

"I was a cadet at the RGMA when they died. They wanted to force me to finish the remainder of my mandatory service. I had to remind them that war orphans were exempt. They even offered to hold my spot until I came around. I'd already come around. I knew I wasn't going to throw my life away."

He held strong to that promise. It was the only thing

that kept him from losing it during the farewells with the cadets who'd become his friends. He'd considered them his family away from home but even they didn't understand his rejection of all things heroic or altruistic. To Keir, there was nothing complicated about it. "What I'm saying, doll face, is that there ain't a person in this galaxy alive that doesn't know about loss. Not to minimize what you feel, but why don't you live a little? At least you get to. Live, that is. Your little friend upstairs. Who knows how long she's got?"

"You make it sound as if she has a terminal disease."

"What no one has died from on Coalition worlds for centuries," Wren interrupted as she walked into the galley with Mawndarr. "But that people on our worlds do so with regularity. Because my father spent money on war and not medicines. He and all the warlords before him did the same. They're my terminal disease. If I die it will be because of that." She took a seat at the table, then sniffed the air. "Something smells delicious."

Vantos shook his head. "On that pleasant note, let's eat."

BLOODIED, QUAKING with shock, Aral climbed to his feet—again. He would not flee his father's fists. Never run—that was his mantra. Face the man and fight. For all his determination, it only made things worse. But he'd rather be beaten and defiant than cower in fear of his father's wrath.

Karbon grabbed his shirt collar, lifting him off his feet to throw him into the wall. "Run, boy," the man growled. "Show me what a coward you are."

Aral climbed back to his feet, swaying some. Being hit in the head shook up his equilibrium. The key was *not to let Karbon see. The more weakness he showed the longer the beating.*

*"Fool boy, you need to learn when to stay and when to give up." Karbon was slapping him with both hands, alternating top, bottom, left and right, so that Aral never knew from where the blow would come. Instinctively, he used his hands to protect his head, face and gut. "Don't you see the lesson I am trying to teach you? Worthless piece of freep—go. Get out of my sight, I say. Run away!" The back of his father's hand sent him crashing to the ground. "You won't beat me."*

*Slowly, gingerly, for his body was a million points of agony, Aral picked himself up. Sometimes a week or a month would go by without provoking his father's rage. More than that when his father was on space duty far from home. Each time Aral hoped he didn't return. But the man always did. Just as Aral survived the beatings when his father, drunk on sweef, let his temper go too far, Karbon enjoyed victory after victory over Coalition ships. He seemed invincible.*

*Perhaps his father thought him invincible, too.*

*"Run! You have to know when, boy. Know when to give up."*

*Aral once more stood. His nasal passages were swollen nearly shut. Blood ran down the back of his throat. One eye was so puffed up he couldn't see out of it. The other turned his father's face into a blurry purple rose.*

*"Again, Aral? I'm giving you the chance to get away. To retreat. Back down and this will be over. Why don't you?"*

*Because running would give his father power—over*

*him. Over everything. His father wanted him to flee, but
his legs refused to take him. His father wanted to break
him, but he was no longer whole. He wanted him to cry,
but the tears had dried. He was closed up, safe inside.
No one could open the door.*

"Aral!"

*The scene shifted. He was in an unfamiliar building.
Wren stood at the opposite end of a corridor. A bright
light shone above her head. Then he saw four more
lights, one by each shoulder and each foot.*

*Her violet eyes were haunted and wide. Afraid.*

*She needed him. He started to run to her, haltingly
at first, then faster. The corridor seemed infinite. The
longer he ran, the farther away she seemed to get and
the brighter the lights until they all drowned out the
small silhouette of her body.*

*White light engulfed him. Too late, he thought. He
shouldn't have let her go. He'd lost her now. Lost her
forever...* "No," *he bellowed, falling to his knees.* "Wren,
don't leave me."

"Aral. Please—*wake up!*"

He sucked in a mighty breath and jerked upright.
He'd fallen asleep. Wren was leaning over him, her eyes
pools of worry. The sight of her washed and lovely and
dressed in borrowed night clothing brought him up
short. She was so beautiful. "You're here." His voice
cracked with relief. "I thought I'd lost you."

"Is everything okay?" Vantos was nearby, looking
disheveled, clearly dragged out of bed by Aral's nightmare. This ship was far smaller than *Nevermore*, and
with no real privacy. They'd have heard every blasted
thing. Kaz hurried up behind him.

"I'm here," Wren told them. "I'll stay," she repeated to Kaz when his second hesitated to leave.

He nodded at her, and she left him alone with Wren on a mat on the floor in the aft section of Vantos's ship. A turning point, he thought, going from the hands of a friend to a wife. Wren would be with him through thick and thin. Through war and peace. Through grief and healing. For better or for worse. This, by far, was worse.

He should have told her of his impending madness. How hard he fought not to end up like Karbon. And how weary he became sometimes of the struggle. But he was too far along in his plan to derail it. For years he'd planned and plotted to destroy the empire, annihilate his father and rescue Awrenkka, bringing her under his protection. He'd pursued his plans to the point of obsession. Now she was with him and he realized he didn't know what *to do* with her.

Because he still hadn't ended his personal war, a war declared on a long ago day when he saw his school teacher murdered by a monster. His war with Karbon.

*"Fool boy, you need to learn when to stay and when to give up. Don't you see the lesson I am trying to teach you? Stubbornness equals stupidity to persevere for the sake of persevering."*

Giving in equaled letting go. Moving on. He'd told Kaz to move on. Apparently he couldn't take his own advice. Or Karbon's. Repulsed, he rose from the mat. He would not be reduced to the level of taking his father's advice. Blast the dreams. "How much did you hear?"

"Enough to know you had a terrible nightmare."

Urging him to run after Wren before he lost her. The five lights were dangerous. The dream told him so. If he took her to the treasure he'd expose her to more danger than she was in now. It was as close to reality as any dream he'd ever had.

He stalked to a sink to splash cold water on his face then scrubbed a towel over his face and neck. He fought hard not to throw the towel down then throw her down on the bed. Ever since the ice had been cracked between them last evening, he'd been painfully aware of her presence…the heat of her skin…her scent. And her voice, her manner, her eyes, her little nose—every freepin' thing about her.

"You said you have trouble sleeping. Is it always because of the nightmares?"

"Yes. But I don't recall having this particular dream before." There were many versions of his past. He'd rather see none of them. Unfortunately, he was forced to relive all of them. His skull throbbed. Tipping his head back to stretch his neck, he stifled a groan. His throat ached, too. All things considered, he felt better than how he used to feel following a beating before nanomeds kicked in to wipe out the pain. Too bad the meds never could eliminate the pain on the inside, the pain no one could see. "Did I yell?" The very idea embarrassed him. He'd never showed such weakness in his waking moments.

"Only my name. You begged me not to leave you." She searched his face, her expression worried, tender.

He crossed the room to don a fresh shirt over his tank. He felt the need to keep in motion around her. He wasn't certain what would happen if he stopped.

"You need to go back to sleep. We're going to be at Issenda tomorrow."

"The only way I can is by exercising to the point of exhaustion, or drinking whiskey. I don't care to medicate." Numbing himself like his father did, he'd risk accelerating down the same path.

She lay down on his sleeping mat. "I'll sleep with you."

"Ah, fates. Wren, there's no privacy. There's—"

"Sleep with you. Not anything more." She sighed. "Sabra was right when she told me that males had simple minds—sex and food, and that's all."

"That's far from the truth." Wasn't it? "Sleeping with me is dangerous for another reason. I thrash about in my dreams. I may hurt you."

That won him a withering look.

He heaved a sigh of defeat. Feeling a smile on his lips, he lay down next to her, on his back. She removed her glasses, then dropped her head on his chest as she slid her arms around him. He embraced her, carefully at first, then with increasing relief. She'd come to give him comfort. By the fates, he'd take it.

And so they lay there, Wren tucked close. Having her near steadied him as no meds, no shot of whiskey or even hours of brutal exercise could. None of those avenues brought a sense of safety, the knowledge that he wasn't alone. His thoughts floated back to his childhood on the estate. The beatings he cared not to think of, but afterward, made pretty again by nanomeds, he'd run out to play with Kaz and Bolivarr, both of who remained inexplicably untouched by Karbon's cruel hand. He'd run to them to be made human again in his soul.

Wren made him feel human again in his soul.

Aral stared at the ceiling, feeling warm and hollowed

out, and oddly reassured. It wasn't just her physical closeness; it was something else. Something more.

Something totally outside his experience.

Sex for him had always been a purely bodily pursuit. He'd never remained with a woman afterward, let alone actually spent the night with someone. Refusing Wren's attempts to sleep with him had been a kneejerk reaction, a compulsion to distance himself that had become habit over the years. Yet it felt natural wanting to hold her like this, good, and right, somehow. They belonged together. Perhaps that's what they saw in each other's eyes that long ago day.

Judging by the sound of Wren's slow, even breaths she'd fallen asleep. Carefully, he turned, holding her against his body. He let his eyes close, hoping perhaps sleep would come.

Sometime later—his sense was that it was hours later—the ship's wake-up chime sounded, rousing him and Wren from bed.

"Did you sleep?" she asked.

He paused, thought about it, and let out a quick, quiet laugh. "I did." He lifted up on an elbow, leaning over her as she drowsily searched his face, trying to see him without her glasses. "Sleeping with you could well become a habit."

Heat radiated off her powerful little body, and his loins tightened. His initial intentions were not sexual, but her sheer proximity, her scent, her curves, her mouth, it was overwhelming, to say the least. "Other things may be habit forming as well," he confessed, winning a grin from her as he ran a hand up her thigh. The muscles in her legs flexed at his touch. Someday, he wanted her to know the pleasure those strong thighs could bring them both, wrapped around his hips as he made love to her.

"Aral." She sighed and brought her hand to his face, tracing his features, "seeing" him. He lifted her hand and pressed his lips to the heel of her palm. He followed the ridge of her tendons to the pulse on the inside of her wrist and felt her shiver. Her other hand slid around the back of his head to pull him closer, her lips parting.

"All right—everyone up!" Vantos was marching through the ship, banging on a pan to rouse them. "I've got Issenda on my scopes. No time to dilly-dally. This ain't a hotel—"

He came to a halt by Aral's sleeping mat. "Well," he said. "I stand mistaken. Happy honeymoon."

This time Wren turned red. Aral brought his mouth to her ear. "Let him think what he wants. Let everyone."

A datapad dropped onto the mat. "Got the morning news. I think you two lovebirds might be interested. I know I was."

Aral took the pad and sat up. "Bloody hells." For a few blissful moments he'd forgotten about the galaxy they'd left behind. Now reality returned to slap him in the face. "Mission: Origins Seeks to Unravel Mystery of Ara Ana." He scanned the text as he wrapped his mind around their new dilemma. "Ara Ana isn't a person. It's a place."

"That's right," Vantos said. "And unless our asses get moving the Triad's about to beat us to it."

# CHAPTER FIFTEEN

AS THE *CLOUD SHADOW* neared Ara Ana, Hadley listened with increasing dread to a security bulletin coming from the Ring. Another Borderlands settlement had been attacked. She and her central staff gathered in her office at Bolivarr's request.

Hadley's first officer reacted to the news with alarm. "These are remote outposts—almost as far away from everything as we are." Garwin was understandably nervous. The archaeologist had spent a career avoiding war.

"Copycats?" she asked Bolivarr. The incidents brought back memories of her previous assignment when the *Unity* had pursued a group of Coalition extremists masquerading as Drakken skulling raiders. They'd wanted the treaty to fail by turning sentiment against the Drakken. But that was many months ago. "Or maybe loyalists."

Bolivarr nodded. "The resistance was my first thought, too, but these attacks are deliberate and specific. They're targeting religious sanctuaries only."

"Horrifying," Sister Chara said. "I thought peace would bring an end to the persecution."

Bolivarr shook his head. "I don't think it's motivated by intolerance."

"The slaughter of believers is exactly that." Garwin shook his head. "Your people were committed to genocide."

"My people." Bolivarr's flat tone caught Hadley's attention. His normally placid gaze had sharpened with anger. "My people are your people now."

"My people wouldn't desecrate sisters of the goddess."

Hadley placed her hands flat on the desk. "Lieutenant Tadlock, these are unprovoked terror attacks. Acts of hatred. Battle-Lieutenant Bolivarr is a full-fledged member of this crew, and a Triad citizen, as are we all. As members of my crew, you will treat each other with respect." It reminded her of the conversation she'd had with Cadet Holloway the first day out. Now the adults needed a refresher.

He cleared his throat. "Captain. My apologies. It's just that no coalition-born citizen would do…this."

The rape and skulling of nineteen priestesses. It was, Hadley thought, a deed too horrible to contemplate.

"Monsters did this," the man said.

"Yes," Bolivarr said. "*Monsters* did. My point exactly. I may not know what I was, exactly, but I know the man I am now. I despise the warlord and all he's done. I've made it my life's commitment to see atrocities like this stopped and the creatures who commit them punished and stripped from the face of the galaxy."

Garwin seemed to accept Bolivarr's statement, but the division was troubling. When pressed, her crew tore apart along old scar lines. It had been like that on the *Unity*, despite its lofty name, and it would be like that for years to come, she was afraid.

"That said, I don't think intolerance was the motivation," Bolivarr continued. "We are seeing a systematic sweep of priestess sanctuaries. In each case they ransacked the sanctuary's stash of valuables. Evidence also points to interrogations taking place before the killings. They're looking for something."

"And here we are headed for a planet supposedly loaded with religious relics," Garwin put in, his gaze darting outside as if dreading the sight of Ara Ana.

"No one knows the destination coordinates."

*Thank the gods.* "In light of our destination, and its religious overtones, and the nature and location of the attacks, I've placed the ship on level-two alert as a precaution," she said. She stood, pausing to look at each of her senior staff in turn. "What happened here tonight and across the Borderlands should remind us all why our mission is so important. The birthplace of the goddesses, ladies and gentlemen. We might very well rediscover it." She thought of the day Prime-Admiral Zaafran had called her to his office: *A fable the lost scripture may be and the treasure that surrounds it, but to entertain the promise of such a discovery, to dream of it…it is what our weary, war-ravaged people need. To know the goddesses existed…that they were real. That true goodness exists, Hadley.* "Gods know this galaxy could use some goodness right now. It starts with us. We can't find what we don't know ourselves."

She redoubled her commitment to complete the mission without incident. She would not fail Zaafran. She would not fail this galaxy.

*BORROWED TIME* DROPPED to a landing on the odd little world of Issenda. It was lumpy and small, warmed between two suns, one as primary and the other distant, never letting night engulf the world fully. Wren's deteriorating glasses made seeing the new world around her difficult. It smelled fresh, unlike Zorabeta, and the air was still and temperate. The gravity was lighter here, making her feel as if she could run and leap great distances. There was no time to test her theory. They had to load up on supplies, see a doctor and leave. If they didn't, the Triad expedition would beat them to Ara Ana. Mission: Origins. She'd not be able to complete her promise to Sabra.

Wren, like the others, was dressed as a simple trader. Disguising herself as a priestess when amongst them was not a good idea, they'd agreed. Hefting her gun in her hand, she marched down the gangway, the gravity making her feel a bit dizzy. Aral caught up to her. "Slow down," he said.

"I'm nervous."

"This place is about as safe as we're going to get. We took every precaution."

"About my eyes." She adjusted her glasses, squinting up at him. "I've never seen how everyone else sees."

"That will be a wonderful thing—to be able to see well for the first time. Or are you afraid to know what I really look like? Perhaps my looks will frighten you away."

He actually made her smile. Then her doubts returned. "Will sight give me too much power? Is my vision all that's holding me back from becoming like the warlord?"

"Your heart is good and pure. That's what keeps you from becoming your father."

"You see what you want to see." She couldn't look at him. His eyes would have that tender look she wasn't sure she deserved. She didn't know herself well enough yet. "I know what's inside," she insisted, softer. "And I will keep it from hurting anyone else."

"I know your heart," Aral argued. "And I will keep anyone from hurting *you*."

The others commented on the beauty of the surroundings. If she squinted hard enough, Wren could make out a lavender sky, red, conical peaks that reminded her of the castles she used to build with dribbled sand at the lakeshore as a girl. Some of the red hills wore tufts of trees like funny, feathered hats.

"Twilight here is downright eerie," Vantos said.

"Why?" Wren found the landscape interesting but not frightening. It was then she noticed the shadows across the parched ground: long, dark ones, crisscrossed with fainter ones at an angle. "The shadows look like fingers."

Kaz agreed. "Like light passing through someone's hands."

"In prayer." Vantos laced his hands together. "The heavenly mother Herself prays over Issenda, keeping watch. That's what the sisters here say."

"Is that what you found so eerie, Vantos?" Kaz asked.

"Hells yeah. I was a mixed-up seventeen-year-old boy, and not religious at all. I was terrified thinking the heavens were keeping an eye on me. I behaved while I was here—I had to. It settled me down enough to find a job when I left and actually hold on to it." He whispered. "I'm kind of glad they won't remember me."

Two priestesses waited at the gates to the sanctuary, a vast area of reddish, mud-colored conical huts, squashed versions of the hills. A lively market promised a source of supplies. Incense sweetened the still air.

The sisters didn't resemble the ones she'd seen every-where else. The Order of the Hand of Sakkara, they wore body-hugging robes. Strong and athletic, they flexed arms that were bare from the shoulder down, their skin covered in henna tattooing. One woman had blond hair, thick and unadorned, reaching to the backs of her knees. The other was dark, her skin tone almost too deep for the henna to show, with equally long and curly dark brown hair. Except for long hair allowed to fall free from under silken wrappings, their heads and their faces from the nose down were wrapped in the same silk as their robes, allowing only a view of their eyes, ageless and serene, like the priestess she'd seen on Zorabeta. Nothing would seem to unsettle these women. They were eternally calm. Several times Wren had felt that kind of calm steal over her. Then her inherited temper would run roughshod over it.

"Your instruments of war, please. Place them here. We will watch over them as we do all such items." The blond priestess waved at a polished, flat rock. Vantos had already told them to expect to be disarmed.

Wren had gone from never wanting to touch a weapon to not wanting to let it go. The vulnerability made her stomach ache. Aral pressed reassuring fingers on the small of her back.

"Blessed are all who enter here," the darker priest-ess said, allowing them to pass while her partner observed them. "Welcome back, Vartekeir."

The runner almost stumbled. Her dark eyes crinkled, suggesting a smile. "We remember *all*," she said with-out him having to ask the question. The sister's gaze shifted to Wren, lingering on her long enough to spark alarm. Then she greeted her with a pointed nod and waved their group past.

"She acted as if she's seen me before." Pushing on her glasses, Wren stared over her shoulder until Aral yanked on her arm, tugging her forward. She felt for the pendant snug beneath her bra band and made sure it wasn't showing.

As "godless Drakken," she, Kaz and Aral couldn't be expected to know of Ara Ana, the mythical birthplace of the goddesses. Vantos had been raised with almost as little factual knowledge of religion. "Soldiers prayed twice," he'd explained. "When going into battle and when coming out, first to plead for survival and second to give thanks for it."

Wren took in the sanctuary of Issenda with wonder. The priestesses looked like goddesses themselves, fit and strong. In one area, she saw several women training with long sticks, trying to knock each other off an elevated log. Others practiced martial arts. All of it under the strange shadows. The praying hands.

Sabra would have fit right in. She'd have been so happy here. But her duty to Wren and the warlord never would have allowed it. She'd sacrificed for Wren. She'd died protecting her. The Triad expedition would not keep Wren from fulfilling her vow to Sabra. The Triad would not keep her from atoning for her family's misdeeds. Misdeeds on a grand, almost unimaginable scale.

Kaz and Vantos went to the market to gather provisions for the next leg of their journey. Aral accompanied Wren to the sanctuary's hospital. The closer she got, the more slowly she walked. "It will give you more control, not less," he tried to convince her as they neared the large hut.

They kneeled at the bowl where they were to leave their "gifts," an indirect payment for the procedure. To Aral's funds, Wren added one of the pouches of gems she'd brought all the way from Barokk. It was far more than needed, but not to Wren. Nothing would ever make up for the killings ordered by the warlord, but every small bit helped. Wren kept her gaze trained respectfully on the ground the entire way into the room where the procedure would be performed.

A short, well-swathed sister attendant escorted them to a small, clean room. Like the others here, she used few words, speaking only when necessary.

"She's a bit nervous, Doctor," Aral said as the healer examined Wren's eyes.

"It's a simple procedure. It won't take long."

"What are the risks?"

"Virtually none. The nanomeds are engineered to re-form the lens. If the eye itself was damaged, perhaps then I couldn't offer such an optimistic prognosis, but her eyes are healthy, only the lenses malformed." She smiled at Wren. "You'll be able to see for light years in just a few moments."

"A hundred paces would suit me fine."

Aral clasped her hand. *Easy.*

The doctor applied the nano-drops. Tingling and itching began as the specifically programmed and targeted meds went to work, knitting, stretching and healing. Her eyes watered and stung.

Aral's hand tightened over hers. "Does it hurt?"

"It feels like pinpricks."

"The sensation will soon go away," the doctor said, and handed Aral a towel to help wipe the tears. "Blink.

Keep blinking. Now dry your eyes and keep them closed until I return." She patted Wren on the hand and stood, addressing Aral. "Make sure she does."

"I will."

They were left alone in the quiet room, an ex-battlelord and the daughter of his former leader in the care of a deeply religious sect. It seemed surreal. "I used to think my father was a powerful man and respected across the galaxy," she said quietly. "I thought he did what he had to in order to keep the empire strong and free of religious fanatics who wanted to tear down our civilization. I figured some might not care for him because of that, but he was a good and fair leader." Even now, a tiny part of her held out hope that Aral would agree and dismiss all that she'd heard to the contrary as jealous gossip. All the wickedness she'd begun to suspect in herself would go up in smoke.

"A good and fair leader? Is that what they told you on Barokk?" He made a disdainful sound in his throat.

"I worshipped him." And it mortified her now. "I was never able to live up to his expectations."

"Be glad, Awrenkka. Be proud that you're not someone whose actions he'd admire. And that you never had to dirty your own hands in his demise." He paused. "The Triad wasn't responsible for Karbon's capture. I was. I tracked him down and handed him over to the high command."

He said it matter-of-factly, but it didn't quite hide his struggle with what he'd done. What he'd had to do. She squeezed his hand. "I heard the queen killed my father. Queen Keira. She's my age. Can you imagine how mortified he must have been? I'm not sure how much thought he ever gave to his death, but if I had to guess, he'd have wanted it at the hands of a real warrior. Like you, Aral."

Aral cleared his throat. "Neither man died at my hand." She heard him twisting the towel in his hands. Her pulse skittered nervously. "But because of it."

His voice was thick with sorrow, and even shame. Her throat began to ache. "It was you," she said. Fates. "You were behind the coup. You let the prince pass through the perimeter."

She pulled the towel off her eyes. He pressed it back in place. "Keep it on, Awrenkka."

So he was back to calling her by her birth name. "Because of your actions, my father was killed."

"Yes."

A chill rippled through her.

*He saw to the warlord's death, then married his daughter.*

Hero or murderer?

Or traitor? Until Karbon's escape, Aral Mawndarr was the last battlelord standing. He'd wiped out every last one of his kind.

Her stomach ached. Blind, she gripped Aral's hands with her shaking ones and thought back to the day they'd first laid eyes on each other. It had been the briefest of exchanges, but it had affected both their lives. She'd seen a lost boy, not a man capable of brutal violence. What in fate's name had happened in between that day and now?

"I did it for you. I did it for us all. Despise me if you will, but I don't regret bringing down this empire. I don't know what our civilization started out as, but in the end it was rotten, rotten to the core. Evil beyond redemption. Just as my father was. Karbon." The name made him shudder with revulsion. "He was a monster of the same ilk as the warlord…with one difference. Your father practiced his cruelties on those outside his family. Not so Karbon. In fact, he seemed to derive the most pleasure in torturing those closest to him."

She moved to take off the towel again. "No." He pulled her hand away. "Keep your eyes closed." He pushed to his feet. "One day, he raped and murdered our schoolteacher, if only because Bolivarr and I loved her."

"Aral…" His name spilled out on a horrified gasp.

"I tried to save her, and he…" She heard his breath hitch. "He…"

"No." She lurched out of the chair. Eyes closed, she found him, letting him crush her into his arms. "I don't need to know more."

He took a shuddering breath. "Between the drugs and the beating, I couldn't be revived right away. I nearly died. When I did regain consciousness, he was gone. He stayed away for a year. It was the longest period of time he remained on assignment. It coincided with some of the Coalition's worst defeats, the bloodiest campaigns. But that day I woke, I made the decision to stop him, to *end him.* I set out to punish him like he punished us. His family meant nothing to him. His status, his power, his empire did.

"I was on guard the day the warlord and your half brother died. I'd been passing intelligence all along, for years. I knew the Coalition prince was desperate to rescue his wife, the queen, from their clutches. I allowed the prince's ship through the perimeter. I did this, and I acted alone. I knew where the battlelords had run to hide. I gave their locations to Zaafran. Every last one."

Wren clung to him as tears ran down her cheeks, some from the meds, some that were real. Aral Mawndarr had singlehandedly brought the empire to its knees, a civilization tens of thousands of years old. Thinking that she didn't know her husband very well had become a gross understatement.

"The warlord blamed blindly, punishing others for the losses no one could explain. Battlelords were executed on his orders for the so-called lapses that *I caused*. Sadistic men, their passing didn't sadden me in the least. I used the opportunity to befriend the warlord."

"My father," she whispered, knowing now where he'd go with this.

"I became a favorite. I was a frequent guest in the palace. I advised him. I made him laugh. He thought he'd befriended me as much as the man was capable of having a friend." His voice dropped lower as he slid a hand over her damp cheek, cupping her face. Fates, if only she could open her eyes to see what was in his. "I could have committed my treason without becoming the warlord's confidant. Easily. But there was more I wanted. There was a reason for my madness."

He tensed at that word, his muscles bunching under her hands. "I left my morals at the door when I'd step into that palace. I cheered him his victories, and shared in the celebration. I turned my cheek to all manner of depraved behavior carried out within those palace walls. I was his friend. I tried to do so without compromising myself, but at times…" He paused, swallowing. "At times it was difficult. Then, one day everything I'd worked for, and hoped for, came to be. He offered me his daughter. I took it. That, sweet Wren, I did for you."

His fingers slid into her hair at the base of her skull. "May I kiss you, Wren?" His deep voice sent shivers spinning down her spine. She was his wife, willingly or no; he didn't have to ask. He had every right to take, to force her hand, as was the way of their people, the way of *the Horde,* for thousands of years. He didn't. He asked. It set him apart from all the others, even Sabra. Not once had anyone ever asked what *she* desired.

*"Don't be fooled. The boy will turn out like the father. A Mawndarr."* Sabra's long-ago warning screamed in her mind.

Wren's instincts urged her to flee Aral. This was the trap she'd always feared, what she was certain would be the death of her spirirt: marriage to a battlelord. To a Mawndarr.

Run? Like a scared girl? Where was her courage? There was no freedom to be gained in running, in giving in to her fear. She needed to trust her instincts that told her she could trust Aral. Her newfound strength would make her his equal.

And soon, perhaps, his lover, she thought as his caresses melted the last shreds of her resistance. "Yes," she murmured, "kiss me."

As she held her breath in anticipation and pleasure, he placed one, single, soft-as-a-whisper kiss in the center of her lips. He'd hardly touched her and she was already shaking. He hovered close, his lips grazing her temple. Her blood heated to the boiling point as his lips traced a downward path along her hairline.

"It is time." The physician's melodic voice interrupted.

They moved apart but slowly, reluctantly. Aral kept a hand on Wren's arm to steady her—or was it to steady himself? Her body sang from his tender kiss.

"Open your eyes, child."

Wren used the towel to blot excess moisture. Then, holding her breath, she blinked her eyes open. And gasped. She'd been able to see with the glasses, but not like this. "Oh…my…" There were no words to describe it. What was always muted and blurred before was startlingly bright and clear, *vivid*. Everything looked bigger, closer. She'd never known what she'd missed. *The warlord did.* Yes, this is what he'd kept from her, either through sheer neglect or to keep her under his thumb. Never again. She soaked in the sight of Aral's hard and handsome face. Happiness glowed in his eyes. They weren't black, she realized, but charcoal-gray inside a darker ring. They'd seen so much pain, so much violence, and loss. She was able to put joy there.

"Tell, me, child, what do you see?"

"A hero." Wren smiled. "I see my husband."

ARAL HONESTLY COULDN'T recall the last time he'd allowed himself true joy. A rusty emotion indeed. In Wren's eyes he was a hero, not a lunatic. If only she had an idea how much that gaze meant to him, her first taken without her glasses. He made sure he remembered to take her old glasses from the exam room. What was left of them. He no more wanted to shatter them than he did this moment. "I'll save these for you to remember how far you've come."

Miraculously, her arms rose. He caught her hands halfway to his shoulders and drew her close. His mouth was on hers, and she was kissing him back with the heat of passion. Her skin was hot, her scent intoxicating, her body yielding. The need to hold her close went beyond wanting to console her, and wanting her to forgive him for all his mistakes, all his imperfections, all the invisible inner scars left from boyhood. They shared something, he and Wren, something that ran so deep he struggled to define it. He only knew that he'd never felt this way before. *Could not* feel this way with any other.

Then he remembered where they were—in a sanctuary, in front of *a priestess*. Almost roughly he pulled away before somehow calming himself, cradling her face in surprisingly gentle hands. Her violet eyes were as black as the band dividing twilight and space. As black as sin. He wasn't a believer, but he had every reason to believe a night with Wren would be something close to heaven.

"Thank you, sister," Wren gushed, gripping Aral's hand. "Thank you for my eyes."

Beaming at their joy, the woman simply nodded, smiling, as she waved at the door, signaling that they should go.

IT WAS A NEW WORLD. Wren couldn't help but gasp at the tiniest things as they walked outside. "Everything's so colorful. So clear." Pirouetting, she felt like a newborn child. "I have a lifetime of seeing to make up for."

"And I a lifetime of loving you." With one big hand, Aral cupped the back of her head, sweeping her close. Aral was disciplined and cold, controlled. But it wasn't the way he kissed. How she yearned to feel his hands on her bare skin, his hot mouth on her body. Everywhere. It was said Rakkuu blood ran hot. It was one thing she'd inherited from the warlord that she actually didn't mind having. No wonder her father had kept her locked away on a faraway all-female planet. He worried about *this*.

Perhaps he did, but the reality of her situation dictated having to wait to know Aral more intimately. There would be no normal life for them until she completed her quest.

THEY RENDEZVOUSED with Vantos and Kaz at the gate to Issenda. They buckled, holstered, and stowed their various weapons. "So what do you think now that you can see?" Vantos asked Wren, throwing his arms out wide.

Joyously she soaked in the sight of the sky and the hills, everything. "It's incredible. More than words can describe."

Vantos sucked smugly on a nanopick. "I knew you'd like me once you saw me."

"Boor," Kaz muttered, her dark eyes amused and disgusted at the same time.

"Are the provisions fully boarded?" Aral asked, all business again.

"Yeah. We're done. We're ahead of schedule, but I don't want to jinx anything." Wren started walking away with the men before she noticed that Kaz hadn't followed. She remained with the blond sister, conversing with her, their voices too low for even Wren to hear. For a wild moment she thought that Kaz might want to stay behind. Then, solemnly, Kaz reached for her ruby earrings and removed them, dropping them one at a time into her hand. "There." With a rueful smile, she carefully arranged them on the same polished slab where they'd placed their weapons earlier. "A gift for the sanctuary."

Kaz flicked a moist gaze at Aral, avoiding Vantos's baffled gaze completely as she swept past the men in the direction of the ship.

"My brother gave them to her," Aral explained.

In farewell, the blond sister made the sign of the goddess. "By the stars of Ara Ana, go in peace."

Wren halted so fast that her boot heels skidded on the dirt. This time there were no glasses to worry about jostling off her nose. Her heart bouncing, she turned back to the woman. "Ara Ana," she whispered. "It's the birthplace of the goddesses, yes?"

"Wren, no," Aral and Vantos cautioned at the same time.

"Do you know where it is?"

"We remember all," the priestess supplied.

"We're trying to find it, but I've never been here before."

"No." The sister bowed her head once and with respect. "But your mother has."

# CHAPTER SIXTEEN

ARAL SWUNG WREN AWAY from the priestess, his pistol coming up. Vantos and Kaz had theirs unlocked and ready to fire an instant behind him. "No," Wren cried, lunging at him. "Please."

"She knows who you are." Alarm ripped through him. Fates, not this. Not now. He should not have let down his guard.

"Stop it." Wren pulled on his arm, almost tearing off his sleeve. "Don't!"

*"Don't!"* Into his mind burst the horrible image of him taking his father's shirt in his fists as he tried to pull him away from a sobbing Nanjin, his ill-fated teacher. *"Let her go. Father, please."*

Aral coughed out a curse. Racked with self-loathing and shock at being put in the same place as his father, he pulled back but didn't lower his weapon. "She's a *priestess,* for fate's sake," Wren yelled, her eyes blazing. "She wants to help." Furious, she pushed at Aral, and almost did the same to Kaz. Then she seemed to catch herself, staggering a few steps away to gulp deep breaths.

"Wren?" Was she hurt?

She thrust out an arm. "I'm fine. I...need a moment."

She swiped a hand over her hair, calming herself. "Better now," she whispered, turning back to the group.

"We'd better get out of here," Vantos said, low and easy.

"Agreed," Kaz said curtly. The fear he so rarely saw in her face was back. They were trapped away from their ship and their identities were compromised.

The strapping blond woman had observed the entire spectacle with little outward reaction, and certainly no fear. "Sorry," Wren told her. "I'm sorry for what my father, my people, did."

"They are forgiven. Go. Go now."

"But my mother…what do you know about her?"

"Wren." This time Kaz urged her to leave. But Wren seemed as uncaring of the danger as the priestess was sad.

The woman's facial expressions were hidden by the silk. Only her blue eyes told of her feelings. "If you are here and not her, then…it is not good. I'm sorry." She paused, her voice lower. "You have her eyes. That's how we know." Then she drew herself up to her full height, resembling a warrior more than a priestess. "Go quickly. Go now."

Wren put her hands together, stepping backward as she bowed. "May the goddess be with you."

"And also with you."

Before the woman had even finished the sentence Aral was shoving Wren ahead of him. "We must egress now." No matter what her thoughts about the strange priestesses here, they knew who she was. Unexpected as hells, but it had happened. How? The only people other than himself who knew what Wren looked like were dead, executed for war crimes—he'd made sure of it. Except for Karbon. Impossible. His father didn't keep company with believers. He slaughtered them.

*You almost did.*

He cringed. Fates. He'd never deliberately attacked believers, but in that moment the sister had been an enemy and, had the war-lust of defending Awrenkka overtaken him, he would have.

Wren jerked free of his grip. Proud, drawing her weapon, she pulled out in front.

He strode hard to match her pace. How did such a small woman walk so fast? "That was a foolish risk you took. Had she been a hostile, you'd be dead now."

"But I'm not." Her banked fury simmered. "She knew my mother, Aral. She recognized me because of our eyes."

"Another disturbing turn of events." Wren would be recognizable to some because of her unique eye color. And what had he gone and done? Encouraged her to go without glasses. She would have been better served hiding her eyes. "No more shore excursions for you." He couldn't abide the thought of anything happening to her. "If we need to dock, you stay aboard."

"Not on Ara Ana I won't."

He swore. He'd forgotten all about her guardian's death wish. He'd never keep Wren from it. A sense of frustrated helplessness gripped him. His gut clenched, his lungs hungry for air. He was at the receiving end of his father's fists all over again, a spectator at Nanjin's killing. *No.* This was now, that was then. He took a shuddering breath and separated the two. "I'm going to be at your side every moment, whether you like it or not, Wren. If I have to kill to keep you safe I will."

Her chin jutted out, her violet gaze snapping with

challenge. Then her fury dissolved into something he didn't understand. Slowly, evenly she said, "Then be sure, Aral. Don't press that trigger unless you are. If anyone dies because of me, it will be justified self-defense." Her fingers touched his sleeve, dragging along his bicep before she pulled her hand away and made a small fist. "I want to live, Aral. You made it so. But no more deaths on my conscience. I have a billion weighing on my shoulders, thanks to my father."

They stomped up the gangway. This time the runner had left the security feature off, thank the fates. They had the hatch opened and then closed in seconds. Wren pulled the pendant from her blouse and set it on the navigation console. The glassy black face with its five, piercing lit jewels stopped all of them for a moment. "She knew I had this. It must have been my mother's. Somewhere in her life Lady Seela made it to Issenda. How? Why? As an eligible beauty her movements would have been as controlled as mine were. After her marriage, she would have been in my father's control. How did she find her way here? It doesn't seem possible." She seemed to lose herself in studying the pendant. "If this was once hers, how did it make its way back to me?"

"And how did my brother come to know it?"

Nodding, she turned pleading and determined eyes to Aral. "I want to find out what happened to her the same way you want to know about your brother."

Aral took the pendant and handed it to Vantos. "I would guess that there are coordinates to Ara Ana embedded in nanocoding."

Vantos held it up to the light, then slid it under a

scanner to await the results. "Look at that," he said, leaning forward to look at the screen. "The road map to wealth. Ah yes. I believe I'm about to get rich."

The runner might be celebrating. Aral felt like doing anything but as they accelerated away from Issenda. *Be sure, Aral. Don't press that trigger unless you are.* Wren's demand echoed in his aching skull. How sure did she want him to be? If he hesitated, he'd lose her. He knew it as surely as he breathed. Yet if he killed without any forethought, was he not just like his father?

No. Karbon killed with abandon and with glee.

*He* killed through necessity. Or was his opinion based on point of view only?

Bloody hells. He remained silent, his hand in a fist on the armrest of his chair.

There was a downside to being an undefeated battle-lord, he thought. He did not know how to take defeat. Bringing Wren under his protection had been so irrevocably linked to destroying his father and the Drakken Empire that he'd never envisioned failing. The priestess on Issenda knew Wren's mother. It proved danger lurked around every corner. No matter how many precautions he took, he could be blindsided.

He thought of the nightmare he'd had the night Wren first came to comfort him. Was it a premonition or simply a manifestation of his fears? No matter, he'd lost her. It was a warning he'd better heed.

BOLIVARR APPEARED in the doorway to Hadley's office. In the mode of security officer he was all business, but she knew him well enough to detect the slight amusement lighting up his dark eyes. "Bed-check failure. Two cadets didn't make it back to their quarters for curfew."

"Which ones?"

"Holloway and M-19."

Sighing, she closed her captain's log. "I'll help you look for them. I've been working on reports too long. Zaafran wants images of the surface."

"That's Garwin's job."

"The prime-admiral wants my commentary anyway, in daily reports."

"My guess is that the attacks on the priestesses have him worried. In this planet he sees the intersection of a mission he cares about and religious artifacts he can't afford to lose."

"He needs to have faith in me."

"He does. You're young. You're a favorite. I think at times he sees you as a daughter. That comes with its benefits and its costs."

Daughter, yes. Her previous commanding officer could be almost motherly at times. What was it about her that brought out parental tendencies in senior officers? "I want to be a captain in his eyes, Bo. Not a child." When would that day come? Who knew if the planet they were racing to visit was even remotely connected to Ara Ana, but it was clear she had to excel in this mission to gain any esteem. "If I don't prove myself to Zaafran and the entire high command, I'll be seen as a girl the rest of my career."

Bolivarr gave her a private smile. "I don't see you as a girl."

"Thank the goddess." Her tension released in a soft laugh. "Now, making sure rooks are where they're supposed to be at the required times will help, eh? It's a small ship. How many places can they be?" She paused, thinking of all the trouble teenagers got into. "You checked the boys' bunks, right?"

"That's the first place I looked when they didn't check in for curfew. Short of making a shipwide announcement and waking the sleepers, let's walk the ship." He rubbed her back. "Plus I get to see you before my shift starts and yours ends."

She recalled the times she'd patrolled the *Unity* after hours with Admiral Bandar. Once, the woman confided in Hadley it was how she unwound after her hours on duty, contemplating how she could have done things better, what lessons she'd learned, and sometimes, on the darker nights, saying her personal farewells to crew members lost in battle. Even when peace stuck, the admiral never gave up the custom. Hadley could see why. The hum of a well-run ship soothed her. A ship that she ran. So far all had gone smoothly. Barring a few cadets who forgot about bedtime.

"Are you sleeping better?" she asked Bolivarr.

"Trying. The meds help."

"I thought you said they were too strong."

"That's why they're helping." His mouth thinned. Faint shadows were still visible under his eyes. "They blank out my dreams. No dreams equals no night waking."

"Doc said if they interfered with your REM sleep, he was pulling you off them."

Bolivarr brought his finger to his lips.

"Bo…"

"You don't know what it's like," he said a little too sharply. Instantly the wall rose up between them. "It's like having someone else's thoughts, Hadley. I guess it's still me, but I don't know *that me*. I don't know if I want to."

"Why?" she asked quietly.

A muscle in his jaw pulsed. "I think I may have hurt someone. *Killed*."

"You were a wraith. That's what you were trained to do." She hated to think about it, but there it was. Fortunately wraiths operated most times as solitary assassins. Mass murder was left up to the warlord and his battlelords. It was all that had saved Bolivarr from being tried as a war criminal. "Of course you killed. Most of the people we know have killed in some fashion, either directly like you or on a huge ship in battle. We're soldiers."

"Then why do I feel guilt over it? Guilt over something I don't remember doing, or why."

They were patrolling the ship without really seeing it. Hadley stopped. "We're going to have to backtrack. I wasn't even looking."

He met her eyes with a sheepish smile of his own. "Me, neither."

His hand brushed against hers, all the affection they could show in such a public place. She searched his face, looking for answers and finding none. "I'm not going to keep quiet about something that's going to hurt you. If those meds make you sicker, then I don't want you to take them. We'll find something else to help."

He nodded, exhaling. "A little longer, Hadley. Give me that."

"All right. I'll be watching you. You were doing really well." Or did he put on a good face? Sometimes it seemed as if she could read him so easily. And other times? His waters ran cold and deep and left her out.

They retraced their steps then resumed their rook roundup. The shuttle docking area was peaceful. In days it would be bustling when they reached the planet they'd dubbed Ara Ana. Laughter and the smell of roasted snap-nuts drew Bolivarr to the pilot ready room. He peeked in the door. Chairs flew backward as three pilots stood, seeing her standing behind Bolivarr. Cards, snacks and piles of queens as bets were arranged on the table. A bottle of liquor was two-thirds full. The fourth pilot was on sleep shift and, she hoped, sober. "Captain," they said, seeing her standing behind Bolivarr.

"At ease."

"Looking for a couple of rooks. The Earth girls," Bolivarr said. "See them?"

"No, sir."

They left the men to their game.

In the main part of the ship, the mid-shifters were already coming on duty, headed for the mess hall for their breakfast. Everyone shook their heads. "Nope, haven't seen them."

"You might see if they're with Sister Chara," the assistant mechanic suggested, standing in line for a helping of ground-meal and fruit. "They were at the service earlier."

"The service?" Hadley lifted a brow at Bolivarr. M-19 wasn't religious, and Ellen was of an Earth sect called Catholic and viewed her services through the comm. Neither practiced as believers. But ever since they'd started work on their special project translating runes with Sister Chara, their interest in the way of the goddess had soared, if only academically. It was hoped the writings would yield hints as to where relics might be found. Of course that was based on a big supposition:

that the planet otherwise known as 95834-UTF was actually Ara Ana. Regardless, what had started out as a special project had seemed to turn into a labor of love.

As they neared the sister's study, the scent of incense lured them closer. Hadley tapped on the door. "Sister?"

From inside the study, a young female voice coughed out a startled curse in Earthling English that Hadley still recognized from Tango's vocabulary. Ellen Holloway, Hadley thought with an exasperated smile. In the next instant, she heard the girl apologizing to the sister for her language.

The commotion had Bolivarr shaking his head. "Well, it's the safest place on the ship they could be."

The priestess opened the door. "My children, I have been a bad member of this crew, keeping the girls here past curfew and not making sure they had their PCDs." Technology was not something at the tops of many priestesses' minds, particularly one as advanced in years as Chara. "They were immersed in their translations, and wanting to hear the old tales. I'm afraid I let it get out of hand."

"The cadets should have known better," Hadley said sternly, but wanting to smile at the sight of the way M-19 and Ellen stood, shoulders pressed together, at perfect attention. "No matter how fascinating the task, duty comes first." She turned to them. "Number one, accountability."

"Yes, ma'am."

"Do you realize I was moments away from initiating an all-ship call to roust you two out from wherever you were hiding?" Bolivarr also managed a frown at the upset girls. "That would have compromised the sleep cycles of a third of the crew, and thus the safety of this ship."

"Yes, sir."

The pair looked positively gloomy.

"Would you care to come inside?" The sister invited them in with a wave of her gnarled hand. After a point the aging process was beyond the reach of nanomeds. Hadley guessed the priestess to be at least 130.

A reproduction of an ancient text lay open on a table. The room was lit dimly, the scent of incense thick. Hadley almost sneezed.

Bolivarr halted by the table. His gaze stumbled over the pages of the open book. The sister watched him carefully. "They've worked long and hard on their translations," she explained as he studied the runes. His face was unreadable, his body tense as he traced the shape of the five marks with his hand.

"The five marks point the way to the inner Keep on Ara Ana," Ellen said, reciting. "'Closed to all but she with a heart pure and true.'"

"Maybe it's one of us," M-19 said, equally dreamy. "We'll be able to open it."

The people of Earth were as prone to believing fairy tales as Taloans, Hadley thought.

"Pure and true means 'priestess' in the old tongue," Sister Chara explained. "Priestesses take vows of poverty. And celibacy."

"On the *Cloud Shadow* it means that those pure and true of heart don't miss curfew," Hadley scolded, girding herself against their crushed expressions. "Soldiers also understand when they have to be confined to quarters as a consequence for ignoring it."

"Yes, ma'am," they chorused.

The girls' sincerity tugged at her, and reminded her a bit of herself. "I love your enthusiasm. But I need to know that when all hells breaks loose, my people are where they need to be—or where they say they are. No matter where you go in your careers, rooks, those you fight with—" she stopped herself, remembering the treaty "—and those you protect peace with expect and deserve the same from you."

Goddess, Hadley thought as she watched them go. She'd just told the prince-consort's niece to go to her room. Although they'd taken the lecture like troupers, it made her feel a bit guilty. She'd been in their boots not so long ago. But she was a young captain, untried; if she looked the other way too often she'd soon lose respect of the crew. Admiral Bandar said that being captain of a ship was a lonely job. Hadley was lucky. She'd tasted only a little of that truth. She had Bolivarr.

He scanned the runes. "What's this one, Sister?"

"It's the symbol for a key."

He nodded. "And this?"

"Keeper."

He tapped his finger on the last symbol, his eyes narrowing. "I know this one. I know what it means. Keeper..." He grabbed a stylus as if about to sketch a picture on the datapad, dropping the stick a moment later to press a fist to his forehead. "Gods," he said tightly. Fist clenched, he gave his arm one quick shake, as if holding an enemy at bay.

She rushed up to steady him. "Pain" he coughed out. "Searing— Gods, those bastards." Swallowing convulsively, he turned regretful eyes to her. "They don't want me to remember," he half whispered. "Every time I get close, every time I feel I'll break down that wall and see, *finally see,* it's like a knife plunged in my head."

Sister Chara made a small sound of horror. Hadley had, too, the first time she'd heard Bolivarr use that expression to describe the inhumane methods of thought suppression practiced on Imperial Wraiths to ensure they never recalled what they weren't supposed to. She supposed it would have been cheaper and less work to simply kill the wraith to keep a secret, but their training took too long. Too much was invested to throw them away. So they turned the wraith's own mind into a vault never to be opened—without killing them.

She rubbed a hand over his back. The muscles were rock-hard with tension. "I know what it means." He gazed at the runes the way a man dying of thirst eyed a glass of cold water held just out of reach. It was the closest she'd ever seen him come to recollection. He was standing at the edge. All he needed was the right trigger to push him to the other side.

Again he recoiled, hissing in pain.

"Let it go for now," she coaxed. "It's not time. Don't force it."

Squinting from his headache, Bolivarr swiped a hand over his face. "I'll make sure the rooks made it back to their quarters. Knowing those two, there's no telling where they might end up." He walked into the corridor, unsteady on his feet.

After he was safely gone, Hadley leaned over the small table, her weight resting on her hands. Sister Chara observed her, her expression one of compassion. "It must be difficult to see him suffer, Captain."

"Very. I don't always know how to help."

"Being there is the greatest help."

Hadley smiled softly. "I hope so."

"Sit, please."

The woman did so herself, leaving Hadley little choice. In a way, it was with relief that she joined the priestess. The woman was a religious figure and Hadley did not have to worry about displaying what could be perceived by others on the crew as weakness. Save Bolivarr. He was her best friend. She told him everything.

"I think your Bolivarr knows much about these ancient symbols—more than even me. I see how the boy struggles, how he wants to know more. And yet doesn't want to. He fears what he is."

Shivering, Hadley leaned forward and tapped a finger at the runes. "Key. Keeper. Tell me what they mean."

"Keepers were the original guards of the goddesses. Heaven's knights. Keys were specially chosen priestesses. They possessed the ability to open the sanctum on Ara Ana. The privilege is passed down through maternal bloodlines like divine blood is passed goddess queen to goddess queen. There were several such family lines at one time. Quite possibly, they're all dead now. The Hordish campaign of genocide played no favorites, child. My research on this subject has been my life's work. It's why I was invited along on your expedition." Chara dropped her voice to a private tone. "Scholars of antiquities like me believe Keys and Keepers existed. *Do* exist. And that there is a clandestine group of Imperial Wraiths who carry on the tradition, chosen and trusted through the centuries to protect the Keys and keep the birthplace safe—and secret."

"So you think Bolivarr may be a Keeper," Hadley whispered, her heart racing.

"Or he hunted them for the warlord, if the warlord knew of them. I don't know which."

*Goddess.* The thought chilled her instantly.

"See, if the warlord wanted to find the birthplace and the legendary treasure he'd need a Key. The way to a Key is through her Keeper, her protector."

"But Keepers and Keys are *Drakken.*" The "godless" Drakken as guardians of the birthplace and its sanctum? "The birthplace is Coalition. It doesn't make sense."

"It does if you realize that the schism was more than simply Drakken and Coalition splitting. It was a rift within the very order itself. In those days it had nothing to do with the two sides we know. Those staying behind in the original Hordish lands didn't want the others fleeing with everything. They refused to let the contents of the sanctum go to one side and not the other. Not until they were assured the galaxy could be whole again. They've kept it under their protection ever since, throughout the entire war."

And now the war was over. Previously forbidden regions were opening up, relics were being recovered after being plundered, hoarded and plain old forgotten for centuries.

Was Bolivarr keeping the ultimate secret? Was Bolivarr a wraith-protector, a Keeper? The alternative was unthinkable.

## CHAPTER SEVENTEEN

A FAMILIAR CHIMING dragged Hadley awake. Then she felt Bolivarr's arms slide from around her waist. Goddess, they were still in bed! Silent and in need of her, he'd come to her quarters after assuring the cadets were safe. He'd made love to her with an almost desperate edge she'd decided not to question. It left them both exhausted. The last thing she remembered was spooning afterward, then—

"Captain Keyren." She groped for her PCD and hooked it over her ear. Even as she spoke, Bolivarr was pulling on his uniform pants. Everyone knew they had a relationship that preceded this mission. They were supposed to keep the intimate aspect of the affair from the eyes of the crew.

"It's me, Garwin."

She winced at the archaeologist's complete absence of military protocol. "Go ahead."

"I thought you'd like to know that we're ready to establish orbit."

Outside the floor-to-ceiling porthole in her quarters, a lovely planet rotated slowly below, closer than ever before. The planet everyone hoped was Ara Ana, perhaps her more than anyone else after last night's revelations.

Cloud strewn oceans cast soft, bluish light into the room. Where day became night over the curve of the planet, equatorial storms flickered like glow bugs on a Talo summer evening. They'd been in sight of the planet for well over a day. Even from that distance she'd been hypnotized by the beauty of the far-flung world. The pull was even more so now.

"I can't reach the security officer," Garwin said.

She snapped her gaze from the scene outside and exchanged a pained glance with Bolivarr. "He's with me. We were meeting late." She winced even as she said it. It was the middle of her rest period. What "meeting" would go that long?

She ended the call. "Flarg."

Bolivarr touched her arm to reassure her. "I should have known better than to let us fall asleep."

She grabbed the edges of his unbuttoned shirt and pulled him close. "But it was wonderful. It's been too long since we stayed the night together."

Bolivarr's mouth curved into a sexy, sleepy smile. His glossy black hair was ruffled from sleep, his cheek creased from the pillow. He moved aside her tangled hair and nuzzled her neck. "Good morning." Their lips touched, lingered, then what promised to be a busy day began.

They finished dressing. Quickly, Hadley brushed her hair into her "battle-bridge" chignon. The ruby earrings glinted in their box next to her bedside. She hesitated, putting down her brush. She'd taken them out to sleep. Every time she saw them, she was reminded that the proposal she'd hoped for from Bolivarr hadn't materialized. They further reminded her that she was pink, not red, in nature. Her intimacy with Bolivarr didn't lack in passion and heat—last night was proof of that—but then again, he knew his way around a woman's body. She gleaned the luscious benefits of that experience, yes, but from whom did he get it? *Silly thoughts.*

Useless thoughts. She put them out of her mind as she placed the earrings in her ears. There was a planet to explore.

On the bridge, they found Garwin's team already at work using onboard equipment to locate likely sites for their initial exploration. There was a lot of terrain to cover.

The archaeologist stood hunched over a data screen with Sister Chara at his side. Hadley slowed, not expecting such perturbed expressions when moments ago all had been routine.

"Captain, there seems to be evidence of a prior visit to this site."

They clustered around the images. Garwin magnified them until they could almost see the leaves on the trees. "Someone's landed here at some point in the recent past."

"And launched." Bolivarr traced a finger around a clearing. "Fairly recently—or at least since it last rained. It's charred…here…all around the ring."

Hadley studied the landscape. She'd had plenty of tracking experience on Talo. "You can still see the paths from boots crushing the grass." The paths wound in curves and circles. "They were looking for something."

"The sanctum," Sister Chara breathed.

Disappointment dragged at Hadley. It was like receiving a gift and finding out it had already been opened. She'd wanted to be the first here. She wanted to be able to give Zaafran his wish of proving goodness existed— and before anyone else could. She straightened her spine and placed her hands behind her back. "We'll gather a team and go down to the site." Quieter, she said, "If these visitors were looking for something, I hope to goddess they didn't find it."

THE JOURNEY TO ARA ANA took *Borrowed Time* many days. Even though the nanodata in Wren's pendant contained what appeared to be precise coordinates for the planet, it wasn't until crosschecking with legend and rumors and three experienced spacefarers' best guesses that they were under way.

Each night she slept with Aral on his mat. Their closeness remained chaste but by no means dull. They had to be careful. There was so little privacy, and every sigh or moan would carry on the small ship if they weren't careful, but they'd quietly spent more hours kissing than she could count. Kissing and touching that left her ravenous for more.

His nightmares occurred but with less intensity, and he was no less ashamed of them. His atrocious past kept him in its grip no matter how hard he tried to escape it: torture, insult done to his body through drugs and beatings by the man who was supposed to love him, or at least care for him. She imagined him as a boy standing up to Karbon Mawndarr. That would be a nightmare come to life. No wonder his sleep was shattered. "Why only you and not your brother, Bolivarr?" she asked him as he held her close.

His body went rigid. She came up on her elbow, her hand on his face, not allowing him to escape the question. His eyes were dark and narrowed and rife with anguish. "Because he couldn't break me."

The sentence lingered in the shocked silence between them. "He wanted to break you—why?"

"Because he *couldn't*. He tried for all the years I was with him. I think he realized the only way he could do so was to kill me. He stopped short of that, as I stopped short of killing him." He exhaled, his eyes narrowing further. "If he'd hurt Bolivarr, I would have killed him, Wren. And by the fates, Wren, if he so much as touches you, I won't stop to think, as you want me to. If he raises a hand to you, he's done. No question. No second thoughts."

He dragged her close, at first out of pure need, then out of desire. The kiss deepened with mutual urgency. His hands slid over the swell of her breasts before starting another luscious, downward slide. She urged him on with equally hungry hands.

"I want to make love to you," he whispered, gasping as their mouths separated. "All night, and wake with you in my arms." His lips brushed over hers. "To stroke you and kiss you until you were ready for me once more." He buried his mouth in the crook of her neck, making her sigh. "Then as you went about your day, you'd carry the memory of me between your legs."

As he whispered his carnal words, he began to touch her, bringing her to pleasure. It was not difficult; his erotic promise had already carried her halfway there. Within a few breaths she was pressing her teeth against his shoulder to muffle her moan. Grabbing her wrists, he started to mount her, then a shudder ran through his body and he wrenched his mouth from hers. Breathing hard, he swore. Her eyes opened wide. He gave her little time to ponder the acute expression on his hard, noble face before he lowered his head between her breasts, groaning and quietly laughing out of the frustration she shared. "This is madness. I want you, Wren. I want to make you my wife in every way."

"I'm already yours in every way that counts."

He lifted his head, his eyes questioning and dark with need. She touched his cheek, feeling the hardness of his jaw, knowing the tenderness of the man inside and not how that gentle soul managed to survive what had been done to it. "I love you, Aral Mawndarr."

Emotion played over his face, raw and honest. "I'll see us safe, my love. We won't have to run forever. You have my word."

"Hush now. It's time to rest." She did indeed love him, and feared it. Bad things happened to those close to her. A sense of dread followed her into an uneasy slumber. It somehow came as no surprise when the ship's alarm jolted them from a deep sleep.

"We've got a target on our tail," yelled Kaz into the confines of the small ship.

They scrambled, gathering on the bridge. A blinking icon dragged her attention to the main screen. "Who is it?" Aral demanded.

"Ion signature undetermined."

"Flarg me," Vantos blurted out. "They've got no identification at all."

"Pirates? Rogues? REEFs?" Kaz wondered aloud.

"Or loyalists," Wren warned. Karbon was on the loose. The resistance was a real threat. Falling into his father's hands would be a fate worse than death.

Vantos jumped into his seat. "I'm not hanging around for the rest of the guessing game, boys and girls. They're definitely tracking us. Everybody tied down?"

"Strap in," Aral yelled at Wren. She'd come to know that his fear came out as anger.

Vantos whooped. "Prepare for the run of your life, folks. Hang on."

Turbulence indicated the wormhole entry. The transit was prolonged. The ship shook hard. Wren stifled a moan and gripped the armrests. Her stomach seemed to stretch like rubber, vertigo making her head spin. A few more jolts and they were back in normal space. If only they could stay there.

The proximity alert wailed once more. "The bastard's still with us."

"Jump!" Aral called.

Their pursuer chased them through wormholes, one after the other. Vantos didn't give the ship a chance to recover before making another jump. He seemed to have no sense of self-survival whatsoever. He took risks only a dead man dared. Thank fates for that.

They kept up the pattern until Kaz warned that the fuselage had heated to dangerous levels. "We're leaking fuel and air and fates know what else. This pace is too hard on your ship."

"Keep going." Aral's tone was flat. He wasn't ready to give up.

Vantos drew an exhausted hand through his hair. "This area of space is riddled with instabilities. If we decide to jump, our best bet is here—" he magnified an image "—via this wormhole. It's old. I'm not too sure it's still viable."

Jumping without looking first. Since when did that bother the man?

"And ready whatever weapons you have," Aral said.

"If they follow us through this wormhole, we'll turn and fight."

"No." With the eyes of the warlord, Wren shook her head. "If we can't outrun them, we'll strike a compromise. A deal."

"No deals," Aral argued.

Vantos echoed him. "No deals."

"Doesn't my opinion mean anything?"

"No," they chorused, Kaz included.

"Not in this, Wren," Aral said. "I know where your heart is with regard to our safety, and the reason for your guilt. It makes it impossible for you to be objective."

She fell back into the chair, glowering fiercely over her hands that she'd once again pressed together under her chin.

*I understand your need to atone for your father, but I will not allow you to commit suicide.* Aral bit back the words. She'd argue and they needed all their concentration on their pursuer.

The runner readied his weapons. "I've got a small bank of missiles and a couple of relativistic bomblets—should we need them."

"On *this?*" Kaz's expression showed her disbelief.

"This crate you mean? Yeah. Thanks to a nice, unexpected trade bonus from an illegal arms dealer in the Borderlands." Vantos's hands flew over the panels as he put the weapons online. "I managed to wangle a nice little profit off the record, taking arms in place of some of the money. I sold most of it afterward, keeping a few things for my ship. You never know when you might need a bomblet or two, right?"

Aral hoped to the fates they didn't need any now.

The transit alert rang. "This passage isn't too stable. I've seen some like this before, though. I think we can make it if I hold off just shy of max hyperspeed and coast out the back side."

"Weapons alert!" Kaz cried. "They've armed their plasma cannons."

Aral had fought in many a battle over the years. They couldn't afford a hit. If they made a jump while damaged the forces of distorted space would tear them apart. "Jump now!"

The wormhole entrance wavered. It shrank then bloomed, filling the forward screen. The stars began to distort. Entry was imminent. Aral made a fist. They would make it. They *had to*. Just as they made the jump, the wormhole collapsed behind them.

# CHAPTER EIGHTEEN

BORROWED TIME CAME screaming out of the wormhole, warning alarms blaring. It had been a shrieking, jolting ride. How they had made it through a collapsing wormhole at all, Aral had no idea. Whether or not their pursuer had tried to follow was moot. They couldn't.

He shared a glance with Wren. *We made it.*

*"Hull integrity 77%. Plasma loss number two thruster. Low fuel state."*

"Flarg. We've got a hull rupture. We're leaking fuel and losing air."

So much for making it, Aral thought. He homed in on the air-remaining readout. The digits were extrapolated to the ten-thousandth place. The smallest ones were plunging so fast that they were blurred to the eye. Taunting him. One hour and thirty minutes of air. A heartbeat of time in space. *Battlelord, what will you do now?* "Can we make Ara Ana?" With all the jumping through hyperspace they'd done, they were practically on its doorstep.

"Only if we don pressure suits. I've got three. The women get two. Mawndarr—we will flip a queen to decide which one of us gets to breathe."

"Absolutely not," Wren said.

At the same time Kaz shook her head. "We're a crew. Either we all put on suits or none of us do."

Vantos looked positively touched for a moment, then schooled his features. "If we abandon ship we can make it in the escape pod." He magnified the still invisible planet many times until it filled the screen. "There you are, beautiful. At last." Then he turned back to them. "It'll be a one-way trip, boys and girls."

Kaz took the news as stoically as ever, but as he watched she lifted a hand to touch her ruby earrings, a way she sometimes seemed to connect with Bolivarr when under pressure. But the earrings were gone. And he was gone.

*"Life support reserves critical. Fuel state low."*

They had no choice. Wren found Aral's hand. He leaned close to her, his forehead pressed to hers. "I wish I could have done more for you, Wren. I wish we could have run away like you wanted."

"Ara Ana is where we're supposed to go."

"And not be able to leave?"

"We'll find a way out," she whispered.

"From the laser-fryer into the fire," Vantos growled suddenly, drawn by an incoming call. "We've got a welcoming party."

"Unidentified trader vessel, this is the TAS *Cloud Shadow.* We copy your distress signal. Do you require assistance?"

They jolted at the sound of strange voices after so long. TAS, Aral thought. That meant a Triad Alliance ship. Bloody hells. "It's the Mission Origins vessel." Not only had they beaten them to Ara Ana, they were offering them rescue.

ENSIGN MORGGIN, assistant security officer, hurried over to where Hadley stood with Garwin and Bolivarr searching for signs of inhabitation. "We've got a target emitting a Mayday. It has a trader signature. Triad. No visible threat. It's an old AG-250. Tiny, a crew of one to six, max. They're down to emergency levels of fuel and air, Captain."

"It's a long way from home for a triad trader."

"They could be our treasure hunters," Garwin postulated, looking quite possessive about his hoped-for discoveries as he frowned at the damning images.

Everything plundered, hoarded and tucked away in a thousand years of upheaval was now fair game—and irresistible for trader types with old ways of earning money drying up as fast as border skirmishes.

Bolivarr shook his head. "I'd be surprised if they're one and the same. That ship isn't made for long-distance hunting. Close-in maneuverability, yes. They're crazy to be out here."

Already the cadets, on the bridge for the orbital entry, were speculating excitedly about the turn of events. "They're probably lost," Holster said to a burst of derisive laughter from the other rooks, all clearly feeling full of themselves for having spent so many weeks in space.

"We have a duty to rescue them." Hadley turned to Bolivarr. "And quickly. Send a shuttle."

"I'll go."

No, she mouthed silently. The incident in Sister Chara's quarters was too fresh. He'd taken meds for a severe headache even as they'd left her quarters. He had no business flying in that condition.

"We're still on level-two alert," he reminded her,

trying hard not to lean on his cane. "I highly doubt these idiots were involved in the attacks of the religious settlements, but I can't take that chance. Especially now with signs someone beat us here. I want to question them."

"You can question them here."

Although he knew the reason, he seemed to struggle with her order, hating to admit to what he perceived as weakness—his tenuous health—especially if it interfered with his assigned duties. He must have seen she wasn't intending to back down, either. Or that she was indeed the captain of this ship. With a locked jaw, he nodded. She hid the shiver of relief that went through her. He hated worrying her even more than feeling shame of his physical and mental condition. "I'll send the shuttle with extra crew—armed, then," he said. "I take over once they're back."

"Approved."

Morggin called from his station. "Captain, the traders have abandoned ship. We're tracking the escape pod."

"Raise the alert to three," Bolivarr said.

Hadley nodded. "I concur."

Bolivarr left to supervise the shuttle preparation, and Garwin to organize the first of many surface visits. With security mobilized and the threat level raised to three, a sense of purpose swept through the ship—and her. Finally they were seeing some action. A rescue mission would only add to the excellent training for the cadets, even if it meant bringing aboard a group of scruffy, directionally impaired traders from their ramshackle ship.

WAITING IN THE ESCAPE POD for rescue, the Drakken looked as if they were on their way to their execution. Maybe they were, Keir thought.

Blast it all. He tossed aside the nanopick he was chewing to listen to Mawndarr's briefing. "On that ship we're going to have to watch every word we say, everything we do. Three of us are at risk of being convicted for treason. Vantos, you're the only one with a choice of sides."

"Sides? You think I'm going to spill the beans? If they find out she's the warlord's daughter, there's nothing to stop them from splitting the bounty between them while my frozen body drifts out the nearest airlock. No treasure, no bounty. Not a good deal for ol' Vartekeir. Look, I got us into this, I'll get us out."

He felt Wren's grateful gaze on him. "Nope, not hero stuff. Don't even think it. It's still about the money. It's always been about the money."

But it had become more than that.

Fates. He jammed a hand through his hair. He wasn't responsible for her or any of these Drakken. He owed them nothing. But blast it all, common decency told him he didn't deliver them into the Triad's clutches and take the spoils.

*"That's hero stuff, Vantos."* He cringed, thinking of Ellie's words back on Zorabeta. Like then as now, doing something nice for a pretty girl who just happened to be the warlord's daughter who'd lured him into her little snare telling him fifty-millions queens was pocket change didn't sound like hero stuff to him. Nope. He wasn't involved. No, just offering temporary assistance. The Triad never did anything for him. He owed them nothing.

"Look, we've got a watertight alibi. We're traders

who got lost scoping out possible new routes. We tried to jump our way back and cooked the ship."

"They're scientists," Kaz said, dismissing the Triad crew as nonwarriors the same way she'd once dismissed him. "They won't care. They're hunting artifacts."

"That *we* happen to want," Vantos said. "Our treasure."

"My treasure." Wren stared them down with her best imitation of the warlord's stare. It was surprisingly effective.

Mawndarr wasn't any happier about it than he was. Keir was a trader at risk of losing the deal of his life. And Aral? His wife.

The Triad shuttle coasted close. "Standby for tow." The closing of a mechanical arm over the pod reverberated with a clank. The stars started moving again as the shuttle turned to return home—with them in its jaws.

"A battlelord, his second, the warlord's daughter and a blockade runner hitch a ride on a Triad shuttle," Keir said to the grim group. "It sounds like the beginning of a bad joke."

Aral sat with Wren held close. Keir couldn't see her face. It was buried against Mawndarr's chest. Mawndarr, an infamous battlelord, unrecognizable in his incarnation as a trader, cradled the warlord's daughter so tenderly. He hadn't seen such easy intimacy since his parents. This was why humans sought out someone else, he thought, feeling his loneliness and blasted well not wanting to. It was why his parents fell in love and took a gamble on spending a lifetime together. No, not just for the sex. For *this*—to be able to open yourself to another. To know someone had your six. Always.

He realized Kaz was watching him, her dark eyes

curious. "Do I get a hug, too?" he asked, half hoping she'd cave in.

Kaz snorted softly. "Trader trash."

"But you say it with the utmost affection."

Her lush lips lost some of their stiffness. "Yes, actually. I do. But don't read into it."

"I thoroughly intend to." They regarded each other in the pod's snug confines. Keir leaned a shoulder insolently against the inner wall—or, rather, he leaned his shoulder as insolently as a man could in the total absence of gravity.

Shaking her head, Kaz made her way to a seat. With a firm hold on the handgrip behind his head, Keir tried to keep his legs from floating up in front of his face and obscuring his view of one hells of a cute ass moving under standard-issue trousers he was sure weren't designed to spark the imagination. But despite all reasonable efforts to assure a different reaction, Kazara Kaan did spark his imagination—in a decidedly un-commerce-like way.

Kaz drew the straps over her head. The movement sent her short hair swirling around her face like ink poured in water. *Don't try to get close to me.* The sentiment was written all over her face.

"Don't you have something else to do, Vantos?" she asked.

"A good-luck kiss would be nice."

She made a choking noise. He'd actually startled a laugh out of her. Imagine that. The woman who had treated him with unrelenting, absolute disdain from the moment they'd met, a battlelord's second who reserved the lion's share of her respect and regard for Mawndarr, and who saw the fact that he'd quit the military as instant points against him. Even if that military service would have meant fighting as her enemy. To her, civilians were as boring and necessary as the supplies stashed in a cargo hold. As meaningless as chem-toilets. "So, you like me now."

"I hate you."

*Liar.* "It makes you a challenge."

"I told you—I don't want to be involved with anyone, Vantos."

"Keir. Sexy beast is fine, too."

Her expression chilled further but two spots of pink appeared on her cheeks. Oh, yes, he was breaking down the walls. It made the humiliating tow-in to the Triad ship almost bearable.

She focused on him again, this time as if sizing him up. For what purpose, he had no clue, but that gaze did something to him. He wanted to be with her, he decided. At least give it a try. It completely and overwhelmingly went against everything he stood for. Not only for what she was, a Drakken, but for who he thought *he* was. His standard operating procedure told him one thing, but when he was in this woman's company, the rest of him was telling him something completely different....

Keir closed his eyes and leaned his head back against the uncomfortable seat for the duration of the trip. He'd lost his ship and just about everything else that mattered. He wasn't going to throw away his bachelorhood, too.

A LOUD, HOLLOW CLANG left Aral with no doubt they'd been released from the shuttle's tow claw. "We've been deposited in their cargo bay," he explained to Wren.

"From hauling cargo to being cargo," Vantos muttered.

A voice on the comm instructed. "Disembark and proceed through decontamination. Leave all weapons behind."

Vantos popped the hatch. With an ear-popping cold rush of air, they stepped into the cavernous cargo bay. It was as if they were alone on the ship. From the cockpit of the shuttle, a gloved hand motioned toward the decon tubes. Aral nodded his understanding and the pilots replied with a friendly wave. So far they'd been treated with cordiality and understandable reserve. It said a lot about the captain of this vessel. It was a well-run ship.

He held fast to Wren's hand as they stood in the decon mist. They were a married couple. It was the one part of their reality that he wanted as part of their ruse. It would ensure they were able to share quarters.

The doors opened to a larger bay filled with supplies of various kinds. He and Wren exited first as Vantos and Kaz then stepped into the decon chamber behind them.

"Welcome to the *Cloud Shadow.*"

A young, pretty blond woman greeted them. With his battlelord's observation, he noted the captain's stripes decorating her sleeves and labeled her instantly as inexperienced in her role but sharp, her confidence a thin veneer over her uncertainty in her new position.

Her steps faltered, and she paused, giving Wren no more than a quick friendly glance but staring outright at Aral in definite recognition. His heart accelerated. Had Zaafran sent a picture around? Witness descriptions from Zorabeta, or of his father, Karbon?

No. That wasn't it. Her eyes held no threat. Only shock. Wren must have noticed, too. Her hand squeezed his in warning as the captain turned to a tall, lean golden-skinned man striding into the bay to join them. He flashed a smile at them, his gaze only momentarily tripping over Aral.

A smile Aral knew. A gaze he could never forget—or mistake. *Bolivarr.* Aral made a quiet, choked sound in his throat as his ears rang with a rush of roaring blood. His brother was alive!

# CHAPTER NINETEEN

ARAL GRASPED his brother's hand in greeting, too hard, loath to let go, wanting to crush the man into an embrace.

Bolivarr's smile wobbled. "Do we know each other?"

"Yes." Pressure built behind Aral's eyes. *Fates, yes.* "It's Aral."

No recognition flooded Bolivarr's eyes. No accompanying shouts of joy. Aral shoved aside the crushing disappointment. To his brother he was a complete stranger.

He wanted to bellow in rage as fury coursed through him. What did the monsters do to his brain? Whose side was responsible—the Coalition or the Drakken? Or those who didn't want the secret of the five marks getting out? He sent an accusatory glare to the priestess standing in the group. An ancient, she didn't recoil in fear. She met his regard straight on.

Heart thundering, Aral tried to tell himself it didn't matter. The only thing that was important was that Bolivarr was alive.

The captain had moved closer to Bolivarr as if to protect him. Her stare had intensified; she saw the resemblance between them. She'd seen it the moment he'd stepped out of decontamination.

Aral gripped Wren's arm, drawing her close. "My

brother. Fates, Wren," he whispered in her ear. "He's freepin' here."

Her violet eyes opened wide in astonishment. In the next instant he knew she saw what the captain and what Bolivarr saw but couldn't fathom—their resemblance.

By the time Aral turned back to his brother, Bolivarr's expression had changed. It was clear his brother sensed something now but seemed to be struggling to recognize what it was. *Remember, Bolivarr. Try.* He was using a cane and seemed thinner, and of course five years older. "Aral? I'm sorry. I don't recall meeting you."

Aral simply nodded, and it was as hard as hells to do graciously. He wanted to take Bolivarr aside and shake him. He wanted to demand that he remember who he was. By the fates, how could he not know?

Brain damage. Injury. Thought suppression. It could be a hundred things, all of them agonizing as hells for Aral to accept.

But his brother didn't seem so sure anymore. The longer he studied Aral, the more he appeared to doubt they'd never met. Bolivarr was shaking now, using a cane to support more of his weight. He shifted reddened eyes to the captain as she brushed her fingers over his arm—a fleeting touch, but it told Aral there was more between them than what they were willing to reveal. Fates, Kaz.

Aral spun to where she and Vantos were emerging from decon.

Bolivarr made a raw sound. He'd seen Kaz. Everyone's eyes were on him now, all except Kaz, who in her meticulousness was dusting powdery mist off her clothing.

The captain took over. "Sit down," she advised more

tenderly than a captain normally would. But Bolivarr stepped forward, ignoring her. A muscle in his jaw jumped. Something was happening. His eyes were shining bright. "I know her, Hadley," he whispered and swallowed thickly. "I *know her.*"

Kaz was busy being greeted by a group of teenagers—military cadets, by the look of them. Appearing charmed, she glanced over at Aral, then Bolivarr. Instantly the blood drained from her face. Her look of astonishment, of utter disbelief, of joy, was all the things Aral had felt. But seeing it on her face, knowing what she'd gone through, made it all the more poignant.

Her voice held the slightest of trembles. "Bolivarr?" Aral had never heard anything uttered with such heart-rending joy.

Bolivarr's expression was equally wrenching. The cane bounced to the floor. Both the captain and Aral tried to steady him. He pushed them away, walking forward unsteadily but with increasing control. "Kaz," he whispered. "Kaz."

Aral glimpsed black eyes that were moist with tears of joy. Crying out in joy, she ran to Bolivarr, crashing into his arms, clinging to him as he crushed her close, his face buried against her throat, and leaving the captain to watch the scene with something close to pain.

Bolivarr gripped close, his eyes shut. Then moved her away, his eyes bright. They seemed to soak in each other's features to the apparent delight of the surrounding crew, with the exception of the captain. It was clear she was trying to be pleased for the sake of appearances but her feelings for Bolivarr didn't allow it.

"Well, bite me in the ass," Vantos muttered, jamming a pick between his lips. "Who the hells is that?"

"My brother," Aral said.

"I thought he was dead."

"We all did," Wren said.

As they stood outside the circle of the fevered reunion, Aral felt no less an outsider. He didn't blame his brother. He gave thanks to the fates for finding him again. Alive. He held Wren close, all the more reminded how lucky he was to have found her.

"Aral." He heard his name called in a voice he'd thought he'd never hear again. Bolivarr had set Kaz aside. In Aral's mind's eye he saw the little brother he'd always protected from his father's harsh hand, the boy who never seemed to provoke the wrath that Aral did. *He knew when to fight and when to fold. You were too stubborn.*

Slowly, one limping step at a time, Bolivarr began to walk faster in his direction. "Aral." Was that recognition in Bolivarr's eyes? "My brother," Bolivarr said with gut-wrenching awe. In the next moment they were locked in a hearty, emotional embrace.

## CHAPTER TWENTY

GODDESS, SHE WANTED TO DIE. Hadley told herself she should be joyous that Bolivarr had found his family. She should be profoundly moved by the miracle it presented. She should be experiencing many good and noble things. It was hard to do when it felt as if she'd swallowed her heart.

The woman named Kaz whispered something to Bolivarr, and he threw back his head and laughed. She'd never seen him laugh like that. Bolivarr's brother stood nearby, beaming. The woman with him was shy and quiet, her pleasure in the moment palpable. The fourth trader appeared about as pleased with the scene as Hadley was. In fact, he looked downright miserable.

Bolivarr wiped his shining eyes with the back of his hand. He beckoned her forward, not seeming to see her reluctance to do so. "I would like you to meet Kaz."

Not *I would like you to meet Hadley,* she noted. Putting her friendliest, professional captain face on, she walked up to the couple.

The *couple.* Goddess. *She* and Bolivarr were "the couple." Not Kaz and him. Everything she'd built her life around had come tumbling down.

Kaz beamed at her. Her skin looked made of marble,

contrasting with plump red lips and thick black lashes. There was an air of reserve about her, an ingrained military bearing, and she was obviously of Drakken origin, making her seem a little hard. Hadley was a Talo farm girl with no tolerance for alcohol and a propensity to giggle. Kaz for all her beauty looked as if she could down whiskey shot by shot with her male counterparts and, Hadley was certain, wore ruby earrings. In fact, her gaze did hesitate on the earrings Hadley wore. She seemed surprised to see them in her lobes. She knew in an instant that Kaz wasn't a pink woman. She was a red woman, and she was probably wondering why Hadley was wearing red gems when they were so obviously wrong for her. Where were Kaz's earrings? Surely Bolivarr would have given her a pair. It was why he'd been attracted to them inexplicably in the market on the Ring. He'd unconsciously wanted Hadley to be Kaz.

It was all Hadley could do not to pluck the blasted earrings out. She tried to wrap her mind around how different she and Kaz seemed, yet they both had Bolivarr.

"Bolivarr's been telling me about you, Captain. You served together on the *Unity,* and now here."

As Bolivarr looked on, smitten, Hadley waited for Kaz to mention the other, nonwork things—how inseparable they were, how she'd stood by Bolivarr as he healed from each of the seizures, or of their shared love for giki-fruit ices, the plans they had to get married someday even though they'd never set a date. Kaz was why. She lived in Bolivarr's heart. Although he couldn't remember her, he'd still reserved the space.

"Welcome to this ship, Kaz. We are so happy to have you here. All of you." She turned to Bolivarr. "I wish you two every happiness." She felt as if she wanted to be sick. She'd experienced heartache before, but never like this. She'd fallen hard for Bolivarr.

How passionately they'd made love last night. Their last time. She stifled a groan and did what any captain in this situation would do. She called a staff meeting. "Senior staff—in my office. Now. Morggin, escort our guests to their quarters." As Garwin listened with approval, she told the ensign privately. "And make sure you post guards."

She turned on her heel and left the shuttle bay behind. Left the sight of her lover speaking in hushed tones to the gorgeous, striking woman who'd emerged from decon and did what Hadley couldn't in all the months she'd known Bolivarr. Brought his memories back. As she rode the lift back to the bridge, Hadley kept her hands clasped behind her back. They were wet with sweat and quivering. *You are the captain of this ship. Do not forget it.* She couldn't let the implosion of her personal life get in the way of duty. She had four strangers aboard her ship, evidence of someone trespassing on the site they'd traveled light years to find, and horrifying attacks on innocent priestesses not too far from where they orbited. She couldn't think of her heart.

Goddess, it was going to be hard.

Once again she heard Brit Bandar telling her what a lonely job it was being the captain of a ship. If anything, losing Bolivarr had shown her the cold hard truth of that statement. She squared her shoulders and lifted her chin, hoping her resolve and her spirits would follow her body language.

Garwin followed her into her office. Sister Chara and Doc arrived next. The only one missing was Bolivarr.

She paced, feeling more dread as each minute crawled by. He was her security officer. He should be here.

It was time to be a captain and buck up. Keeping her breathing even, she sat at her desk. The cup that Bolivarr had drunk tea from last still sat on her desk. She closed her eyes and his face lingered now, his dark soulful eyes, his smile that was always somewhat sad. Now she knew why. He had a brother and a lover and an entire other life she knew nothing about. She tried not to think of him making love to Kaz tonight when he would have been making love to her. Her heart swelled and ached.

Her PCD chimed. "Keyren," she said as she always did, feeling nothing like her usual self.

"Hadley, I'm going to be late. I'm with my brother right now. He needed to see me. And...we really need to talk."

*I'm sure we do.*

"I'll be there as soon as I can." He ended the call.

She took a steadying breath and addressed her staff. "The newcomers will be guarded round the clock. Garwin, continue to get your landing team ready. Bolivarr will provide the security detail." If he decided to return to work. "And, Doc, I'd like you to examine him asap. We need to determine what meds if any he'll need now." She turned to her comm. She also needed to report back to Zaafran that the amnesiac wraith was no longer. But as much as duty required that she comply with her orders, she couldn't bring herself to do it just yet. She didn't know what he remembered. If it was war crimes or other atrocities, he could very well be put to death. Her heart froze over, and she realized that there was something worse than losing Bolivarr to another woman. It was losing him to the executioner.

THE BROTHERS SPOKE, heads close, gripping each other's shoulders inside the quarters assigned to them. Then Bolivarr stepped away, his face, a gentler version of Aral's, alive with emotion after the years apart were swiftly summed up. "I have to go." With a polite nod in Wren's direction, Bolivarr left.

Finally she and Aral were alone. "You didn't tell him who I am."

"I said you were my wife."

"A lie of omission. You introduced me as the daughter of a government official." In this world, *wife* or *mate* would suffice. Not in theirs. In Hordish culture a woman was always more than simply her person; she was her lineage, especially if married to a battlelord. She and Aral had discarded much of the tradition and old ways, but some things were still automatic.

"I want to be sure of him first."

"Brother not trusting brother," she said, pained to see it.

"It's been five years, Wren. I don't know where his loyalties sit now." Aral dragged a hand over his face. "We have to be careful. He's a Triad officer."

"He knew from before that you intended to rescue me."

"Yes, but not marry you."

"He's going to figure it out."

"It buys us time to think our way out of this. I'd rather be doing so on a ship in the UT than in a holding cell on a prison barge headed back to the Ring."

"They don't know this planet is the real Ara Ana. We can give them that—I can unlock the sanctum. Think of the joy it'll bring their people."

"It won't change the fact that you're to be arrested on sight, Wren."

"And so are you."

An angry sigh came from deep in his chest. "On a trumped-up charge. Lies."

"Then let's be the ones to stop them first. No more secrets."

Such love for his brother had shone in Bolivarr's eyes. It made it hard for Wren to believe he'd let them be harmed. Then she thought of Ilkka and Sabra, of her father's personal guards and the coup they had allowed. Loyalties changed when tested. She had the feeling that Bolivarr's were about to be exactly that.

AN ENTRY REQUEST to Hadley's office chirped. She'd locked it and wanted no visitors. Her data screen turned on. Bolivarr was standing outside. At first impulse she almost flew to the door. She came to her senses before she acted like a lovesick puppy. Did he come to "talk"? He ought to call it "rubbing salt in the wound."

"Hey, aren't you going to let me in?" He sounded hurt she'd locked the door.

"Enter," she said, and the door slid open. In his Triad uniform he looked as delicious as always. Blast him. She could almost pick up the scent of his skin, spicy and masculine. He shut the door behind him. He appeared different somehow. The sadness in his features had lifted. He actually looked very much in love.

He tried to reach for her hand, but she kept it tucked behind her back. It was damp and shaky anyway. "Do you love her?"

His "yes" speared her heart.

"I'm not *in love* with her like I am you." He squeezed her arm. His expression was incredulous. "It has been a shocking, amazing day."

She suddenly felt incredibly ashamed for trying to divert his attention and force him to make decisions, when all he wanted to do was savor reuniting with his loved ones.

Then he exhaled. "I've known Kaz since I was small. We were best friends. We were lovers when I left to be a wraith."

The words hit her like blows. She stood straighter, pretending they didn't hurt so much.

"She didn't want me to go, Hadley. We more or less broke up then." The next seemed hard for him to say. "But I never came back, and she grieved for me, thinking I was dead. Guilt was the worst of it for her. We parted after a terrible argument and without apologizing. She never forgave herself. And I…" He sighed. "I never gave it a thought because my mind was wiped clean, Hadley. So for her our break-up is five years old. For me it feels like yesterday. I still have to figure things out, Hadley. I admit it."

She nodded, hating that her throat was so swollen that it made talking impossible.

"I do feel something for her." His dark eyes were mournful. "But I'm not sure what, and I need to explore it." He reached for her, bringing his hand to her cheek. "I love you, Hadley. That hasn't changed."

No, but everything else had.

He brushed his knuckles down her cheek. She turned her head, and he dropped his hand. "I really am happy for you, Bolivarr," she managed and meant it. "I've wanted this for you so badly."

"I know that, Hadley. I know." The look of love on his face made her chest ache. He wasn't sure. He needed to sort things out. For a girl from Talo there were few worse things to hear. *You're also a ship captain. Be her.* "Now that you talked about what you needed to talk to me about, is there anything else?"

"But that's not what I came to talk about."

She spun back around. "If not that then what?"

He swallowed. She realized that sweat glazed his forehead. He didn't look ill. He looked afraid. He cleared his throat and said, "I know a secret with the potential to destroy us all."

# CHAPTER TWENTY-ONE

"YOUR BROTHER IS Aral Mawndarr?" They'd been in her office a half hour. Hadley's thumping heart couldn't possibly take another revelation, and he hadn't even gotten to his big secret yet. His upbringing was startling enough. And agony to hear. A sweef-addicted father commanding legions who took out his frustrations on his eldest son, who went on to bring down the entire Drakken Empire.

Her head was spinning. She walked to the window, fingers pressed to her temple. Goddess. Bolivarr was a battlelord's son. Her Bo, a *nobleman*. And she was just a farm girl. Yes, he was raised by an atrocious father, but he was upper crust, out of her league. Little wonder he needed to "figure it out" when it came to her. Her family was tuber pickers. And little wonder, too, that the earrings didn't feel right in her ears. They were more flash than someone with such humble roots was used to.

Bolivarr waited as she wrestled with everything he'd revealed. Blast his patience. Blast him being so calm, so in control when she was not. "You should have told me about Aral right away," she accused.

"I'm here doing exactly that."

"You spoke to him first."

"You're acting as if I've betrayed you in some way."

"You have." Her voice was low and a little unsteady. "There's a warrant out for his arrest. You know that, and yet you didn't do anything."

"Hadley, I haven't seen him for five years. He thought I was dead. What did you want me to do—say 'Hello, Aral, you're under arrest'?"

"If your loyalties were in the right place, you wouldn't have hesitated. You wouldn't be questioning me now."

In the face of her accusation, his eyes turned as cool and smooth as obsidian glass. Her kind and sweet Bo had vanished, leaving a cornered and possibly dangerous wraith in his place. A stranger. She realized how much she truly didn't know about him. "That's unfair," he said.

Maybe it was. Maybe she was transferring her jealousy over Kaz to this critical exchange.

"If anything, gaining my memories back solidifies my loyalty to this Triad even more," he argued. "I know what it's like to live under the warlord's rule. And I know why I despise him so."

She remembered Sister Chara's comment. "Were you a Keeper, or did you hunt them?" Just as she suspected, the question startled him. "The information on Keys and Keepers is documented in the earliest writings of our civilization. When you reacted to the runes, I asked Sister Chara to explain them to me. What were you, Bolivarr?"

"I was neither. I worked for Aral. I knew of the Keepers, though, through other wraiths. I gained the trust of a secret sect called the Hand of Sakkara. They allowed me access to the old books. I was on a quest to find a Key."

"Why?" she asked, unable to keep the fascination from her voice.

"So the warlord wouldn't. Aral and I suspected my father was hunting for her. Possession of a Key would give the Drakken unimaginable power. They'd control the goddess treasure, and the sacred planet of Ara Ana, the birth world of the goddesses. It would have broken the spirit of the Coalition, Hadley. They would have lost the war."

But not before both sides annihilated each other. "What do the five marks mean?"

"It's the sanctum itself. An obelisk that contains revelation of *everything*. To be unlocked only by the one with the blood of the goddesses in her good and pure heart, meaning a priestess. A Key. It was the first hard evidence I found that Ara Ana was real, that the treasure wasn't a myth and—" his voice quieted with awe "—that the Key wasn't a myth. I thought, *I have to find her before the empire does*. But I was being tracked. I passed Aral the intelligence in case something happened to me, then…"

"Karbon found you."

His fist on the desk, his eyes remained trained on his white knuckles. Whatever pain he felt he didn't want her to see. "On Junnapekk, in the Borderlands, he caught up to me. He wanted what I knew."

"Oh, Bolivarr." She clutched at her hands, knowing the story ended in the worst imaginable way. She held back. Helping Bolivarr, rescuing him, was easy when she'd assumed he was a smart and modest soldier. Someone like her. It wasn't the same now that he was a battlelord's brother and one with a great presence to boot—a hero, if what he told her was accurate—who was wanted by Zaafran himself. Now she was harboring a fugitive on her ship! Heaven knew what the other three with him were suspected of. Goddess help her.

When Bolivarr finally met her eyes, he seemed older, less carefree. That one look revealed how much he'd suffered and sacrificed in the name of peace, more than she'd ever done, or people she'd served with over the years who dismissed all Drakken as monsters—and still did. "One of the requirements to be a wraith was to submit to thought suppression. Trauma to the body, or meds, triggers it. My father, he… He lost his temper when he couldn't get what he was after." He clenched his jaw and sucked in a breath so quickly it sounded like a sob. Sickened, she'd never hated anything in that moment more than she did Karbon Mawndarr. "He left me for dead." The anguish in his eyes was nothing compared to what she'd glimpsed a moment ago. This was real, raw. Fresh. "He treated me no different than how he did Aral all our lives. I felt for Aral, I truly did, but I never knew how bad it was. Never, Hadley. I failed him because I never once defended him. He'd tell me to stay back, and I did. I let him defend me. That changes today. Here and now. It's a freepin' travesty that my brother stands accused of helping Karbon escape when he's the last person in this galaxy that would do so." His gaze was hard leveled at her. "I won't allow him to be taken in, not with Karbon out there and traitors on the inside. If those traitors helped our father escape, they'll make sure Aral won't. Karbon's out there, Hadley. Here in the Borderlands. Those attacks on the sanctuaries? It's him trying to find the Key. It's got his signature all over it. I'm sorry, Hadley. I won't hand my brother over." He started removing his rank.

"Wait." She stopped him before he could place the epaulets on the desk. "What are you doing?"

"Making sure you don't take the fall if I go against orders."

She paced in a circle, torn. Knowing what she knew now, she saw that the Triad was clearly in the wrong about Aral. Even the prime-admiral himself had doubts Aral Mawndarr had helped his father escape. She'd seen the officer's indecision as clear as day. But if she disobeyed the orders to hand Aral over, it was treason. She'd lose her ship, her command. And Bolivarr, too.

KEIR SCOWLED as he stalked around his ship now snug in the hangar of the Triad ship. Damage included more than a tank rupture. The entire fuselage was covered with burns, dents and scratches. The former hurt his chances of flying out any time soon; the latter just his ego.

Kaz followed him around the ship, her face paler than ever. Her arms were folded protectively across her chest. Not around Bolivarr, he noted. She hadn't mentioned anything more about the man, and that was fine with him. It wasn't as if he was jealous or anything. Who she took in her bed was none of his business. Unless it was him, of course, and he had about as much chance of that as a snowcicle in hells.

"We'll have her fixed up before you know it, sir." The *Cloud Shadow*'s crew chief was a grizzled, middle-aged bloke who looked as if he'd seen too many battles. Now peace had stuck him on a science expedition crewed by teenaged cadets. "I'm happy to have something to do. Checking coolant levels on the shuttles isn't exactly my kind of work."

"I had to run chem-toilets into the refugee camps. I know what you mean." They crouched down to look at the damage together. "How soon?"

"You itchin' to leave? You just got here."

*He's suspicious.* Keir exchanged a glance with Kaz and put on his best poker face. Hells, yeah, he wanted to be ready to get out if they had to. The only thing between Wren and Aral getting turned over to the authorities was the captain, and only because of her relationship with Aral's brother. Seeing that the relationship was hanging by a tenuous thread at the moment didn't give him a whole load of confidence in this interlude's happy ending. With the treasure on the planet below and the key in hand, more or less, he wanted as many options left open as possible. That meant a ride out.

"A businessman's got to keep on the move," he said. He wasn't going to let a few dings and dents keep him from delivering Wren to the birthplace, and the treasure into his happy hands. "What's your best estimate?"

"Well," the chief drawled. "Maybe by the end of the ship-week."

"Not good enough."

"What you're going to need is to purge the tank, do the repair, then see if it can hold the pressure. There might be other damage. I'll have to check. I like to be real thorough."

Keir got the feeling the chief was going to drag out repairs to avoid going back to the monotony of his daily duties. Keir knew all about that. He couldn't bribe the man to speed things up, either. This wasn't a fly-by-night operation. It was a little ship tightly run by a green captain determined not to make any mistakes.

He rolled up his sleeves. "Sounds like you need a hand. I'm it. I'm an indie trader, ex-blockade-runner. I can fix my own ship. Not meaning to step on any toes, Chief, but I got a schedule to keep."

Or he didn't get paid.

ARAL STRODE BACK to the quarters he'd been assigned with Wren. Bolivarr matched his pace, negating the need for the infernal guards. He felt like a common criminal. *You are, in the Triad's eyes.* "There have been attacks across the Borderlands?" Aral asked, aghast that religious settlements had been targeted.

"Right here in the UT."

"Why didn't you say something?"

Bolivarr coughed out a laugh. "Not you, too."

Aral flicked him a baffled glance.

"Long story. I've been accused of the same all day. I *am* saying something. That's why I'm here, pretending to escort you to your quarters. To *tell you.*" He turned serious again. "The attacks—I told Hadley, too. It's Father."

The sound of the word on Bolivarr's lips sickened Aral. "Let's make a pact never again to refer to the man as 'Father.' Karbon is sufficient."

"He should be called far worse, Aral. You of all people have the right to do so." His voice had turned quieter. Aral knew he was thinking of his own near murder.

"I don't need that right. I'll be happy if I never see the man again. That's all I want."

"As long as he's alive, you won't be free. He'll never let you go free. He'll spend the rest of his days tracking you, and he'll find you. He can do the impossible, just as he got away from his Triad handlers. Now that you have a wife, someone you love, you have to know the risk it brings. He'll take more pleasure killing her than you, because it'll hurt you more."

"Enough." Aral spun around, wheeling his brother into an area of the corridor where they had some semblance of privacy. His gripped the man's shoulder. "Don't speak of that."

"You have to face the fact he'll get to her to get to you."

"I've faced it every moment of every day since I found her!" He fought for control, and it was blasted near impossible. "Because I didn't kill him when I should have. Because I didn't see him dead with my own hands, he roams free, stalking you, Wren, everyone I love. Because I was willing to allow someone else to do the deed, he's organizing a resistance that threatens this peace." With a shuddering breath, he turned away.

"He's still looking for the Key, Aral. He never gave up. Neither did you. And you found her."

Aral jerked his head around. Bolivarr's calm black gaze pinned him. He realized his brother had grown, matured, hardened over the past five years. He'd thought he could hide things from him. He was wrong.

"Wren is the warlord's daughter."

They jerked apart at a quiet sound. Sister Chara, the resident priestess, had just overheard every word they said.

AFTER THE REVEALING MEETING with Bolivarr, Hadley didn't call Prime-Admiral Zaafran. She didn't brief her crew on what she'd learned from Bolivarr. She walked the ship. It was what Brit Bandar would have done. If only she could guess how her mentor would have handled this situation. Turn in an innocent man, or defy her commanding officer's orders?

Damned if you do, damned if you don't.

The ship was busy preparing for the first trip down to the surface. The incoming survivors had distracted them for only a short time from the main aim of this mission. Hadley envied their focus.

Her PCD chimed. "Keyren."

"It's Rayder, ma'am. Just letting you know that the pilot of *Borrowed Time*'s pushing for repairs. He didn't like my time frame, so he's doing them himself. They might be looking to make a run for it."

"Who's with him in the cargo bay?" Her heart chilled with the thought that Bolivarr would run away, leaving her.

"The woman with the real short hair and their pilot. Plus our watchers."

"Make sure the watchers stay there."

"You got it, ma'am. I'm on guard, too."

She thanked the crew chief and ended the call. By design or accident, she'd ended up in the area of the ship where Aral Mawndarr and his crew had been given shelter. Her stomach ached, seeing the door where she knew Kaz would be sleeping. She wasn't there, choosing to assist with the repair of the crippled ship. Not choosing to be with Bolivarr, she noted.

Where was Bolivarr?

Aral's bedroom door was wide open. A guard was posted outside. Silhouetted against the stars was Wren, his wife, gazing at the planet below, one hand spread on the clear-plate.

Hadley hesitated before disturbing her. The woman was an enigma. Underneath her delicate appearance was something as hard as steel. This woman was not to be taken lightly. Curiosity drew her inside—and the hunger to learn more about Bolivarr. She walked in, taking the spot next to her to admire the watery world below. "It's lovely, yes?"

Wren jerked her head around. For a fraction of a second Hadley saw full-on terror in her wide, impossibly deep blue eyes. Then, curiously, a look of resignation and determination overtook that fear. "Ara Ana," she said with feeling.

Hadley let out a small laugh. "Wouldn't that be wonderful? The lost world found. I wish we had the proof of that."

"I do." Wren clutched at something on a chain under her blouse. Torment darkened her eyes. "I have proof this is really Ara Ana. Down there lies the treasure."

Hadley thought of Bolivarr's belief that the birthplace still existed. The belief that had almost killed him. Swallowing, she tried to hide the tremble that coursed through her. "Will you share what you know?" She sensed that demands didn't work with this woman with the intense eyes.

Wren pulled the chain from her blouse. A flat, black oval pendant swung from the chain. Hadley let out a small, very un-captain-like gasp. Five tiny jewels twinkled like stars seeming to have a glow all their own—five lights in the pattern haunting her ever since it had ripped through Bolivarr's mind and started him down the road that had ended today with the return of all his memories, the pattern that had captivated both a bookish priestess and the top military commander of the Triad and launched this mission.

Even as she stared at the pendant, she felt Wren's knowing gaze on her. *"Gods know this galaxy could use some goodness right now,"* Zaafran had said. *"It starts with us. We can't find what we don't know ourselves."*

Hadley made fists to pull her gaze from the alluring piece. "You know how to find the treasure. The revelation of everything. To be unlocked only by the one with the blood of the goddesses in her good and pure heart."

Wren winced. "Yes to the first, no to the last. That part is fable, and not true, trust me."

"Goddess," Hadley gasped. "You're the Key."

## CHAPTER TWENTY-TWO

TO BE UNLOCKED by someone good and pure of heart? Aral saw her goodness, and so had Sabra. But neither understood the nature of the beast inside her. She'd seen what it could do, and it sickened her.

"Yes, I am the Key." If there was such a thing. Wren was amazed she sounded so calm when her heart was kicking so hard against her ribs, when her stomach felt watery and her knees shook. She drew upon that preternatural calm to finish what she'd started. Everything that mattered depended on it. "Have you told the Triad about my husband?"

Blinking, the captain met her eyes. *She doesn't know how to answer without revealing her indecision.* Her silence gave Wren confidence: Hadley Keyren had not yet revealed to her superiors they were aboard.

Thank the fates. She still had time. Words spilled out, belying her composure. "I want to strike a bargain. The contents of the sanctum in exchange for my husband's life."

Was she doing the right thing? In wanting to save the man who'd saved her, was she breaking her vow to Sabra? *"I don't want riches. I want you."* The memory of her last conversation with her guardian haunted her.

*"Find Ara Ana. Make the galaxy whole."*

"Do you realize what may be hidden there?" the captain asked. "The revelation of everything. The original scripture that tells of the origins of the goddesses. Treasure."

"Beyond imagination, I'm told. Yours—the Triad's—if you agree to help me."

And so they stood there, searching each other's faces, the Triad captain and the warlord's daughter, each struggling with shades of gray, answers that were neither right nor wrong. Wren knew she might not have the power to make the galaxy whole, but she could make a family whole, if only this woman trusted her.

Hadley Keyren made a fist, tightened her jaw, cast her sky-blue gaze to the world below for a good long, almost excruciating moment before bringing newly confident eyes back to Wren. The captain had made a decision. Fates, was it the one Wren so desperately needed? Would the beast inside her accept any other answer?

A small nod had Wren exhaling a pent-up breath. "I give you my word," Hadley said. "The treasure of Ara Ana in exchange for your husband's life."

*And mine,* Wren yearned to say. It wasn't her place to beg for her life. She'd never expected to live even this long. She'd simply do as she'd planned since she'd left Sabra behind on Barokk that day. Atone for her family's atrocities.

IN HADLEY'S OFFICE Wren faced down the entire senior staff of the *Cloud Shadow*. "But she's the warlord's daughter," the little scientist named Garwin was complaining to her mortification. "What if she's not telling the truth?"

If the man had an ounce of self-preservation, he'd be more worried about her tendencies to violence than lying.

"You analyzed the pendant," Bolivarr pointed out.

"The coordinates match the primary site of interest," Garwin admitted.

"I'm assigning a security team to accompany your expedition," Bolivarr said, clearly displeased over how quickly distrust of the Drakken aboard resurfaced, even when they shared the same uniform. "I'll stay behind to assure a balance of forces."

A balance of Drakken, he meant. "Keir and Kaz go down to the surface with me," she insisted. "And Aral."

Aral stepped forward to stand at her side. "I'll serve as her protector, not your ship's guards, Captain."

That won Wren furtive, distrustful glances from the security team. Coolly she returned their looks of suspicion, her hands folded in front of her. It was a natural stance for her, one that mimicked Sister Chara's. Odd, that. She hadn't stopped thinking of her mother's time spent in the company of priestesses. Maybe some of it had rubbed off on her in the brief time she'd been in her mother's care—and love.

"Then who's watching him, Captain?" Hann, the lead security guard asked, studying Aral as if sizing up the threat he might pose.

"You are. And he watches you." Hadley glared at the assembled group. "We're a team. We have each other's backs. Distrust ends here—it ends now. We're the Triad—Earth, Coalition and, yes, Drakken. From here on out and into the future, we go as one. Today is the day we prove we can maintain peace. If we split apart here and now, the galaxy will ultimately split apart along old fault lines, too. If you feel you can't participate under those rules, then remove yourself from the sortie. I don't want you on this team."

*And I don't want you on my crew,* the captain's eyes said loud and clear.

Hann's cool gray eyes settled on Wren for a fraction of a second before moving to the pendant she wore securely around her neck. Then curiously he pondered her neatly folded hands, something in him softening. "I'm in," he grumbled.

"In," the other guards said.

"In," Garwin said nervously.

"Good." Hadley nodded, her boot heels snapping together.

Wren felt Aral's protective hand brush across the small of her back. They'd had not a minute alone together since coming aboard this ship, and no hope of time together anytime soon. Turning slightly, she lifted her chin, soaking in the sight of him, feeling his heat, memorizing his scent. Darkening in response, his midnight eyes regarded her. *This is madness,* he'd said, protesting their unconsummated desire that evening on *Borrowed Time.* It would be madness for some time to come, she knew. She had a debt to pay the galaxy before she could have her own life. If repaying that debt didn't kill her first.

"I'm in!" A girl's voice pierced the tenseness in the office. All heads spun in the Earth cadet's direction. "Ma'am," she added seeing Hadley's surprise, throwing in a snappy salute.

The other five cadets stood behind her in clear support.

"The team has already been selected, Cadet Holloway," Hadley said.

"You have no representatives from Earth coming along. Major Richardson is going to be flying cover in a fighter—that doesn't count. If this is an historic occasion, and only the Coalition and Drakken participate, well, it won't feel right unless people from all three sides are there to witness it." The girl's ponytail swung as she stood at attention. Her slightly worried gaze shifted to the others and finally back to her captain. "Ma'am," she said.

Hadley's mouth clamped closed. *Goddess.* Just as she'd thought she'd wrapped up the prebriefing better than she'd hoped, Prince Jared's niece pointed out a glaring omission. The cadet was right: of the Earth personnel aboard, none would be on the surface for the unlocking of the sanctum. As it was, Hadley was going to be in hot water when this was over, no matter what the outcome. She didn't need a public relations nightmare, too.

Ellen's aunt through marriage was Queen Keira, who'd killed the warlord, Wren's father, with a dagger through the heart, assisted by Ellen's uncle, Prince Jared, who'd been let through to the warlord's flotilla by Aral Mawndarr, the warlord's daughter's husband. Hadley swallowed, dizzied by the implications. Not only was she harboring the man wanted in the escape of an infamous war criminal, she'd placed the warlord's daughter under her protection, as well. Now she could very well be risking the queen's niece.

No one said peace would be easy—or uncomplicated. *Goddess help me.* "Permission granted, Cadet Holloway."

The rooks began to whoop, then Ellen silenced them with an angry wave of her hand.

Garwin waved toward the shuttle bay. "Let's go make history," he said in his tremulous voice.

Indeed, Hadley thought, and yet again several hours later as she leaned over the holovis, tracking the shuttle down to the surface. Ocean covered eighty-percent of it. The continents were small, islands really, scattered across blue-purple water as if a god had flung a handful of gems across its surface. On one of them she'd bet that the goddess treasure would be found, bet everything— the safety of her crew, her integrity as an officer, the very future of the galaxy.

Wren had the key, Bolivarr the sketch of the obelisk, and all of them the terrible knowledge that Karbon Mawndarr wanted both. "Fates," she muttered. Would the Key find the sanctum before their enemies found them?

A warm hand covered hers. She jumped back. "Bolivarr," she scolded under her breath. *We're not alone,* she mouthed, throwing an angry chin in the direction of the buzzing activity on the bridge.

He appeared utterly unapologetic. For the past half day he'd been acting less uncertain when it came to her. Now it was she who'd put their relationship aside for the successful completion of this mission. Failure meant no future—with or without Bolivarr. Being Bolivarr's possibly spurned lover was counterproductive. "There are no ships in the vicinity," he reminded her. "Fighters are escorting them to the surface. The high command has no new reports of terror activity."

"Very good, Battle-Lieutenant."

It had been a long time since she'd called him that, and the flicker in his eyes reflected the snub. He backed away and let her be captain. She had to be. Too much was at risk.

Garwin's perky voice jangled her nerves. "Origins One has landed."

Hadley's throbbing pulse pounded out a staccato beat of anticipation. *We have to win this or everything is lost.*

"Go with the goddess, Origins," Sister Chara murmured, clasping her gnarled hands in front of her.

ARAL SCRUBBED A HAND over his bristled jaw as they trekked inland from their beach landing. Overhead the sonic booms of patrolling fighters didn't quite lend the feeling of security they ought. He was married to a woman entrusted by the goddesses to unlock their treasure. And he was the incarnation of evil in the opinion of all but the most enlightened in the Coalition. "This is an historic day," Kaz said, observing his scowl with her usual wry amusement. "What kind of face is that?"

"This is the face you're going to have to endure until we're off this planet." Then he refocused his attention on the task at hand, a dirt-side mission when all his prior experience was at the helm of a ship. He couldn't forget that. He was as out of his element in this as he was when Wren was in his arms, her lips on his...

He forged on ahead, armed himself to the teeth, prepared and imminently ready to fight to the death to see Wren through this trek and back. *As long as he's alive, you won't be free. He'll never let you go free.* He shoved aside Bolivarr's warnings about Karbon. He mustn't allow the man to distract him now.

Hefting an impressive plasma rifle, Vantos walked on the other side of Wren, trudging with the team into the woods. "I get paid extra for this," he grumbled. "Don't forget it."

Kaz reacted with a quiet snort as they began an uphill climb toward the seaside cliffs where it was said the pendant pointed.

Wren climbed the hill along a path that had already been tamped out of the spring grass by other feet. Stranger's feet. Would she unlock the sanctum only to find it empty?

As they topped the hill, the sea stretched out before her. The sun was warm on her head and shoulders. The pendant was humming, warm and glowing. "We're close," she whispered as if anything louder would disturb the peace of the lofty glade. She pushed ahead, now leading the way into a clearing and the remains of an ancient village. Then, ahead, a group of crumbling spires cast shadows. "Heavy damage to the site," she heard Garwin reporting back to the ship. "All five towers. There's evidence they tried to break in. Gouges, plasma burns." Then he went silent and Wren's heart skipped a beat. She followed his gaze and that of the others to the smallest of the towers, the least impressive. Like her, she thought. "This is it," she said. On the crumbling structure she could just make out the indents of five marks carved in the stone but scoured by countless years of wind and rain.

The treasure.

"Be still, my profiteering heart," Vantos said in awe.

Garwin asked Wren, "Are you *sure?*"

"Yes."

Ellen, the Earthling cadet, murmured, "To be unlocked only by the one with the blood of the goddesses in her good and pure heart."

Wren's excitement fizzled. "It will have to be opened

by me, I'm afraid," she said wryly. "By the one with the blood of the goddesses on her hands, not in her veins."

The girl's eyes shone as she regarded Wren and shook her head. "Not your hands. You can do it." Her open gaze held none of the prejudice of the two older societies in the Triad. Ellen truly believed Wren was capable and even worthy of this act.

A glance at Aral told her the same. "Win our freedom, my love," he murmured.

Their freedom, yes. The freedom he'd never believed in before she'd convinced him otherwise.

She stepped forward and raised the pendant, holding it as it vibrated and sang. A deep grating rumble shook the ground. Rocks crumbled and fell from the structure. For a panicked moment she feared she'd bring the entire obelisk tumbling down. Then a seam opened in the rock and the rumbling ceased.

It was dead silent except for a few annoyed birds protesting the disturbance. The archaeological team rushed forward. They heaved on the rock door, trying to get it to move. It fell over heavily, raising a cloud of centuries-old dust. On the floor in a shaft of light lay a golden box. The treasure. Bodies surged forward.

"Halt! She needs to go inside first," Vantos yelled.

"You—stand back." One of the security guards inserted himself between the runner and the tower. "This is ship's business."

"What the hells? This is my business, and you're just along for the ride."

"He's right," Aral said. "Wren goes inside before anything is touched by any member of your crew."

Hann unlocked his weapon. "This is not your cruiser,

battlelord." Resentment etched lines around his mouth. "Stand back."

Protectively, Kaz moved closer, her rifle held at the ready, drawing the nervous reactions of the other guards and one of the scientists, whose pistol shook in an unsteady hand. "This is our treasure, Drakken," the man said.

All Wren saw was his gun coming up. She swung out a foot and kicked it from his hand. Fists held tight to her chest, she spun and floored him with another kick. Gunfire deafened her, a single shot.

"Stop," Garwin was screaming. "Gods be damned— *hold your fire!*"

Gripped in Aral's calming arms, Wren sucked in deep, angry breaths. Fury pulsed white-hot in her skull. Ellen was watching her with a look of shock and admiration. The beast had reared its head, Wren thought, shame filling her. She didn't want the girl to admire her actions. She didn't understand the danger they represented. She carried violence on her genes, and those genes were wanted by the resistance to breed more warlords.

"What the hells is going on down there?" Hadley was yelling.

"Report," Bolivarr demanded, also from the bridge.

"Let me see your hand, Vantos," Kaz cried.

The runner was standing hunched over, his left arm tucked to his chest. "It's about time you asked to see more of me, doll face."

"Your hand, runner."

"Show her, Vantos," Aral said.

"I'm fine." Vantos was sweating. Blood had soaked his sleeve. "Just a scratch."

Scratch, hells. Vartekeir Vantos had been shot.

## CHAPTER TWENTY-THREE

HADLEY RAPPED sharp orders through the comm. And one by one they followed them. On Hadley's command, hefting their rifles, Aral and Wren dived into the sanctum. Garwin took control of the *Cloud Shadow* crew, ordering Hann to pull in his guards and disarm the one whose stray bullet had struck Vantos. "You and you," Hann shouted, "cover the sanctum. No one goes in or out until they say."

So he'd decided to obey his captain and the expedition leader, Wren thought, watching the men defuse the situation. It wasn't hard to hear the note of distaste in his voice at having to do so. Her people and his were too recently enemies for the alliance to be automatic, much less comfortable. Knowing who'd sired her had made his struggle even worse. Kaz attended to Vantos and his wound while Garwin commed Hadley and Bolivarr back on the ship, working together to get everyone calmed down.

The heat of embarrassment burned her face. Out of habit she started to push on glasses that were no longer there. It showed how much she'd changed over the course of the past weeks, and yet had not. Once again she'd loosed the beast inside her, but had pulled back before she did anything worse—or permanent—like shooting someone. It was little consolation. Seeing the looks of fear, of hatred, in the crew outside the sanctum reminded her acutely of the impossibility of being seen as anything but a product of her bloodlines. In that, she was still dangerous. Being with people who saw her as Wren and not the warlord's daughter had been a dream come true. At the same time she'd grown complacent. Everyday ship's guards turning into a mob was a cold dose of reality.

It was time to do what she'd vowed to do: take possession of the treasure and use the contents for the good of the galaxy.

*"My blood is your blood. My DNA is your destiny."*
*You're wrong, Father.*

Her destiny was *this*.

She turned from the chaotic scene outside to the cool, musty interior of the sanctum. Her mortification over the recent violence faded at the sight of the golden chest.

Aral followed, walking backward. His wary scrutiny was on those remaining outside as if he expected the situation to deteriorate at any moment. Kaz was out there, and Vantos, though injured, wouldn't hesitate to defend them. But he'd take none of it for granted.

"It smells old in here," she said, soaking in the wonder of it all. Sunbeams speared the still air, turning ordinary dust motes into glitter. The chest was the most obvious object in the obelisk. As her eyes adjusted, she saw deeper into its reaches. Tucked into shadowy nooks were items of breathtaking loveliness.

"The treasure," she breathed. The closer she moved

to the chest, the more her pendant vibrated. "Something's happening."

Buzzing was like a hundred tiny bees resonating in her body. Her teeth and bones hummed, matching the frequency. "Something's happening *to me*."

Aral's eyes, dark and intense, searched her face for signs of trouble or trauma. She had no doubt that if he saw anything that scared him, he'd have her out of here in an instant. But he saw her awe, and matched it with awe of his own. Even Aral, a skeptic when it came to the goddesses, a man raised to be a warrior, saw the wonder of this holy place.

That wonder swelled inside her—not at all like the beast with its pulsing fury and desire to hurt, and not quite like the liquid pleasure that flooded her with Aral's caresses. No, this was a different sensation entirely, and definitely not *of her.* It felt foreign to her body.

She turned over a hand to study it as she had the first time she'd been administered nanomeds. "The pendant knows this chest." She made a fist and dropped her hand. Her body sang. "My body knows it, too. Something's happening to me."

"You are the Key. You are the only one who can open that chest. Those responsible for sending you here saw to that."

Garwin and some of the others clustered at the entrance now, recording images of the moment. It seemed invasive and somehow disrespectful, and yet it might delay her execution if not stay it if there was proof she'd helped to unlock the treasure.

Wren paused, her hands on the lid. *To be unlocked only by the one with the blood of the goddesses in her good and pure heart.* Wren didn't feel good and pure. Her blood was too cursed. It was vile and wicked, and…

But the Earthling, Ellen, saw her as Wren, the doer of good things, not the warlord's daughter, the carrier of evil. And in Aral's eyes, she was the love of his life. His wife. It was enough to give her the strength—the heart—to make this moment worthy of all who'd placed their hopes in her, a small girl with a big reputation.

She grabbed the lid and hoisted it high. Her heart pounding hard, her mouth long since gone dry, she gaped at the open chest, trying to come to terms with the fact it had actually opened.

For a heart-stopping moment she thought it was empty. The two items inside took up little room: a sealed urn and a thick old book. Runes decorated the cover. As she ran her fingertip over the embossed, old-fashioned surface she trembled with realization. "This isn't just any book, Aral." She cracked it open. It was very likely the lost scripture the Coalition believed was hidden there. And she, a Drakken, was chosen to rescue it.

Carefully she replaced the book and turned her attention to the urn. Someone's ashes. Whose?

"Freepin' hells." Aral stopped her hand. "The chest's been compromised."

"How?" Garwin blurted. "What?" He scurried inside and crouched next to them.

A modern-day datapad, covered with dust, had been hidden under where the urn had sat.

"May I?" Garwin started to reach for the datapad.

Wren shook her head. "The data is meant for me."

She opened it, releasing a voice that echoed in the hollow chamber. "Ah, sweetling, your presence means you survived to do as you were destined. You will ask, how did you come to be here?"

Sabra! *Oh, my fates.* Wren's hands opened. The datapad clattered to the stone floor.

Dismayed, Garwin cried out and snatched it up, and Wren stole it back, her hands shaking almost violently, causing the voice coming out of the unit to wobble. "It's my guardian's voice. How?"

"Your mother was a priestess of the highest order, child," the recording of Sabra continued.

Lady Seela, a *priestess?*

"She was a Key—one of only a few blessed with guarding the knowledge of the origins of the goddesses. The goddesses left this and more behind when they fled their birthworld. It has been the responsibility of the Keys to guard its existence since the days of yore. As it has been the responsibility of the Keepers to protect the Keys. I, sweetling, was your Keeper."

Wren almost dropped the datapad again. Aral helped her catch it. His fingers found the nape of her neck, gently massaging the knotted muscles there to calm her.

"The warlord didn't know your mother was a Key, only that she was a powerful priestess. He married her by force in hopes of empowering his line with her holy blood. He felt she defied him by bearing a daughter. A man's seed determines gender, yes, but the warlord believed she had special powers and *chose* to deny him a son."

Sucking in a harsh breath, almost a sob, Wren clutched the datapad to her chest.

"She fled with you to a world called Issenda. There she reunited with her people, the sect of the Hand of

Sakkara. She would have left you there to be raised, but wraiths found you both and returned mother and child to the warlord. She sickened and died. Indirectly, the warlord was responsible for her death, yes, but I don't think he intended it. Your father was a very superstitious man. He feared her powers too much. He feared being cursed."

"In the end he *was* cursed," she whispered to the datapad as if talking to Sabra herself.

"I hope that we are listening to this together," Sabra said. Wren squeezed her eyes closed to blunt the ache of tears. "But if not, and you are here, I was able to do as I vowed as a Keeper."

Wren dropped her gaze to her hands clutching the datapad. Around the base of her index finger was a thin black band imprinted with dye in her skin. Interlinking eagles: the pattern was extremely common for a Drakken to wear. Yet the eagle *for her* was symbolic of so much more. It was her family crest, and had been for eons, even before the galaxy split into two warring sides. Now Sabra was telling her that her own mother had dedicated her life to serving those goddesses. It shifted Wren's vision of Lady Seela radically. In her imagination she'd always been a rather helpless, fragile, ornamental beauty. Now she was a gorgeous and powerful priestess imprisoned by an ambitious warlord in a sham marriage.

Wren wasn't bad. She was good.

Her power wasn't evil. It was strength.

*The revelation of everything. To be unlocked only by the one with the blood of the goddesses in her good and pure heart.*

I am good.

"I am recording this message in your second year of life at your mother's dying request. I only wish she were here to see you. She wanted nothing more than to see you grow up. She loved you, sweetling."

Wren touched the urn. Her mother's ashes were contained within.

"Now you will complete the final leg of your journey that Lady Seela could not. Her destiny is now yours, child. Deliver the lost scripture to the Goddess Keep. In the name of the goddesses I so say, Awrenkka. Make the galaxy whole."

Wren rose on quivering legs, holding the heavy old book close to her chest. *The lost scripture.* Now found, she thought, feeling the responsibility weighing on her shoulders and in her heart. It was her duty to return it to the people. Her destiny. "The Goddess Keep. That's the palace on Sakka."

"The heart of the Coalition, the capitol," Aral said angrily. "You're wanted for treason. They'll put you to death."

"If that makes the galaxy whole, so be it."

"Wren…" He lifted a not-too-steady hand to her cheek. "I don't want to lose you."

Her face almost crumpled, seeing the unshed tears in his eyes. She whispered, "I hope you don't have to."

"They won't hurt her," Garwin insisted with all the certainty of a scientist at the culmination of his life's work. "Not knowing what we do now."

"They were ready to do just that outside," Aral argued, adjusting his rifle. "Knowing she was the Key."

Garwin held up the image recorder. He aimed it at the sky, swiping his thumb over a tiny red light. It changed from red to green and back again. "The record has been sent ahead of us—to the ship, and, at the captain's discretion, beyond. No one will be able to argue what happened here today."

But others would welcome the news in a whole different way. To the loyalists, her blood had just doubled in value.

## CHAPTER TWENTY-FOUR

THEY WERE FINALLY ALONE. Aral sealed the door to their shipboard quarters while Wren sat on the edge of the bed they'd not yet had time to share in the way she wanted. Instead of taking the opportunity to kiss her and hold her, he paced like a caged jungle predator. All because she was forcing him to Sakka and the heart of the Coalition, and he was certain they'd never get out alive.

"If it's meant to be, Aral, we'll have our life, our future. If not…"

"How can you leave it up to fate? That's like the believers, handing everything over to the will of the gods." He made a fist. "I believe in taking a proactive approach to life. I won't sit back and place my whole existence in someone else's hands."

"Not even mine?"

Her quiet question stopped him. He seemed to want to use a harsh tone, puffing out his chest, then his tenderness for her took over and he calmed. "You've completed your promise to your guardian. Now it's time to complete my promise to you—see you to safety. I won't leave it up to fate."

She patted the bed. "Come lie with me for a while. Remember the nights on the mat?"

His mouth softened. "How could I forget?"

"We won't have long to rest before we have to join the others. I...I want to know what it's like to be married to you. In every way."

She huffed out an annoyed groan when he continued to frown, pushing off the bed to walk to his side. She brushed her knuckles over his warm cheek. "If it's battle you miss, then make me your next campaign. I want a coordinated frontal attack, a well-planned invasion. Maybe even a surprise ambush."

She was the virgin, yet *he* turned red. Then he laughed, shaking his head. "I can be an idiot sometimes."

"Yes, you can."

"For as long as I planned for you to be with me, now that you are, I don't know what to do with you, how to be a husband. I wasn't bred to be one. I had no examples."

"I have even less of an idea how to be a wife. Although I thought we were off to a good start on that sleeping mat."

Her hands curved behind his neck, massaging his knotted muscles and making him utter a sigh, his eyes almost fluttering closed. Then he jerked back.

"It's not wise, taking this time. Not now. Not yet."

"Why not?"

He brushed his thumb over her cheek. Her body reacted instantly with a flurry of tingles. She swallowed her sigh as he bent his head to brush his lips over hers. A slow and tender exploration. Her tingles became a roaring blaze. "I'll fall more in love with you than I am already."

She leaned closer, her lips a breath away from his. "And is that so terrible?"

"It is for a man terrified of losing you."

"We can't live in fear. That's no way to live. I don't know how much time I have left but I don't want to do it running scared. Is that what you learned in battlelord school? To run?"

His face turned hard. "As long as he's alive, we'll never be free. He'll never let us go free."

"Karbon?"

"Yes. Those were Bolivarr's words to me. He's right. If I had killed him when I had the chance, then perhaps we wouldn't be having this conversation now."

"Karbon is not in this bedroom. I will not stand for it." She grabbed his collar, pulling him down to her. "It's me and you, Aral. No one else." She gentled her voice. "Show me you feel the same. Show me." She pulled him down to her mouth, kissing him hard.

His resolve crumbled in the face of her onslaught. Smiling, she left him no escape. Marrying a battlelord had been her greatest nightmare. Sabra had warned her away from the Mawndarrs, telling her that even Aral would mean the death of her. Sabra never knew about their shared glance the day Aral visited Barokk. Wren had otherwise told her guardian everything. Why not that?

Because she'd had so little she could call her own. Aral Mawndarr was hers.

She thought he'd reach for her blouse to undress her, or perhaps lead her to the bed. Instead he caught her around the waist and pressed her close enough to feel the hard contours of his body. The sheer potency of his masculinity was dizzying, and her physical reaction? Immediate. Her skin warmed, and she tingled low in her belly. Holding her gaze, he lifted her hand to his lips, pressing them to the heel of her palm, and then the inside of her wrist. Goosebumps prickled her arms. "Slowly. Gently. It's your first time."

"I won't break. And you've already seen my enthusiasm." She cupped her hands behind his rear and gave him a firm little push just to prove the point.

His pupils dilated, turning his black-gray eyes even darker. The dimple in the center of his jaw deepened as he let out a quiet male laugh that sent delicious shivers all the way to her toes. "In spades." Another shudder coursed through his body as he pressed her close, one big hand cupping the back of her head. Her sense of smell hadn't lessened with the return of her vision. His unique scent filled her nostrils, spicy and exotic. On a primal level, she smelled his arousal. And felt it. His kiss was hot, hard with passion as he guided her backward to the bed. A heartbeat later she was lying on top of his powerful body, her knee wedged between his muscular thighs, his hand resting possessively on her back, as if ensuring she didn't escape.

Hells, she wasn't going anywhere—not in the midst of this. Madness, she thought, as they threw off their pants and shoes, and everything else not buttoned or tied down.

She soaked in the sensations of his eager exploration of her body, and hers of his. She slid her arms over his shoulders, her head tipping back, trembling for that first feel of him entering her. His hard body trembled, muscles shifting as he fitted himself inside her, ever so slowly joining their bodies. She was so ready that already she could feel her inner muscles contracting, squeezing him. Fates. A pulsing pressure began to build, deep inside her as he moved, so carefully at first then with more passion.

She moved with him, her blood running hot, losing herself in the sensations. "Wren." He seemed to be clinging to the barest shreds of control. "Slow," he warned. But by the fates, she couldn't. It was too late to hold back.

Afraid she might cry out and alarm someone outside in the corridor, she pressed her teeth against Aral's heaving bare shoulder. He hissed a breath between clenched teeth. Hearing him at the limits of his control both frightened and fascinated her. Skating along the edge with him, urging him on, she felt lightheaded and aroused and a little bit out of control.

Her belly contracted and her hips writhed. He caught her moans with his mouth as she arched her hips, her entire body rocking with pleasure. Then, with his own release still quaking through him, Aral wrapped her in his arms in a way that said she was now finally, inarguably his.

The vengeful battlelord tormented by nightmares and the warlord's forgotten, freedom-loving daughter—it sounded like a disaster in the making. But it was the best thing that had ever happened to them both.

KAZ FOLLOWED KEIR DOWN to the bay to see *Borrowed Time.* "You've seen better days," he said, running his good hand over the dented, charred hull.

"You're one to talk. You're looking about as banged up as your ship."

"That's what I was talking about—not you." He held up his injured hand. "It was only a graze."

"A graze?" One of those perfect inky brows of hers rose. "You have a hole right through the center of your hand."

"Bah. Cosmetic."

"It's going to put you out of flying for a while until they knit up those tendons. That's not cosmetic."

"Now you struck me in the heart, fair maiden, reminding me I can't fly."

"Fair maiden? What happened to doll face?"

"Fair maiden suits you better. Kind of like sexy beast suits me."

She rolled her eyes.

"Yeah. You're a fair maiden, all right. The beautiful princess who never wants to be rescued."

"I don't need to be. I can take care of myself."

"It's not so bad letting someone else do it sometimes."

Her brows drew together, her mouth pursing as she studied him curiously. He suddenly envisioned kissing away that skepticism, and everything else, including all that high-collared, perfectly tailored clothing she liked to wear—that she looked blasted fine in, but he still had to wonder if she wore anything lacy under those militaryesque outfits. And if she'd mind if he unfastened those lacy underthings with his teeth—right before he proceeded to devour the rest of her as if she was the best flargin thing he'd ever tasted.

He stopped himself before his brain ran any further down that path, or she'd be wondering just why his trousers seemed to be becoming uncomfortably tight. He gave the patched-up fuel tank a once-over. "They got themselves one hells of a mechanic. It's almost as good as new." He stopped under the wing, pretending to inspect the leading edge next. "So, I'm thinking out some new ways of doing business. This was but one treasure left behind when the flargin galaxy split up. The same happened all over these worlds. Sister Chara even said so. That stuff's ended up in private collections, illegal museums, and even on some blasted arrogant loyalist's yacht. And what about the treasure still where they left it? Riches for the taking." He rubbed his hands together, then winced and swore.

"Vantos, you should be resting that paw."

"Yeah, yeah, I will. But let me finish. I say we head out and see what we can find. Sure, the Triad will want it, but we'll get a percentage of what we recover for our trouble.

"You're serious."

"As a shot-up hand. It wouldn't take long to build up the business, especially if we're the first ones out there. And it definitely won't take long to build up our profit."

"'We'? 'Our'?"

He gave her his best grin. Well, it used to work for charming other women. He could tell by the tiny flicker of interest that it did Kaz, too. She just didn't want to admit weakness. A weakness for him. "I'm proposing to you, Kazara Kaan, for blasted sakes. Do I have to spell it out?"

"Proposing? Proposing what?" All the blood had drained from her face.

"A business arrangement. We hunt treasure and get paid a share of what we find. It's better money than hauling toilets. And what have you got tying up your schedule now, with Mawndarr all married?" And Bolivarr cozy with his captain, he almost said, but shut his trap seeing Kaz's hand started to lift to where her earrings used to be. Started to. And didn't. "Don't you want to try something new?" *Try me?* "What do you say? See how we— I mean, the arrangement works out."

When she looked up at him, it was with interest. "You drive a hard bargain, Vantos."

"Keir."

"Keir," she conceded in her husky voice. Then she shrugged. "Peacetime doesn't have much use for battle-lord seconds. I've been looking to start a new chapter in my life. And I liked flying your ship."

She meant she liked flying *with him*. But he'd go easy on the vernacular for now.

The rest could be negotiated.

A STAFF MEETING with her senior officers was Hadley's first order of business after the team had stored all the items recovered from the sanctum, save the urn with Wren's mother's ashes and the blessed scripture. Fresh from a tense meeting with Hann, who'd headed up the team of security guards sent to the surface, Bolivarr stormed in a few minutes late. He gave her a glance that assured her he'd taken care of the problem.

"Prime-Admiral Zaafran on incoming screen," Hadley's comm officer announced.

"Put it on."

The prime-admiral appeared, not sitting at his desk as he was in many official announcements, but standing in front of it, his arms folded over his chest.

Uh-oh, she thought. She was in trouble.

"Greetings, sir," she said.

"I watched the holovis you transmitted, and read your report, Captain."

The silence roared. Or was that her pulse?

"Congratulations. Your mission has succeeded beyond measure. Beyond anything we—I—could have hoped for. The queen and the prime minister also extend their congratulations for a job well done."

Relief rippled through her. "Thank you, sir."

"A job well done, yes. If reckless." He glared at her, letting the last word sink in. Then he sighed and walked back to his desk. "There has been another attack. This time on Issenda."

"Issenda!" *Goddess.* It was the world where Wren's mother had tried and failed to hide from the warlord.

"They could easily have targeted you," Zaafran scolded. It hit her that he was possibly more worried than angry. "The attackers were fought off with little loss of life. This time we were lucky. Next time…"

Hadley squared her shoulders. "We're heading home immediately." Bolivarr nodded his approval. His thinned mouth broadcast his unease.

"Report to my office upon your return, Captain Keyren." Under the scrutiny of the miss-nothing blue eyes of the Triad's top commander, Hadley felt a little smaller. "Yes, sir."

"And, Captain?"

"Yes, sir?"

"Gods-speed. Get home safe. And without your trademark recklessness."

Less than a month as captain and her reputation was already firmed up in the worst possible way. She cringed.

"Hadley," Bolivarr said after the screen went dark. "Aral put down on Issenda for supplies *before* those so-called terrorists struck. *Borrowed Time* wasn't attacked. They were chased away. The only reason the unmarked ship didn't finish the job was because Issenda was the real target." Bolivarr held her gaze as he theorized with certainty. "They let *Borrowed Time* escape because what they wanted was on Issenda. Or so they thought."

"The key," she hissed. "The attackers thought she

was on Issenda." A likely place, it made sense. "Terrorists or the resistance?"

"Try Karbon Mawndarr."

Hadley ground one fist into the other. "If he learns Aral is on this ship, and the warlord's daughter is, too." She turned her gaze to his and thought of the vicious beating he'd endured on Junnepekk. "Goddess, you're in danger, too, Bo."

He paused midbreath. She cursed herself for letting the pet name slip. "Based on what happened to Aral with that mystery ship, we're not taking chances being out here where they can find or recognize us. We are officially out of here. To your stations, gentlemen." As the staff filed out to their positions on the ship, she followed.

"Hadley."

She shivered. "Don't do that."

He reared back. "What?"

"Make your voice all low and rumbly like that. It gives me the tingles."

His smile turned quite roguish, for Bolivarr. "I like that I still do that to you."

"Of course you do. You never stopped. That's why it hurt so much when you put us on hold while you *figured out* your feelings for me. And, I suppose, Kaz." She started to leave. Again he stopped her.

"My feelings were never in doubt," he said. She saw his upset, his fear of losing her in his expressive eyes. Whereas his brother held more of himself in check, Bolivarr let everything show. Including his love for her. "I wanted to make sure I did the right thing."

"You didn't have to put me aside to do that," she whispered. Blasted tears threatened to well up. "I've been thinking. I deserve a whole man. Meaning a man who doesn't take pieces of himself away at will. You're either with me or you're not. No in between."

He ran his hand up her arm. It made her tremble, blast it. "You mean so much to me that I screwed it up. I made a mess of things when it was opposite my intention. Of course you deserve a whole man. It's why I never felt worthy of you when I had no memory of my past. You're amazing, Hadley, an incredible woman. I want you to have all of me." His fingers spread on her back and he forced her closer, his gaze direct and glowing with his feelings for her. "But I want all of you in return."

"You have all of me." Her voice cracked, and she swallowed thickly.

"No, I don't. But if you marry me, I'll have more than I ever dreamed possible—"

*"Marry?"*

Her hesitation caused pain in his dark gaze. "If you'll agree, Hadley, I'll spend a lifetime convincing you it was the best decision you ever made."

"You won't have to." Her smile was soft, her eyes moist, the most emotion she dared while on the bridge under scrutiny. Inside, however, her heart bounced with joy. "I already know you're the best decision I ever made. Bolivarr Mawndarr, the answer is yes." *Yes, yes, yes.*

The ship's claxon went off, grating and loud. For a split, naive second, she thought it was in celebration of their moment.

Then, "Target onscreen—gods, I can see them with the naked eye" came over the comm from the bridge and she knew she was very badly mistaken.

# CHAPTER TWENTY-FIVE

"ENEMY TARGET ONSCREEN, Captain."

Hadley detected the panic in her weapons officer's voice. Déjà vu dragged her back to the day she'd won her captain's wings. Only, this was real. As she'd learned that day, there was no time to give in to terror, hers or anyone else's.

"It's the same ship we encountered near Issenda," Aral informed her as he and Wren returned to the bridge.

Vantos shook his head. "You're not going to be able to outrun him. Even I couldn't."

"Noted."

"Ship in sight." Menacing and silent, a vessel flew up alongside them. It was almost as if the craft wasn't there at all. The fuselage was solid black. No marking of any kind broke its pristine surface.

"If that's Karbon, he spent our inheritance on a new ship," Bolivarr muttered to Aral.

The proximity siren sounded, alerting them that the distance between the ships was becoming dangerously small. They were close enough now to count every porthole.

Wren gasped as her pendant suddenly warmed as it had in the sanctum, tingling her skin where it made contact. "Aral, you use the expression 'interrogated' when you say another ship's computer has asked for our identification."

"That's normal procedure. It's how we know who's out there. Friend or foe."

"I think that ship just interrogated *me*." She had been tracked.

"They're hailing us, Captain," the comm officer yelled.

"Let it through."

A man appeared, immaculately groomed and dressed in Drakken red. He searched out Wren with a cold, appraising stare, warm compared to the void of empty space outside. "There you are, Awrenkka." White still streaked the midnight-black hair he wore in a neat ponytail, perhaps a little more than when she'd first seen him a decade ago. He was still as regal, still as handsome, with the same cruel set to his jaw and mouth. Still as arrogant and condescending in manner as he was the day she first saw him.

"You are trespassing in Triad space," Hadley said. "State intentions."

Karbon chuckled, shaking his head. "We can make this hard, young captain, or we can make it easy. Which do you prefer?"

"Me? Hard." She turned to the bridge once more. "Launch the fighters. Launch everything we've got."

"My ship's got some teeth," Vantos said.

Hadley sighed. "Launch it, too."

"Woo. Now we're talking. Coming, Mawndarr? It's time our friend learned his lesson."

Wren turned to Aral in dread. The idea of losing him had been hard before they'd made love. She couldn't touch it now. Aral grabbed her shoulders, bringing his mouth down over hers for a swift, hard kiss. "I love you. I'll never have a real life with you until I do this."

"Do what? Where are you going? Aral!" He gripped her shoulders, urging her to understand. Then he strode off, leaving her alone.

ARAL STORMED to the shuttle bay, Vantos in tow. He had a plan. *Borrowed Time* was in working order, but not necessarily his runner. Of all the times he needed the man in top shape, this was it. Except the runner had a wounded hand. The fates, it seemed, enjoyed throwing wrenches at him. *"As long as he's alive, you won't be free. He'll never let you go free."* Bolivarr was right. In her name he'd finish what he should have done long ago.

"I'll fly," he told Vantos.

"You've never flown an AG-250," Vantos protested. "I've got so many retrofits on this crate the retrofits have retrofits."

"I'll manage," Aral said dryly.

"Don't wreck my ship, Drakken."

"I had the chance a dozen times in the past—why start now?"

"You fly. I'll talk you through it."

They threw off the hooks attaching *Borrowed Time* to the floor. Flying out to distract Karbon was a desperate, last-ditch maneuver. It had to work. He had to rid the galaxy of a bonafide monster.

HADLEY TURNED TO WREN and took a deep breath. "I know this won't be easy, but if you want to help you can start by distracting Mawndarr."

Wren shuddered, but slowly nodded. A quick look at the communications officer and Karbon was back on screen.

At second glance, he wasn't in good shape. The signs of sweef addiction showed, despite the meds he was likely taking to combat it. There was a telltale glassiness in his eyes, a false brightness to his teeth, an overall sense of physical rot she sensed more than saw in this man who'd left Bolivarr for dead. Who'd skulled priestesses. Who'd sufficiently tormented a boy, his own son, so as to make his nights as an adult a living hells. Aral would forever be scarred inside. She could hope only to offer him some peace, her unconditional love his salve. It didn't make up for what this man had done to him.

The beast inside Wren awoke. Instead of burying it, she let it come to life. She could control it. There was no need to fear it. It was as much a part of who she was as her hands or her hair. She unleashed its fury for the first time without hesitation. "I am going to blast you the hells off this plane of existence."

His head jerked at the sound of her voice. Disbelief that she'd spoken up blazed in his eyes.

She stepped forward, planting her hands on the center console. "As you said, we can make it hard, Karbon, or we can make it easy. Your choice." Her face was her father's, her glare the warlord's.

Its effect wasn't lost on Karbon. "Come with me and realize your full potential as my mate. Rule this galaxy at my side."

"Monsters belong *under* the bed, Karbon, not *in* my bed."

His face flushed red. He lunged forward, mirroring

her stance, his big hands on a similar console on his ship. His expression was as ominous as an approaching whirl-storm as his ship bore down on *Cloud Shadow,* weapons arrays glowing.

Just then, Aral and Vantos streaked across their bow. In his distraction, their flyby caught Karbon off guard.

Wren could see him bellowing at his crew to arm the plasma cannons. It was the last thing she heard before a blinding flash of energy flashed outside and the screen went blank.

"He's hit." Bolivarr's eyes shone with intensity, but his voice was curiously subdued. She knew Aral suffered the same struggle. No matter how much of a monster, no matter how bitter the blood, Karbon was still their father.

"The ship is intact," called the engineer. "I repeat, the ship is intact."

"Arm plasma cannons," Hadley said. Her eyes narrowed. She was intent on finishing Karbon off before he could regroup and rearm.

"Plasma cannons armed," the weapons officer announced.

"Fire." Her calm command resulted in a huge double explosion. Energy blinded her. She grabbed for the seat to keep the violent quaking from throwing her to the ground as shrapnel collided with the ship with deafening thumps.

When the debris cleared, Karbon's ship was gone. Could it be true? Had they done it? Had the man been so arrogant to not expect his demise?

Apparently, yes. Hadley heaved a huge breath.

Kaz pumped her fist. "Good shot, Captain."

Hadley flashed her a grateful glance. "Well, the men softened the target."

"Where are they?" Wren asked, her heart suddenly in her throat at the eerie silence.

"*Borrowed Time,* report!" The bridge crew was silent waiting for the men to answer Bolivarr. Alarms wailed distantly through the damaged ship, but no cocky trader's voice, and no Aral.

Not like this, Wren thought. *This isn't how it ends.* Kaz moved next to her and took her hand, squeezing as the crew searched for the missing ship.

A burst of static erupted over the calm. Then Keir's voice. "*Cloud Shadow,* this is *Borrowed Time.* We had a little personal encounter with a hunk of molten luranium. We're gonna need a tow."

## CHAPTER TWENTY-SIX

THE CEILING OF THE PALACE, the Goddess Keep, soared almost to the heavens themselves, Wren thought, holding the old book she'd recovered from the goddess's birthplace. Her lush, silver gown, gorgeous and undoubtedly expensive, rustled as Aral walked at her side, he, too, decked out in finery—a suit that faithfully followed the hard lines of his body. Silver was the color of the robes of the highest priestesses, and the family color of the ruling family on Sakka. She found it curious but an honor that the palace tailors chose to clothe her and Aral in the hue.

It also made them both feel a little more confident that they wouldn't be arrested immediately following the ceremony.

His hand brushed over her arm, tenderly, even a little possessively, something he'd not fully ceased to be. But then, he was a product of their culture as much as she was. Along with Vantos, Kaz, Hadley, Bolivarr and the crew, they formed a solemn procession as they made their way down the long marble path to present the scripture to the goddess-queen Herself. Wren quaked at the thought. She was the warlord's daughter, and though cleared of crimes, her family and theirs had spent millennia battling each other.

Finally she reached the queen, Queen Keira's mother. The woman was startlingly beautiful, with masses of black hair lit by reddish strands, much like Wren's

Wren dipped her head respectfully and offered her the book. "I have returned it in the name of peace."

The queen took the volume, her eyes widening with wonder and awe as she opened to the first page, turning to the next and the next; Wren and her party waited, the audience of thousands waiting in the wings to see if the book met the queen's approval. "The revelation of everything," the woman whispered, looking up. "Unlocked by the one with the blood of the goddesses in her good and pure heart."

*Goddess?* Stunned, Wren almost pushed on her glasses out of awkwardness before remembering they were long gone. "How?" she managed.

"Your mother, Lady Seela, was of a lost bloodline descended from the goddesses themselves, as is my family. As are you, child." The queen's hand smoothed over the pages of the book. "There are many other revelations to be discovered in the pages within, but this is one I thought you would like to know."

Sister Chara stood off to the side, looking a bit amazed herself, but no less than Aral. "You're going to be insufferable now," he said in Wren's ear.

She simply groaned, whispering back, "More DNA to live up to."

THEY GATHERED AFTERWARD in Prime-Admiral Zaafran's office, an event attended by most of the highest-ranking members of the military and parliament. The man seemed moved almost to tears seeing Aral. He gripped his shoulder, soaking in the sight of him. "M," he said.

"Z."

"Aral, there are no words to adequately express the Triad's gratitude for your acts of bravery. Not one, not two, but countless deeds over years of loyal work. And this latest—" he looked at Wren, his eyes warming "—your *personal matter,* was something quite wonderful for us all."

He turned, reaching for a shiny object resting on a cushion held by one of his assistants. "We hereby award you the Medal of Freedom," he said. "In the Triad, it's our highest honor." As Wren watched, her heart swelling with joy, he pinned the commendation on Aral's chest. Then they embraced, heartily pounding each other on the back in masculine fashion.

He then turned to Hadley, calling her forward, followed by Bolivarr, giving all promotions in rank. It was a glorious day.

"I'm not sure what your plans are, Aral," Zaafran said later over drinks. "But your expertise is welcome."

"My expertise is war," he said. "It's peacetime."

"We never stop preparing for war. It's how we prevent it."

"I thank you," Aral said, sliding his arm around Wren's waist. "But we hope for a quieter existence. Planetside."

"Do you have a location chosen as yet?"

"Yes, in fact."

"Earth," Wren put in. She caught Prince Jared's niece Ellen grinning at her. "It's far from here, and a shrine." Owing to its being the birthplace of Prince Jared, Queen

Keira's consort. "We'll be able to enjoy greater accep-
tance, and less recognition there."

The admiral nodded, understanding.

A new life, she thought, in the Earthling land called
Australia. Advised by the prince's family, they'd chosen
a private stretch of beach on the western side of the continent, far from prying eyes.

*Three months later*

WIND FILLED THE SAILS of the small boat, pushing it
swiftly across the water off the Australian coast where
Wren and Aral were building their home. Aral dropped
the sails when they were far enough from shore. Wren
carefully unwrapped the urn containing her mother's
ashes, and unplugged the lid. She'd thought long and
hard about whether to scatter her mother's ashes on
Issenda or here. In the end, she'd decided that it was
only right that they finally be together. In her heart, she
knew it was the right choice. The sun gleamed on Aral's
bare chest as he made his way to stand next to her. Her
hair whipped around her face as she turned away from
the wind, tipping the urn to release the ashes. They flew
away in the breeze, disappearing into the air and water.
"You're free now, Mother."

Aral's arm looped over her shoulders as she pulled
another item from her bag. The pouch of gems she'd
intended to use to bribe Keir and secure passage out of
Zorabeta had never been used. Gems that Sabra had given
her. They were her only tangible connection to her
guardian. In lieu of ashes, she'd scatter the gems at sea
to honor her. "You were the mother I never knew, dear

Sabra. You taught me what love was. Else I may never have known." Tears in her eyes, she tossed the gems out to sea. *In making the galaxy whole again, I became whole.*

Aral moved behind her, holding her close, his chin on her head. His fingers laced over her stomach, his marriage tattoos blending with hers.

"You would have known of love," he argued sometime later as they drifted on the water. "I would have come for you no matter what, and we'd have fallen in love."

She smiled, turning in his arms. "My lost boy."

"Lost...and found." His handsome face lit with mischief, a quality emerging more and more as his nightmares ceased to haunt him. "So, what do you say, goddess. A swim?"

She stripped down to her bikini, a scandalous garment by highborn Drakken standards. Whooping, she dived after him, following him into the water soaked in warm sunshine. The battlelord and the warlord's daughter were finally, inarguably free.

### ACKOWLEDGMENTS

For everyone who stood by me and put up with me
throughout the writing of this book (that some might call
a labor of love, but I would put the emphasis on labor)
with special mention, thanks and love to Connor and
Courtney, George, Carolyn, Tara and Linnea. I could not
have gotten through it without your patience! Special
hugs and thanks to Kendra, Carolyn and Linnea for
early reads. And muzzle kisses to Tala, the world's best
doggie. We'll do that agility course now, I promise!

From *New York Times* bestselling author

# Gena Showalter

Enter a mythical world
of dragons, demons and nymphs...
Enter a world of dark seduction
and powerful magic...
Enter Atlantis...

Catch these thrilling tales in a bookstore near you!

**THE NYMPH KING** • Available now!

**HEART OF THE DRAGON** • Available January 2009

**JEWEL OF ATLANTIS** • Available February 2009

**THE VAMPIRE'S BRIDE** • Available March 2009

"Lots of danger and sexy passion give lucky readers a
spicy taste of adventure and romance."
—*Romantic Times BOOKreviews*
on *Heart of the Dragon*

## HQN™

We *are* romance™

**www.HQNBooks.com**

PHGSAT2009

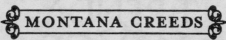

# REQUEST YOUR FREE BOOKS!

## 2 FREE NOVELS
## FROM THE ROMANCE/SUSPENSE
## COLLECTION PLUS 2 FREE GIFTS!

**YES!** Please send me 2 FREE novels from the Romance/Suspense Collection and my 2 FREE gifts (gifts are worth about $10). After receiving them, if I don't wish to receive any more books, I can return the shipping statement marked "cancel." If I don't cancel, I will receive 4 brand-new novels every month and be billed just $5.49 per book in the U.S. or $5.99 per book in Canada, plus 25¢ shipping and handling per book plus applicable taxes, if any*. That's a savings of at least 20% off the cover price! I understand that accepting the 2 free books and gifts places me under no obligation to buy anything. I can always return a shipment and cancel at any time. Even if I never buy another book from the Reader Service, the two free books and gifts are mine to keep forever.

185 MDN EF5Y  385 MDN EF6C

Name _____ (PLEASE PRINT) _____

Address _____ Apt. # _____

City _____ State/Prov. _____ Zip/Postal Code _____

Signature (if under 18, a parent or guardian must sign) _____

### Mail to The Reader Service:
**IN U.S.A.:** P.O. Box 1867, Buffalo, NY 14240-1867
**IN CANADA:** P.O. Box 609, Fort Erie, Ontario L2A 5X3

Not valid to current subscribers to the Romance Collection,
the Suspense Collection or the Romance/Suspense Collection.

**Want to try two free books from another line?**
**Call 1-800-873-8635 or visit www.morefreebooks.com.**

* Terms and prices subject to change without notice. N.Y. residents add applicable sales tax. Canadian residents will be charged applicable provincial taxes and GST. Offer not valid in Quebec. This offer is limited to one order per household. All orders subject to approval. Credit or debit balances in a customer's account(s) may be offset by any other outstanding balance owed by or to the customer. Please allow 4 to 6 weeks for delivery. Offer available while quantities last.

**Your Privacy:** Harlequin is committed to protecting your privacy. Our Privacy Policy is available online at www.eHarlequin.com or upon request from the Reader Service. From time to time we make our lists of customers available to reputable third parties who may have a product or service of interest to you. If you would prefer we not share your name and address, please check here. ☐

BOB08R